AURORA
CV-01

Ryk Brown

CHAPTER ONE

Dayton Scott sat in front of the big picture window that looked out from his study across the sea of lights in the city below. He had sat in this same chair many times over his seventy-two years. He could still remember sitting on his father's lap, looking out this same window as his father read to him. He remembered how much smaller Vancouver had been back then. It had just started to bloom, like a rose that had opened up just enough to show its true colors. Nothing more than a distant clump of lights in the night back then, but still a beacon of hope for a world just starting to be reborn. Now the lights filled the entire valley below. Now it was a blazing symbol of prosperity, of accomplishment, and of anticipation of things yet to come. He could still hear his father's voice telling him, *"Things are already changing, Dayton. By the time you're my age, everything will be completely different. It's a great time to be alive, my boy!"*

His father had been right; everything had changed. Things he couldn't have imagined in his wildest dreams had not only come to be, but were no longer considered wondrous. When he was born, they had just started flying around in propeller-driven aircraft. Now they were building faster-than-light spaceships that could take them away from Sol and out to the long-lost colonies of Earth. But that sudden, meteoric rise in technology had come at a price. And it was a price he was desperately trying to prevent his world from having to pay.

"Dayton," his wife beckoned as she entered the room. "We have a house full of guests and you're hiding in here?" When he failed to offer a response, she became concerned and moved across the study to stand at his side. "What are you doing?"

"Just looking out the window, my dear."

"Dayton," she teased, "are you nervous?"

"Maybe just a tad," he admitted.

"Whatever for? You've given a million speeches in your lifetime."

"But none as important as this one," he sighed.

She could see the worry on his face. "You'll do fine, I'm sure," she promised, placing a comforting hand on his shoulder.

The senator smiled at her, placing his hand on hers, about to say something when a knock came at the door. "Yes?"

The door opened to reveal a nondescript man in his mid-thirties. He was dressed in a plain dark suit and wore a small transceiver in his left ear.

"Senator?" he asked before spotting him in the chair. "It's almost time, sir."

"I'll be there momentarily." The senator rose from his seat and put on his dress jacket.

Mrs. Scott straightened her husband's jacket and adjusted his tie. "As handsome as the day I married you," she attested before giving him a kiss.

"Did he show up?" the senator asked.

"Oh, you know Nathan. I'm sure he's lurking around here somewhere, hiding in the shadows, checking out all the pretty young girls in their fancy dresses."

He knew she was lying. She hadn't seen him, and

she was just trying to keep his mind off the painful subject. He had hoped that the academy would've changed his son for the better, but he was beginning to think that his youngest had already become the man he was going to be.

"Come on, honey. Time to dazzle them with your charm," she teased as she walked him to the door.

* * *

It was a beautiful summer night with clear skies that revealed an ocean of stars overhead. The south lawn of the senator's palatial estate was packed full of guests, all dressed in their most fashionable evening attire. Some were still finishing their dinners, but most were milling about, talking in little groups as they tried to see or be seen. In the background, an orchestra was playing selections from the senator's youth, inspiring some to ignore the evening's agenda and start dancing, despite disapproving looks from the older, more conservative guests.

The orchestra suddenly stopped mid-chorus, breaking into the upbeat theme song used in the senator's last campaign. The attention of the crowd suddenly turned toward the top of the stairs that led from the south entrance of the main house down into the courtyard. As if by magic, and in perfect time with the music, two pale blue spotlights snapped open at the top of the stairs revealing the senator and his wife. Again in time with the music, the senator thrust his right hand up into the air in triumph, a gesture made popular at his last victory party. The crowd broke into cheers and thunderous applause, while the senator took his wife's hand and began their journey down the staircase. The spotlights captured every step as they descended, waving to the crowd, occasionally making a special effort to point at those guests they knew best. It was an absolute frenzy of excitement, albeit a perfectly choreographed one.

As the senator reached the bottom of the stairs, his wife let go of his hand and turned to her left, disappearing into the darkness as her spotlight faded out right on cue. The senator broke into a jog, peeling off to the right, looking fit and full of life despite his age. He made his way onto the stage and over to the podium, arriving just as the music reached its climax.

"Thank you!" he said, repeating himself several times while he waited for the applause to die down. "Is everyone having a good Founders' Day?!" he yelled, whipping them back up into a thunderous roar. He continued waving at the crowd another full minute before the ovation finally died down enough for him to be heard.

"Good. I'm glad everyone is having a good evening. It's an important day in the history of our world, and it should be celebrated." The senator looked around the crowd as the last of the applause fell silent. Finally, he launched into the main body of his prepared speech, his tone changing to one more befitting the topic.

"Long ago, humanity was tossed back into a period of darkness and despair the likes of which were unseen in human history. For over a thousand years, our ancestors struggled to survive in the wake of the most devastating disaster ever to befall humankind. A plague of biblical proportions nearly wiped humanity out of existence, leaving only those blessed with a natural immunity to survive and start over. But the great bio-digital plague did more than reduce our populations. It did more than destroy our civilizations and our infrastructures. And it did more than take away our science, culture, and technology. It took away our unity as a people. It took away our common dreams and goals. In fact, it took away our very will to carry on..."

The senator paused for dramatic effect, scanning the faces of the guests standing on his lawn, until he felt that the moment was right to add one word. "Almost."

"For despite the hardships, and despite the pain and suffering, despite the thousands of mass graves and the countless suicides in the face of utter despair, humanity found a way to carry on. We joined together in small groups at first, scratching out a meager existence. And in time, things got better. In time, we forgot. We forgot the horror, the despair, and the tragedy. But with each new generation, we also forgot ourselves: who we were, where we came from, and what we had once been. We even forgot that humans just like us were struggling in much the same way on worlds *we* had colonized out amongst the stars."

The senator paused again, making eye contact with a few faces in the crowd. He knew that each person whose eyes he met equaled another vote.

"For centuries on end, we merely existed, making little to no attempt to reclaim that which had been lost. Eventually, as our populations grew, necessity again became the mother of invention. Slowly but surely we began to move forward, to rebuild. But we had to relearn all that had been forgotten. We had to conduct the same experiments, the same research and development, and suffer through the same countless failures as we slowly progressed. Until that fateful day of discovery, the day we learned that everything we once were had not been lost, but had only been misplaced. It was the day that humanity would regain all that had been taken from us. It was the day the Data Ark was discovered!"

"Jeez," the young man mumbled as he sipped his cocktail. "You'd think he had been there himself." He finished his drink, setting it back down as he gestured to the bartender for a refill before turning back to face the stage. From his position at the end of the bar, he could see across the sea of supporters—'his father's flock' as he liked to call them—all mesmerized by his oratory.

"There you are." A young woman leaned against the bar next to him, tucking in close to keep the evening breeze from chilling her bare shoulders. "How long have you been hiding out back here?"

"Since the moment I arrived." He turned to face her, giving her a small kiss on the cheek. "How have you been, sis?"

"Nice choice of attire there, Nathan," she said, noticing his dress uniform. "Just couldn't pass up a chance to stick it to the old man, huh?"

"Yeah, well, you know what Pop always says. Missed opportunities..."

"...are lost advantages," she finished for him. "Don't remind me." She picked up his drink and took a sip, her face puckering at the bitterness of the alcohol. "Since when do you drink the hard stuff?"

"How else am I going to get through this?"

"You talk to Mom yet?"

"I've been trying to avoid that."

Nathan's sister looked to the right side of the crowd, spotting her mother standing to one side, talking to a small group of people. "There she is." She started to jump up and down, waving.

"Stop it!" Nathan grabbed her arm, pulling it back down as she giggled. She had always enjoyed pushing his buttons. "Are you nuts? She'll see us." He looked toward his mother, trying to determine if she had spotted them. She was speaking to an older gentlemen and a young blond woman, and as best he could tell, his sister's wave had gone unnoticed.

"Who's the blonde she's talking to?"

"Relax, little brother. She's not your type. She's some scientist or something," she explained. "So, are you ready for the media circus?"

"For the what?"

"The media circus. You know, the press? The paparazzi?"

"What are you talking about, Miri?"

"Haven't you talked to Dad yet?" she asked, somewhat surprised.

"Been trying to avoid *that* even more. Why?"

"Oh, nothing," she lied. "Never mind," she added, deciding to let her younger brother be surprised like all the other guests.

"What? Tell me," he demanded, noticing the sly little smile on her face. He had seen that grin too many times in his life and knew full well it meant trouble.

"Shush! Your father is giving a speech," she teased.

Nathan turned back to the bar and picked up his drink. "When isn't he giving a speech?" he muttered to himself, taking another sip.

"Founders' Day is the moment in history when humanity finally took responsibility for its future. As a whole, we made a commitment to ensure that all of the reclaimed technological wonders of our forefathers would be used wisely, for the betterment of all humanity, and not just the few that could afford them. The founding of the Ark Institute and the tenets upon which it was based would one day lead to the creation of the very republic which provides for and protects the entire population of the Earth today! It was that moment, that one perfect moment, that simple clarity of purpose that quickly brought all of the people of Earth together in a way that had never been done before. The knowledge bestowed upon us by the Data Ark has done more to change and improve our lives over the last century than all of the centuries of darkness that came before."

Senator Scott paused again, this time more so to take a sip of water than for dramatic effect. "But those same improvements can easily lure us back into that very same darkness and despair."

"Man, he is *really* laying it on thick tonight. What's he running for this time?" Nathan looked at Miri. Her smile had grown larger. "You're kidding me!" He had suddenly realized what she had been smiling about. "Are you serious?"

Miri just laughed at him. "You should see your face."

Nathan turned to the bartender again, "Bring me the bottle."

"Oh, come on, Nate. It won't be that bad."

He took the bottle from the bartender and poured

himself a double, tossing the entire contents of the shot glass down his throat before refilling it.

Miri continued laughing. "What are you trying to do, pickle your liver?"

"Haven't you heard? They can grow new ones now." He picked up his glass and tossed down another shot. As he grimaced from the burning sensation of the alcohol, he noticed a young woman stepping up to the other end of the bar. "I think I could use a distraction."

Miri looked past him at the new arrival. "Naw, I don't think *she's* your type either."

"When are you going to learn, sis? Until proven otherwise, they're *all* my type." Nathan turned to his sister as he straightened his uniform. "Wish me luck."

Miri reached up and began straightening his tie. "Luck, little brother, is something you've always had plenty of." She spun him around to face the woman and gave him a little push to send him on his way before departing herself.

Nathan strode confidently toward the woman, emboldened by the two double shots of alcohol he had just consumed. She was a beautiful woman, mid-twenties with long brown hair. Nathan immediately noticed that the fit of her evening gown told of a figure that was well maintained. She was busy ordering a refill of her shot glass as he stepped up to her.

"Evening, Miss. May I buy you a drink?" Nathan was trying to muster as much charm as possible, which wasn't easy considering the amount of alcohol he had already consumed.

"It's an open bar..." She stopped short as she turned to look at him, her irritated frown suddenly

9

changing into a look of bemusement at his dress uniform. "Sure, soldier boy," she giggled. "Knock yourself out."

"Actually, I'm not a ground pounder, ma'am. I'm an ensign." Nathan pointed at the rank insignia on his uniform's shoulder boards. "I'm in the fleet. You know, up there?" he added, pointing toward the night sky.

"Oh, of course. Terribly sorry, Ensign." She picked up her fresh drink and slammed it down in a single gulp.

"You seem a little upset, ma'am," he commented, noticing the way she was slamming down her drink. "Something wrong?"

"You see that tall, blonde jock-type over there? The one kissing every fat political ass he can stick his lips to?"

Nathan looked around but failed to see who she was talking about.

"Well, you probably can't see him right now, 'cause he's still down on his knees puckering up."

"I still don't see..."

"I mean, he should be over here kissing *my* ass! I mean look at it!" She stood up and turned so Nathan could see her tightly wrapped behind. "My ass looks great in this dress! Don't you think?"

"Yes, ma'am," Nathan agreed enthusiastically.

"Damn right! I look hot in this dress!"

"Damned hot!" Nathan decided it was best to play along for now, since it was already going much better than he had hoped.

The woman realized she was ranting and stopped, motioning for another drink. "So, Ensign, what's your story? No, let me guess. You're shipping out tomorrow, right?"

"Something like that."

"And this could be your last night on Earth." She quickly looked Nathan up and down.

"Possibly."

"Well, Ensign," she announced as she tossed back another drink. "This is your lucky night. I've got a score to settle with mister butt-kisser over there and you might be just the right guy to help me settle it." Her expression suddenly turned from one of anger to one of seduction. "Think you can find us some place a little more private?" she cooed as she stepped closer and ran her fingers through his hair.

"Yes, ma'am," his smiling turning into a grin.

"Those who want to build up our fleet in order to better defend the Earth are only inviting that which they fear most! If the Jung believe us to be a threat, they will undoubtedly respond to that threat *before* it is too late!" the senator declared, pounding the podium at just the right moment to emphasize his point. "Should we spend on defense? Yes! Should we have warships in space? Of course! But they should *not* be given the capability of faster-than-light travel, for that is exactly what the Jung fear, an enemy that can reach out and attack them where they live! We need to stop this insane build-up immediately! We need to seek out the Jung leadership and establish a peaceful dialog in order to ensure the safety of not only the Earth, but the entire solar system! I honestly believe that if the Jung government sees that our *only* concern is to rebuild our world and coexist peacefully with the other human-inhabited systems in the core, they will see no cause for aggression!"

The senator paused one last time, looking to his wife for that unwavering look of support that she was always there to provide, and he got exactly that look from her on this night.

"What we need is sane, sensible leadership, and not fear-mongering. What we need is someone who will put the needs of the people of this nation, and of this world, first. What we need is someone who is more concerned with the rebuilding of this country and this world, right here, right now, and not the building of others."

In a nearby anteroom, Nathan finished tucking in his shirt and put on his jacket. He paused to gaze at the woman's reflection in the mirrored tile over the mini-bar as she pulled her evening gown back up over her perfect body. She knew he was watching her reflection, but she didn't seem to mind.

"Zip me up?" she asked playfully.

Nathan turned around and stepped up to her as she turned her back to him. "I'd rather *unzip* you again, ma'am," he admitted as he zipped up the back of her dress.

"Now, Ensign," she teased as she turned to face him, "I think we've settled the score with that schmuck enough for one night. Besides, don't you think we should get back before the senator finishes his speech?"

Nathan was admiring her from behind as she headed for the door when it suddenly dawned on him. "Wait, I don't think I ever got your name." He didn't really care; it just felt like the polite thing to say.

"Oh, that's sweet, really," she giggled, "but I

don't think names are necessary." She began to walk away, turning back slightly to look at him as she took hold of the door knob. "Let's just say that I'm doing my part for our boys in uniform, and leave it at that." She flashed him a sly smile, opened the door, and left the room, leaving the door standing open behind her.

From outside, Nathan could hear his father ending his speech.

"And that is why I have decided that it is time for me to run for the office of President of the North American Union!"

The crowd outside exploded in excitement at the senator's startling announcement. Nathan just rolled his eyes.

"You have *got* to be kidding me."

* * *

"Nathan, honey," his mother called as she approached him at the bar. He had already finished half the bottle and was bound and determined to finish the rest in short order.

"Hello, Mother," he greeted, trying to sound sincere.

"I knew you'd show up," she declared, kissing his cheek. "I hope you didn't miss your father's speech."

"No such luck," he mumbled, picking up the bottle.

"Oh, put that bottle away, Nathan," she scolded. "You know how your father feels about that stuff." She grabbed a candy from the bar and handed it to him. "Here, sweetie. Have a mint."

She stepped back and looked at him in his dress uniform. "Oh, Nathan, I have to admit you do look handsome in that uniform. But did you have to wear it tonight of all nights? You know how your father feels about the fleet."

"Founders' Day *is* a patriotic holiday, Mother. And as you can see," he defended as he gestured toward the crowd, "I'm not the only one in uniform."

"I know, dear. But you *are* the only member of the Scott family in uniform. Now come on, honey," she added as she straightened his tie. "Let's go make nice for the cameras."

Why are the women in this family always straightening my tie?

The journey through the mingling crowd was as painful as Nathan had remembered it to be from his father's last campaign. It was a never ending stream of "yes, ma'ams" and "yes, sirs" along with stories about sons they all seemed to have that were his age or daughters they thought he should meet. Only this time, there was a new twist. It seemed that every old fart he greeted felt obligated to tell him a story about their days in the service. Of course, Nathan played it all off masterfully, just as his father had taught him. But it was all so pretentious and pointless. He really wished that he had gotten the chance to finish that bottle before his mother had found him. Instead, he would just have to distract himself as best he could with the image of that sexy little brunette as she slipped her dress back on.

But then he saw his father up ahead talking to the other politicians in his party. And he saw the look in his father's eyes when he spotted Nathan, in his uniform, dutifully following his mother through the crowd. It was that same look of disappointment that he always seemed to get from his father.

"Nathan! So glad you could make it, son!" the

senator exclaimed as Nathan and his mother approached. Nathan knew his father was just putting on a show for the crowd. The man could've been a professional actor.

"How are you doing, sir?" Nathan asked in perfect military fashion.

"What's with the *sir* crap?" his father exclaimed, holding out his arms. "Give your old man a hug!" He wrapped his arms around Nathan and gave him a warm embrace. As expected, without missing a beat, his father turned them both to face the nearest camera for a shot that would surely reach every link on the Earth-Net within seconds. It should have been no surprise to Nathan that his father would take an irritant and turn it into a photo-op. Nathan flashed a toothy smile for the cameras, unnaturally posing for the customary few seconds to allow all the photographers and videographers to collect their content. Nathan hated this part of his father's life. But even more so, he hated how he had become so accustomed to it that he played the part automatically without any forethought. It was something he definitely was not going to miss.

"Senator Scott!" one of the reporters hollered over the barrage of questions already being shouted at them. "How do you feel about your son's enlistment, considering your position against the EDF?" Nathan stole a glance at his father, knowing he would be quick to disarm the potentially embarrassing issue.

"Why, I'm as proud as any father could be!" he said. His statement had been made with such conviction that Nathan almost believed it himself. "What father wouldn't be proud of a son that had the courage and fortitude to take a stand for what he believed in?" The senator turned directly to the man asking the question and, more importantly, to the reporter's cameraman. "And just for the record, I want to make it perfectly clear that I am *not* against the Earth Defense Force. I simply want to restrict their capabilities to sub-light operations only so as not to provoke the Jung Dynasty into any undue actions. We still have a long way to go in the rebuilding of our *own* civilization before we start dreaming of colonizing other worlds again."

Perfectly played, as usual, Nathan thought.

"Ensign Scott," another reporter shouted, surprising Nathan. "How do you feel about your father's position on the military?"

It was an over-simplification of an extremely complicated question. But that didn't seem to matter to Nathan, as he blurted out the first thing that came to mind. "My father serves the people in his way, and I serve them in mine." Nathan turned away from the cameras to retreat to safer ground, his father following behind him as he placated the press with a few more sound bites on his way out.

"Jesus, Nathan," his father exclaimed as he followed him into the study, his protection detail closing the doors behind them. "I see you're still just blurting out whatever is on your mind."

"They don't care what's on my mind."

"Oh yes they do. They care about every word, every syllable, every action. Hell, they're even analyzing your body language these days... anything they can take and twist into something that will swing votes their way."

"It never seemed to matter much before." Nathan loosened his tie and took a seat on the sofa.

"You were *fifteen* during the last campaign. Nobody cared what you thought at that age," he pointed out as he paced around the room. "Besides, I was only running for the senate back then, not the presidency of the most influential nation on the planet. Hell, the last three North American presidents were selected to serve as the leader of the United Earth Republic. Someone has to lead this world safely into the next century. If I can win this election, then I'm almost certain to be sitting in Geneva within a year. Then I can really do something to help keep us safe."

Suddenly, the memory of his anonymous sexual encounter in a room down the hall no longer seemed a pleasant distraction. *I really should've gotten her name.*

Nathan immediately felt the need to defend himself. "Since when did you have aspirations to the presidency? I thought you always said that the real governing was done at the congressional level."

"I've said a lot of things over my lifetime, son. Not all of them have been entirely accurate."

This came as a surprise to Nathan, who couldn't remember his father ever admitting a mistake so easily.

"But things *have* changed drastically since we learned about the state of the core systems. The Jung *are* a real threat, and the population in general doesn't take it seriously because the enemy is over twenty light years away!" The senator stopped pacing and leaned against his desk, facing his son. "We've advanced so quickly over the last hundred years that people aren't ready to think in terms of light years. It's still an impossibly distant place to them."

"But if you *do* see the Jung as a threat, then *why*

are you so against expanding the fleet? I would've thought that *you* of all people would support us. Hell, you were all for getting us into space when you were my age."

"As I said, things have changed," his father repeated. As usual, Nathan was being shortsighted. It was a failing that his father had recognized in his son at an early age. It wasn't that he couldn't see the big picture; he just never bothered.

"What's changed?" Nathan begged. "What has changed so much that it would cause you to do a complete turnaround in such a short time?"

His father took a deep breath, letting it out slowly as he rose from his perch and strolled over to stare out the window again. His son was right. The change in his position on the buildup of the Earth Defense Force had completely changed over the last four years. And it had caused a tremendous rift to develop between them. The irony of it was that deep down inside, he knew that his *true* position had *never* changed. It was only his *public* position that he had been forced to change. He only wished that he could find a way to make his son understand without exposing the truth. "It's complicated," he finally resigned.

Nathan wanted to press further, but he knew that 'it's complicated' meant that his father either didn't want to, or couldn't, talk about it further.

"I have no delusions that you and I are ever going to agree on this," his father admitted. "Just do me a favor, will you son? No more public shots across my bow until after the election?"

As if on cue, his mother entered the room to end the dispute. "There you are," she said to her husband as she entered. She suddenly noticed Nathan sitting on the sofa. "Oh, Nathan honey, I didn't see you." She kissed her husband on the cheek, noticing the tension in the room. "Am I interrupting?" she asked, knowing full well that she was. Over the last few years, she had developed an uncanny knack for entering the room at just the right moment to break the two of them apart. It seemed impossible, but somehow Nathan was sure that she did it on purpose, and for just that reason.

"Don't worry, sir," Nathan assured his father as he rose to leave. "I'll behave."

"Nathan," his mother scolded at his attitude.

"It doesn't matter anyway. I report for duty on the Reliant tomorrow morning and she's scheduled to be under way in a few days for border patrol out in the Oort ." Nathan kissed his mother's cheek and gave her a polite hug so as not to mess up her outfit, in case there were more pictures to be taken. "After today the press won't have access to me for at least a few years. That should get you safely through the election," he promised his father as he reached out to shake his hand. "Good luck, sir," Nathan announced in a show of good faith. The strange thing was he actually meant it this time.

"Thank you, son." His father took Nathan's hand, placing his other hand on Nathan's shoulder. Despite their differences, the senator dearly loved his youngest child and was prouder of him than Nathan would ever know. And though he hid it well, the news of his son's impending departure on a relatively dangerous patrol both shocked and worried him deeply. "Smooth sailing, Ensign."

Now Nathan too was shocked. For it was the first time his father had called him by his rank. It felt as if he had finally accepted Nathan's decision to enlist, despite his father's repeated objections. "I'll try to keep in touch," he promised as he turned to leave.

"Yes, please do," the senator mumbled, more to himself than anyone else in the room.

For a good minute after Nathan had left, the senator and his wife said nothing.

"You have to do something, Dayton," his wife finally insisted. "You can't let him go out there. We might never see him again." There was genuine fear in her voice.

"I'll try, honey," the senator promised as he put his arms around her. "I'll try."

* * *

Nathan stood at the edge of the driveway waiting for the car that would take him to the airport to catch the next shuttle back to the academy. The party was still in full swing, with the orchestra playing even livelier than before. He could've stayed longer, maybe even gotten lucky again. But after his father's big announcement, he preferred to lie low until he could get back to safe ground.

He had grown up in a politically active family, and he had tired of it years ago. That had been one of the reasons he had joined the fleet, for it would get him about as far away from all of this as humanly possible.

There had been few options that had appealed to him. His degree in pre-plague history could have landed him a decent career as a professor, if he had continued on for his doctorate. But then he still would've been subject to the constant scrutiny that resulted from his father's public service. And he simply couldn't imagine dealing with that for the rest of his life.

His sisters all had their own careers, and later had all married and started popping out kids in an effort to build the Earth's population back up to true industrial levels. But he had grown tired of school, tired of family, and certainly tired of politics. And if he had hung around much longer, that's probably where he too would have ended up.

The fact was he had needed a change, and a drastic one at that. Military service had never even been a consideration in the past. But the idea of joining the fleet and living out in space, only making it back to Earth every few years? Well that was enticing enough that one slightly drunk night with his buddies was all it had taken to get him to sign ten years of his life away, even if it had meant another four years of school before getting off the planet.

The academy had gone by quickly, and it had been far more interesting than college had ever been. The physical and combat training had been fun as well. Nathan had never considered himself to be athletic but had discovered he was far more adept at such activities than he would have thought possible. He never considered himself a 'super-soldier', but he could hold his own with most of his class.

It had been the simulations that had given him the most trouble. At first, they had been more about hands-on training than anything else, and in that he had excelled. But when they started testing his ability to make command decisions, he felt awkward and unsure of himself. In more than one simulation, he had failed to act quickly enough to avoid abrupt and catastrophic conclusions.

Nevertheless, he had passed his practical exams

in the command simulations. His roommate at the academy often joked that Nathan's unusually consistent good luck had gotten him through the sims. And Nathan knew that his friend had been at least partially correct.

So he had graduated the academy and had been rated as both a navigator and a pilot. He was looking forward to his upcoming duty on the Reliant. She was the fleet's oldest cruiser, and although she had never fired a shot in anger, she had seen several patrols, having been in service for more than a decade. With a crew of over 300, Nathan would be just another name on the ship's roster, probably serving on a backup flight crew on the least favored rotation. And that was fine with him.

"Well, well, well," his brother's voice came from behind. "If it isn't Ensign Scott, the prodigal son, returned home to stir up family dissent one more time." Eli was a good twelve years older, and he and Nathan had never gotten along.

"Hello, Eli." Nathan was biting his tongue, trying to remember if there was ever a time the two of them had talked that didn't end poorly. "What have you been up to?" He was trying to make meaningless small talk, hoping to avoid an argument long enough for his ride to arrive and make his escape.

"Funny you should ask that, Nathan. I should be spending time with my wife and kids, enjoying this wonderful Founders' Day celebration. But instead, I spent the better part of an hour bribing a photographer to give up his rather suggestive photos of you and that slut you screwed in the anteroom tonight."

"Still running image patrol for Dad, huh, Eli?" Nathan knew it was the wrong thing to say even as it passed his lips. Eli had always wanted to follow in their father's footsteps and enter politics himself, but he had not been the son blessed with the natural charm required for public life. So the senator's oldest son had been forced to spend his career chasing their father and putting out his fires. It was a sour pill for Eli to swallow, and Nathan was sure that it had always been the primary cause of their ongoing feud.

"At least I'm not trying to ruin it," Eli accused. "So, who was she?"

"None of your damned business."

Eli was obviously exasperated at Nathan's attitude. "Why did you even show up, Nate?"

"I was invited." *Hmm, sarcasm, another bad choice.*

"Still the troublemaker, I see."

"Better than being a kiss-ass," Nathan responded in a matter-of-fact tone. He was already on a roll, so he figured there was little use in stopping now.

"I would've thought the academy would break you of that habit."

"Funny how that habit only seems to surface when I'm around family."

"Then why don't you do us all a big favor and just stay away? Or at least keep your attitude under control until after the election. Do you think you can do that much for your family?"

Nathan wanted to say something more, a lot more. In fact, what he really wanted to do was to punch Eli right in his smug mouth. But there were cameras everywhere, and the car that would take him away from this circus once and for all was pulling into the long, circular driveway.

Nathan turned around and stepped up to Eli,

standing right in his face and giving him a stone cold stare, the same one he had learned to use when standing at attention during inspections at the academy. It took Eli by surprise and for a moment he was unsure of what to expect. He had never before seen such a stern look in Nathan's eyes.

Nathan took his brother's hand firmly and shook it once. "Give my best to your family, Eli." He let go of Eli's hand and gave him what appeared to onlookers to be a brotherly hug. Eli's hands dangled at his sides in disbelief as Nathan whispered in his brother's ear, "So long, asshole."

Nathan released his still shocked brother and stepped aside to smile and wave at the cameras that were watching from the walkway near the main house. Then he turned and got into the back seat of the car that had just pulled up behind him.

And that is the last time I'll have to play that game.

CHAPTER TWO

Despite a slight hangover, Nathan arrived at the Academy Flight Complex bright and early. The previous night's events had only served to remind him of how desperately he wanted to leave it all behind and start anew. Today, he would leave the surface of the Earth, not to return for several years. It was the perfect way to begin his new life.

The complex was unusually busy that morning, as most of the graduates from the academy's North American campus were also departing for new assignments. As he worked his way through the crowd, he saw many familiar faces, as they bid farewell to fellow graduates and underclassmen. It had been a long four years for them all, during which most had formed significant bonds.

The graduates were leaving everything they knew behind, only to be cooped up inside big, metal, high-tech boxes hurtling through space. It was both exciting and frightening at the same time. All these young men and women, from every walk of life and every corner of the North American continent, each for their own reasons, had left their lives and their loved ones behind. They had endured exhaustive education and grueling physical training. And many of them had failed along the way, forced to return home in disgrace.

And it wasn't just on this continent. There were similar scenes playing out on fleet academy campuses in both Europe and Asia. Each of them was turning out hundreds of graduates per year. Still, it was only a fraction of what was needed for the Earth to build an adequate defense, for the Jung controlled the resources of four of the six core worlds, as well as many of the lesser colonies out on the fringe.

Despite the risks, volunteers came in droves each year. And those not accepted to the academy contributed in other ways: as ground forces, trained to defend against surface assault, or as workers and technicians, who built the ships needed to defend the Earth from space. But they all shared the same sense of purpose. They were defending their burgeoning homeworld as it rose from a thousand years of darkness and despair.

As he waited in line to check in, Nathan thought about his academy roommate, Luis. They had become the best of friends during their time at the academy, and Nathan was quite certain that he would not have graduated had it not been for his friend's support. Luis had been assigned to the Intrepid as a Tactician and Weapons specialist. Since the Intrepid was not due back for a few weeks, he had chosen to spend time with his family in South America before departure.

Nathan had envied Luis in that sense. He had such a strong and supportive family. They had been from a relatively remote and impoverished area, so they had yet to reap the full benefits that the knowledge found on the Data Ark had already bestowed upon the more populous regions. Had it not been for the exhaustive efforts of fleet recruiters, Luis's unique gifts might never have been added to the fleet's growing ranks, and Nathan would've missed out on a very important friendship.

"Next!" The voice interrupted Nathan's reminiscence.

"Ensign Scott, Nathan R," he reported to the officer at the check-in desk before reading off his service number. "I'm scheduled for the next shuttle up to the Reliant."

The duty officer punched in Nathan's information, pausing to compare his face and description against the one displayed on his computer screen.

"I'm sorry, Ensign, but it seems there's been a slight change in your orders," the officer reported.

"Sir?" Although this kind of thing was not uncommon, it still caught Nathan by surprise.

"You're still scheduled for departure, but not to the Reliant." The officer looked up at Nathan, smiling. "You've been reassigned to the Aurora."

"The Aurora? But I thought she wasn't even in service yet."

"They bumped up her trials. She'll be under way within a week or two. That's probably why you got reassigned. She needs crew and the next class won't graduate for six months."

Nathan wasn't sure what to think. He had been studying the specifications on the Reliant for weeks. He had even spent extra time in the simulator familiarizing himself with her flight characteristics. He didn't know anything about the Aurora, as most of her specs were still classified.

The duty officer noticed Nathan's dismay and tried to help. "Hell, you should be happy. The Reliant's a slow old girl. She can barely make half light. I hear the Aurora's FTLs will get her up to ten times light. You're going to be traveling faster and farther than anyone has in nearly a millennium!"

"Yes, sir," Nathan responded, bewildered by the thought. He had wanted to get away from Earth, and this would surely do it.

* * *

The Orbital Assembly Platform was the largest structure to be constructed in space since the recovery began. Positioned in high orbit, the platform was capable of building or repairing two ships simultaneously. Nathan remembered that the facility had been constructed more than a decade earlier, just after the Earth had learned of the Jung Dynasty's takeover of the core systems. Since then, the platform had produced six Defender-class warships, starting with the Reliant.

Those ships had since seen a few upgrades, including improved sub-light propulsion systems as well as more powerful rail guns. Many had wanted to fit them with the new faster-than-light propulsion systems that had been constructed using designs found in the Data Ark, but it was a hotly contested issue on Earth these days.

The compromise had been the construction of two new ships, the Celestia and the Aurora. Both were in the final stages of construction and were due to begin their shakedown cruises within a few months. These new Explorer-class ships, while still well armed, were designed to serve as ships of exploration and diplomacy, as well as providing defensive support if needed. It was believed that this new class of ship would appear less threatening than the older Defender-class ships. Hence the United Earth government felt more comfortable giving them the ability to travel at superluminal speeds.

It had taken several hours for the passenger shuttle to climb up to the platform's orbit. For Nathan, it had been a difficult and uncomfortable journey. Besides being slow, these older shuttles were cramped, poorly lit, and poorly ventilated. And the ensign next to him still smelled much like the spirits he had consumed during the previous night's Founders' Day celebration. The only way Nathan had to pass the time was to stare out the viewport at the Earth below. And to make matters worse, the shuttles were not equipped with artificial gravity plating, since they spent no more than a few hours at a time in weightlessness. Despite numerous zero-gravity training exercises, Nathan had never quite gotten used to the sensation of floating, and neither had his stomach. Luckily, he had managed to make it through the flight without having to use his emesis bag. And he was quite relieved when the shuttle touched down on the flight deck and rolled into the hangar bay, the familiar sensation of gravity sweeping over him.

As Nathan entered the boarding area, he could see his new home, the Aurora. She was smaller than the Defender-class ships by as much as a third. He could only see the upper half of her from this deck, but he could already see that she was far sleeker in her design. Nathan found himself drawn to her, moving away from the boarding line to stand closer to the large viewports where he could gaze upon her more closely.

She had a long snub bow that spread out in a gentle curve on its way aft. Around her middle, her lines tapered inward briefly before flaring back out to make room for her oversized main propulsion section. Nathan could not help but notice that her disproportionate drive section looked like it had been stolen from a larger vessel and slapped onto her stern.

Starting at her bow, the topside of her hull rose at a gentle slope, angling upward on its way aft and up from her sides toward her centerline until she abruptly became flat on top. It was like a gentle hill with a flattened summit. And on the aft side of this hill was a sharp drop into which the opening to the flight deck was situated.

"Reporting for duty?"

"Huh?" Nathan turned around and saw that everyone else had already boarded and he was left standing alone.

"Are you reporting for duty, Ensign?" the officer at the boarding desk repeated.

"Oh, yes, sir. Ensign Scott, Nathan R." He saluted smartly.

"Ah, yes. A member of our freshly appropriated crew." The officer checked his display before continuing. "Very well, Ensign Scott. Your quarters are on C deck, cabin one-fourteen. I suggest you stow your duffel and report to the quartermaster on E deck to pick up your duty gear. There's an orientation meeting in the main briefing room on B deck at fifteen hundred. If you hurry, you should have time to grab some chow before then."

"Yes, sir." Nathan instinctively went to salute again, but the officer held out his hand instead.

"Welcome to the crew, Ensign."

"Thank you, sir."

Nathan picked up his bag and headed through the large open hatchway onto the boarding ramp. The ramp was enclosed in a tube that extended from the platform out to the Aurora's main boarding hatch. The upper half of the tube was clear, giving Nathan an unobstructed view of the ship outside as he approached.

Like most ships in the fleet, the Aurora's undersides were dark gray and her uppers off-white. As he walked through the dimly lit tube, Nathan could see dozens of workers floating about outside in the vacuum of space. Clad in bright red spacesuits, they went about performing various assembly tasks on the exterior of the ship. In addition to the workers, there were several work pods, each looking like large coffins with windows and arms. Attached to the ends of long, spindly, articulated arms, they moved pieces about the ship to be fitted into place by the floating red workers.

As he neared the end of the boarding tube, he could see the hull of the ship around her boarding hatch. To the left of the hatch were the ship's name and registry number, 'UES AURORA, CV-01.' Nathan paused, staring at the name, feeling the need to appreciate the moment.

"Touch her," someone said from inside the ship.

"Excuse me?" Nathan looked through the hatchway and saw a stern-looking master chief watching him from just inside. He was dressed in combat fatigues, with Special Operations patches on his shoulders and a gun belt around his waist.

"Touch the outside of the ship before you set foot on her," the master chief explained. "It helps remind you what she is, makes her real."

Nathan looked at the master chief like he was crazy. "Are you kidding me?"

"Hell, no! Every soul serving on this ship has to touch her outsides. It's bad luck if you don't." The chief paused, waiting for Nathan to follow his advice. "Go on!" he said abruptly, startling Nathan. "She ain't gonna bite ya!"

Nathan reluctantly touched the hull of the ship just below her name. He didn't actually believe the master chief but figured it couldn't hurt to play along. The hull was smooth and cold to his touch, its finish perfect and untarnished. And surprisingly to Nathan, it did seem more real after touching her, like she was alive.

"That's eight out of ten!" the master chief laughed to the clerk behind the security desk just inside the boarding hatch. "I'm on a roll today!"

Nathan frowned at the master chief as he stepped through the hatchway and onto the ship, walking through the airlock and into the entryway. "Ensign Scott," he reported to the clerk sitting at the security desk. "Requesting permission to come aboard."

"Don't feel bad, Ensign. At least he only told you to touch it," the clerk said, smiling. "He got me to lick it."

Nathan smiled at the thought. "How do I get to C one-fourteen?"

"First left, then follow the corridor around the hangar bay to the far side of the ship. And welcome aboard."

"Thanks."

Nathan made his way down the corridor as it wrapped around the inside of the ship over to the far side of the hangar bay. Every so often, he would have to step through an open hatch to pass through the various bulkheads used to compartmentalize the ship in case of sudden decompression.

The corridor itself was not abnormally narrow,

with enough room for several people to pass by at least three abreast. Yet it felt much more cramped, possibly due to the maze of conduits and pipes that were always ducking in and out of walls as they snaked their way throughout the ship.

The inside of the Aurora was no more colorful than her outside, with the usual dark gray floors and light gray walls. The ceilings were medium gray, but very little of them were visible due to all manner of ducting and conduits. As he moved between compartments, he kept checking the navigation signs posted above each hatchway and on overhead support beams. Although the ship's internal layout was pretty simple, the last thing he wanted to do was get lost on his first day aboard.

As he neared his cabin, Nathan passed a tall, muscular fellow leaning against a wall as he flirted with a Middle-Eastern woman in medical attire. The man cast Nathan a quick glance, checking to make sure he wasn't outranked. Satisfied that he did not have to salute, the fellow continued his conversation as Nathan passed. A few more steps and Nathan found his cabin, stepping inside.

The cabin was small with just enough room for a bunk on either side and a couple of lockers built into the wall between them. Up against the far wall at the foot of the bunk farthest from the entrance was a small computer desk. Above the desk there was a large view screen built into the wall in a manner that made it seem more like a window.

The hulls of all EDF ships were composed of several different layers that, together, were nearly three meters thick, so windows were not possible. Instead, view screens were designed to act as virtual windows to the outside. Each of them could display the view from any of the hundreds of cameras scattered along the outside of the hull. In addition, they could be used as computer terminals or entertainment displays. The viewer in this compartment was set to its default view, which was of the space directly outside. Nathan stepped closer to look out the virtual window. He knew it was really just a live camera feed, but the incredible clarity made it nearly impossible to tell the difference. Through it, he could see the trusses of the assembly framework that surrounded the ship, as well as the Earth itself as it rotated below.

After a few moments gazing out the viewer, Nathan moved over to inspect the bunks, noticing that each of them also had a viewport built into the wall. The bunks had additional storage compartments above and below, and were equipped with a roll-down privacy door that also enabled the bunks to seal and pressurize in an emergency. In the event of a sudden decompression of the entire section, the occupant could survive inside their bunk for days while they awaited rescue.

The room was spartan, cramped, and had obviously been designed so that nothing would get tossed about during abrupt maneuvers. But the designers had been thoughtful enough to make it as comfortable a space as possible.

Nathan saw that someone else's duffel bag was already on the bunk nearest the door, so he tossed his duffel onto the empty one against the opposite wall.

"You must be my new roomie!" a voice boomed from behind.

Nathan turned to see the same dark-haired man from the hallway. He had a full head of thick, wavy hair and steely blue eyes. He was a bit taller than Nathan and was obviously stronger. "Yeah, I guess so. Nathan Scott," he introduced himself, extending his hand.

"Vladimir Kamenetskiy," he announced proudly in what Nathan recognized as a Russian accent. The animated Russian man shook Nathan's hand vigorously as he continued. "I am engineer, first class. And, I am computer systems specialist," he added proudly.

"Well from what I've seen so far, you're going to be busy for the next few weeks."

"Yes, yes. It is wonderful. This ship has so many interesting systems," he exclaimed. "I am like kid in candy store, yes?"

"Yeah, I can see how you would be."

"Yes, yes. This is true. Did you know this ship has *four* antimatter reactors? And the engines, oh, they are incredible!"

"Really?"

"Yes! But do not get me started on this," he warned. "What is it that you do, Nathan?"

"Helm and navigation."

"Great! I fix it, you fly it!" he announced, slapping Nathan on his shoulder. "We will make a good team, you and I!"

"I guess so," Nathan agreed, as he turned to start unpacking his bag.

"No time for that, my friend. We must report to the quartermaster, for we are not properly dressed for this ship." Vladimir pointed to the Fleet Academy patches they still sported on their sleeves.

Nathan followed his new roommate's suggestion, leaving his bag on his bunk. "Lead the way, roomie."

"Excellent!" he exclaimed as they exited the

cabin.

Nathan followed him out of their cabin and down the corridor, his excitable new roommate rambling on about the engines as they walked. *This is going to be interesting.*

* * *

The main briefing room was filled with the sounds of conversation as the newest members of the Aurora's crew talked amongst themselves and waited for orientation to begin. Being a good-sized room, it had several rows of chairs in order to accommodate the fifty people in attendance.

"Attention!" the Officer of the Deck ordered. Everyone in the room quickly stood tall and straight with their eyes fixed forward, as Commander Montero, the ship's executive officer and second in command, entered the room.

"At ease," he ordered as he stepped up to the podium. "Be seated." The commander paused to allow everyone a moment to get situated, scanning the faces in the room. He was a tall, lanky man with a rugged face and strong dark eyes. On the way to the briefing, Vladimir had told Nathan that the commander had a reputation as a stickler for details and had probably read all of their personnel records prior to their arrival.

"Good afternoon, everyone. I'm Commander Montero, your executive officer, and I'd like to welcome all of you aboard. The Aurora is the first of the fleet's new Explorer-class ships, which means that she will have plenty of bugs to work out. But she is also a state-of-the-art design, based upon the most advanced concepts and technologies yet found in the Data Ark."

The commander picked up a remote and dimmed the lights. An image of the ship's design faded in on the view screen built into the wall behind him, replacing the ship's shoulder patch design that had been there only moments before. As he spoke, the display faded from one image to the next, revealing the Aurora's overall design and layout through a series of perfectly crafted schematics and illustrations.

"As you all probably know, the Explorer class was conceived for an entirely new mission profile. Unlike her predecessors, who were designed to stand their ground and slug it out with an enemy, the Aurora is built to move. She is very fast and highly maneuverable. She can strike quickly and hard, and then make a quick escape. Her designers like to say that she can get out of trouble faster than she can get into it. On the surface, she is a ship of exploration and diplomacy, but at her heart, she is a considerable tactical platform that can be used in just about any combat role. And she will be the fleet's first ship with faster-than-light capabilities."

Until that moment, rumors of the Explorer-class ships getting FTL capabilities had been just that, rumors. Now that her executive officer had just confirmed it, an excited murmur began to rise in the briefing room. The commander expected this reaction, pausing for a moment to let the whispers die down before continuing.

"The Aurora is primarily a carrier vessel, and thus is designed around and in support of her flight decks. I will not be reviewing any specifics during this briefing, as I expect that each of you will be spending quite a bit of time getting to know her over the next few weeks."

The lights came back up, and the display on the wall faded back to the Aurora's shoulder patch design. Commander Montero looked around the room again, observing their reactions before continuing.

"Normally, it would be another couple of months before this ship would be starting her shakedown cruise. Hell, we weren't even scheduled to start taking on crew until next month. But Fleet Command, in all its infinite wisdom, has decided to step up our launch date by a good two months. Exactly why, I do not know, so don't bother asking. What I *do* know is that we've got two months of work to do and only two weeks to do it in. And on top of that, I have to find the time to train all of you so that we don't crash and burn this baby on our first lap around the solar system."

"Now, I'm going to turn you over to Lieutenant Commander Kaguchi, who will call out your section assignments."

Lieutenant Commander Kaguchi, a stout Japanese officer in his late thirties, stepped up to the podium and began calling out names and duty assignments. Vladimir watched for every person called, as if he wanted to connect names with faces. Nathan just sat quietly, waiting to hear his own name.

"Kamenetskiy, Vladimir!"

"Yes, sir!" Vladimir answered.

"Engineering, main propulsion and power. Report to Lieutenant Commander Patel."

"That's what you wanted, right?" Nathan whispered, as the lieutenant commander continued calling out assignments.

"Yes," Vladimir answered, hiding his excitement.

"Then you're happy, right?" Nathan was a bit confused by his new roommate's lack of emotion.

"Of course."

"Sure couldn't tell by looking."

"Believe me, inside, I am very happy. I am overjoyed." A grin came across Vladimir's face as he looked sideways at Nathan and winked.

"Nash, Jessica!"

"Yes, sir!"

"Special Operations and Intelligence! Report to Master Chief Johansen."

Nathan turned his head in the direction of the woman's voice, as it struck him as familiar. He had just about given up trying to see her face when suddenly the ensign blocking his view leaned back, revealing the same brunette he had met at the party the night before, only this time she wasn't wearing a tight little evening dress; she was in a duty uniform sporting Aurora shoulder patches, just like everyone else in the room.

"Oh shit," Nathan whispered as he slumped back in his seat, trying to avoid being spotted.

"What is wrong?"

"I know her."

Vladimir looked in the direction of Ensign Nash. "You know this woman? She is very beautiful. You must introduce me." Vladimir straightened up, raising his hand as if to wave to her.

"What are you doing?" Nathan protested, grabbing Vladimir's hand. "Are you crazy? She'll see us!"

"I thought you said you know her?"

"Well, I don't mean I know her, know her. I mean I *know* her."

"Nathan, please. You do not make sense."

"I mean, I met her, last night at a party. We'd

both been drinking..."

"Ah, then you *know* her!" Vladimir realized. "Then you *definitely* must introduce me."

Nathan peeked toward her to make sure she hadn't noticed them. It was a big ship, and if he was lucky, there was a chance that...

"Scott, Nathan!" the commander called out.

"Yes, sir!" he answered instinctively.

"Helm and Navigation! Report to Captain Roberts."

Nathan sank back down in his chair, peeking toward Jessica just in time to see a mischievous smirk on her face. "You have got to be kidding me," he mumbled.

"I think I may have underestimated you, my friend," Vladimir whispered as he patted Nathan on the shoulder.

"Taylor, Cameron!"

"Yes, sir!" the woman a few chairs down called out.

"Helm and Navigation! Report to Captain Roberts."

Nathan leaned forward slightly to see past Vladimir. She was a few years younger than Nathan, with shoulder-length brown hair. She was of medium height with angular features and appeared to be quite disciplined and business-like in her manner. Even though her gaze never wavered from looking at the podium, he was sure she could see him. As Nathan turned his eyes forward again, she stole a quick glance, sizing up her competition.

Having completed calling out the assignments, the lieutenant commander stepped away from the podium, allowing Commander Montero to finish the briefing. "The next two weeks will be difficult.

Besides your accelerated training regimen, you will also be called upon to help with some of the finishing work within your respective departments. Then, upon completion of your training, some of you will be promoted to head your teams. In turn, you will be responsible for training the next group of graduates due out in six months. Until that group is trained, this ship will be operating on a skeleton crew of one hundred instead of her standard complement of three hundred, so the long hours will continue well after your training has concluded."

The commander paused, stepping out from behind the podium and leaning against it in order to strike a less formal posture with his new crew. "Captain Roberts and I are both aware that we will be asking a lot of each and every one of you over the next six months. But you are Fleet Academy graduates, which means you are the best our planet has to offer. Only the best get into the academy, and only the *Best of Class* get assigned to ships like the Aurora."

That last statement gave Nathan pause. He had done all right at the academy, finishing thirty-second out of a class of five hundred, but he knew for a fact he wasn't *Best of Class*, especially considering the problems he experienced in the command simulations. He had felt lucky when he was looking at being on a backup graveyard flight team on the Reliant. But now he had a shot at becoming the lead helmsman for the newest, fastest ship in the fleet? Not only did he feel like he didn't deserve it, but he wasn't sure if he even *wanted* the responsibility. That's when he started to suspect his father's handiwork in his sudden reassignment. But why? What did he hope to accomplish? Was he trying to force him to accept responsibility, like he had been preaching to him his whole life? Or maybe, he was setting him up to fail, hoping that he'd give up on a life in space and take a nice, safe posting back on Earth. That would certainly please his mother. All of a sudden, Nathan wasn't so sure his plan to leave it all behind and start over was going to work as well as he'd hoped.

The commander returned to his place behind the podium before continuing. "Until further notice, the duty hours of this ship are zero eight hundred to twenty-two hundred. There will be no days off until after the first test flight in two weeks. All crew report to your department heads to begin training. Dismissed!" Commander Montero stepped away from the podium and exited the briefing room, with Lieutenant Commander Kaguchi right behind him.

Vladimir suddenly turned to face Nathan, excitedly demanding, "You must give me details." Now that the briefing was over, he was dying to know more about Nathan's tryst with Ensign Nash.

Nathan turned to him, all set to share the events of the previous night, when he noticed Ensign Taylor hurriedly making her way out of the briefing room. Suddenly, he felt the need to follow her. "Vlad, my friend, gentlemen do not kiss and tell." Nathan got up and left, patting Vladimir on the shoulder on his way out.

"Gentlemen? What gentlemen?" Vladimir turned to his departing roommate. "But we are roomies, Nathan!" But it was too late. Nathan was already on his way out the door.

Nathan entered the corridor outside the briefing

room just in time to see Cameron turning the corner down the corridor to his right. After breaking into a jog, Nathan caught up with her as she was heading up the ramp to the command deck.

"Ensign Taylor," he said as he caught up to her. She barely reacted to his presence, not slowing her stride or missing a step as she ascended the long ramp. "Hi, I'm Nathan Scott." Nathan offered his hand as he fell into step alongside her.

"I know who you are, Ensign," she answered. Although Nathan hadn't expected any particular type of response, her absolute lack of interest or emotion *was* a bit surprising, as was her disregard for his offer of a handshake.

"Really? So who am I, then?"

"Ensign Scott, Nathan R. Graduated from the North American Fleet Academy, thirty-second in your class despite rather mediocre scores in command simulations. Specialized in Piloting and Navigation. Studied Earth history at a private college. Son of Senator Dayton Scott, who just announced he is running for president of the NAU." She flashed a fake smile at him. "Did I miss anything?"

"Yeah, you left out that I flunked chemistry in secondary school. How is it you know so much about me?"

"I make it a point to know who I'm working with."

"Well, that's encouraging—I think." There was no response for an awkward moment. "So, I guess we'll be working together."

"In a manner of speaking." She was either being coy or rude. He wasn't sure which just yet.

"So it's kind of exciting, huh?" he asked, trying desperately to strike up some kind of friendly conversation with her, but he didn't seem to be having any luck.

Cameron couldn't figure out if Nathan was trying to size her up, hit on her, or was just being polite. It made her wonder if he even realized what was at stake. One thing was for sure; she was *not* going to let her guard down around him.

"The XO was laying it on kind of thick back there, wasn't he?" Nathan fumbled. "All that *Best of the Best* stuff."

"*Best of Class,*" she corrected.

"Huh?"

"What he said was *Best of Class,*" she reiterated as they came to the top of the ramp and turned towards the bridge.

"Whatever," Nathan muttered. He was pretty sure now; she was just rude.

Cameron glanced at him for the first time since he'd started talking to her, put off by his cavalier response. "Look, Ensign, I don't know if you realize this, but you and I, we're in competition with one another."

"Hey, I'm not looking to compete with anyone," he defended. "I'll be happy if I just don't screw anything up."

Cameron stopped short of the entrance to the bridge, turning to Nathan to confront him. "Let me spell this out for you, okay? It takes two people to fly this ship, a helmsman *and* a navigator. And the helmsman is the senior member of that team. The first one to take the helm will probably end up lead pilot, in command of all three flight teams once this ship is fully staffed. Get it?" she said, stabbing him in the chest with her pointed index finger to emphasize her point.

"Look," Nathan assured her, "I don't care who's

in charge. I just wanna do a good job."

"Great, then you won't be disappointed when you're sitting second seat to me."

Nathan stopped dead in his tracks, stunned by her brazen attitude. That's when he noticed that she was headed for the captain's ready room. And all of a sudden, Nathan found that he *did* care about the lead pilot position. In fact, he cared about it more than he ever could've imagined. So much so that he ran to catch up with her to make sure that they met the captain together, as equals.

Cameron entered the captain's ready room slightly ahead of Nathan. The room was larger than one might expect, considering the way that every spare centimeter had been maximized throughout the rest of the ship. There was a single desk that faced the bow, with the captain sitting in his chair behind it, studying his display screen. Two guest chairs sat in front of the desk, with a couch along the forward bulkhead that appeared to be more comfortable than Nathan's bunk. Directly to the left of the doorway, mounted into the forward bulkhead was a wall-to-wall display screen that, at the moment, showed what looked to be the view from someone's beach house overlooking a secluded stretch of beach along some tropical shore down on Earth.

Other than the display screen, and a few certificates and degrees, the room had yet to be decorated. However, on the waist-high counter behind the captain, there were pictures of his wife, two grown sons who were both dressed in fleet uniforms, and a daughter posing with her husband and three children.

Captain Roberts appeared to be in his late fifties, with a full head of wavy gray hair and a slight widow's peak. His face was rugged and square, with an air that spoke of considerable time spent outdoors. He had an intelligent demeanor about him, punctuated by dark blue eyes that always seemed to be calculating something. Every look seemed to have a purpose, seemed to be registering something in his brain. He glanced up at Nathan and then Cameron, sizing each of them up in a single look before returning his attention to his desktop display. All that Nathan knew of him was that he had served as the executive officer on the Valiant prior to taking command of the Aurora.

"Ensigns Taylor and Scott reporting, sir!" announced Cameron. Nathan silently cursed himself for not taking the lead and introducing them instead of letting her do the honors. But then again, she had entered the room first.

"At ease," the captain said, his focus still on his display.

Nathan and Cameron both assumed the standard pose, feet slightly apart with arms behind their back.

After what seemed like an eternally long and uncomfortable pause, the captain finally began to speak without looking up at them. "Ensign Taylor," he said, addressing Cameron first, "graduated fifteenth in your class at the European Academy."

Nathan felt his first strike; her fifteenth ranking far surpassing his measly thirty-second.

"Scored perfect marks in all courses and exams, exemplary performance in all simulations, handling every situation according to protocol. Comments from your training officer state, 'Shows impressive command decision-making capabilities.'" The captain looked up from his display at Cameron. "I am impressed."

"Thank you, sir," Cameron replied smartly.

Captain Roberts looked back down at his display, and after a single tap on the screen, his expression soured. "Ensign Scott," he continued, "with you, I am not so impressed."

Strike two, Nathan thought.

"Average marks, barely passing on the command sims, and numerous reports of severe *bending* of the rules, as well as some rather unorthodox approaches to a few of those simulations." The captain leaned back in his chair, looking Nathan over and sizing him up. "*Your* training officer wrote, 'Shows interesting command potential.'" Captain Roberts thought about that one for a moment. "Interesting command potential," he repeated. "Not quite sure what that means." The captain leaned forward again. "We'll have to revisit that one another day."

Cameron had to fight to keep a satisfied smirk from forming on her face.

The captain rose from his seat and walked around the end of his desk, coming to rest in a semi-sitting position on its leading edge, much like Nathan's father had often done. "I suppose my XO has already given you his *Best of Class* speech. So I have to wonder, Ensign Scott, if you're asking yourself, 'How the hell did I get here?' Did the captain piss off some brass hat up at Fleet Command? Did the Reliant's XO take one look at your sheet and say, 'No way I'm taking this guy.' Or maybe it was your daddy, the senator, who pulled some strings to get his baby boy reassigned to a less dangerous mission."

"It had crossed my mind, sir," Nathan admitted.

"Honesty?" the captain said with mock surprise.

"Good, I like that. I can work with that." He rose from his desk and moved back around behind it. "The fact of the matter is it doesn't matter. You're here and I have to make the two of you into a top-notch flight team. And I've only got two weeks to do it. So here's the deal. For the next two weeks, you two are gonna eat, drink, and sleep in the flight simulator. When you're *not* in that simulator, you'll be running scenarios in the command simulator. And if you think the simulations at the academy were hard, Ensign Scott, wait until you see the scenarios my people come up with. They'll make you cry like a baby."

The captain sat down again. "In the end, one of you will take the helm, and the other will take the navigator's chair. Whoever takes the role of pilot *will* be promoted and *will* be in charge of the team, and eventually in charge of all the Aurora's flight teams. But let's make sure we're clear on one thing. Regardless of who takes what role, the two of you will learn to work as a team. Is that understood?"

"Yes, sir!" they responded in unison.

"I don't know if Fleet *meant* to give me two polar opposites to fly my ship or not. Let's just hope that you two will learn to draw on each other's strengths and make up for one another's weaknesses."

The captain took a deep breath and leaned back in his chair again. "I will be watching every minute of every simulation the two of you run." After that, a smile came across the captain's face. "By the way, my name is Captain William Roberts. Welcome aboard."

Neither of them moved or uttered a sound. Cameron was not moving because she wasn't supposed to move until she was dismissed. Nathan, on the other hand, wasn't moving because he was too nervous to do so.

"Dismissed," the captain finally ordered.

Nathan turned and led Cameron out of the ready room and onto the bridge, continuing into the corridor before he finally stopped, leaned against the wall and let out a sigh of relief.

"This is going to be easier than I thought," Cameron bragged as she passed by.

Nathan watched her walk away, thinking, *What a bitch.*

CHAPTER THREE

Something was wrong. Nathan was pulling the joystick to the left to try and line the ship up to dock with the station, but for some reason, the ship was starting to roll to her right. "What the hell?"

"I'm reading an unknown failure in the bow maneuvering thrusters, port side," Cameron said.

"No kidding! I'm telling her to roll left, but she's rolling right."

"Well stop it," she ordered, as she struggled to try and figure out what was wrong.

"Stop what?" Nathan quickly took his hand off the joystick, startled by Cameron snapping at him.

"Stop maneuvering."

"I'm not touching anything." Now Nathan had both hands hovering in the air over his controls.

Cameron's eyes were darting about her console, as her fingers danced across the smooth, touch screen surface in an attempt to deal with the problem. She knew something was wrong. She just had to figure out what it was and then come up with a solution. "The thruster is firing on its own."

"Well shut it down and switch to backups." Nathan was well aware that she already knew what to do and that *telling* her to do it was unnecessary. But they had not gotten along since day one, and he wasn't sure exactly how to deal with her when he was at the helm, so he had been forced to choose the only logical course and just tell her everything, just to cover his own butt.

"Working on it," she assured him, more calmly now that she knew what needed to be done. "It's not responding. The right roll thruster is still stuck open and firing."

"Get it shut down, Cam. We're going into a roll."

"Backups are not responding."

Suddenly, an alarm sounded, followed by a computerized voice. *"Collision warning. Collision warning."*

"Range to station?" Nathan requested after the computer voice alerted him to the additional problem. They were coming dangerously close to the station. If they didn't slow their rate of approach soon, the thrusters would not be powerful enough to keep them from colliding and causing massive damage.

"Twenty kilometers," Cam responded after glancing at the range readout. She immediately turned her attention back to the thruster problem. "I still can't get it to stop firing."

"Cut the fuel flow," Nathan suggested.

"Already tried, no good. I'm jettisoning the entire maneuvering pod."

"What?" Nathan's eyes went wide. "What the hell am I supposed to maneuver with?"

Cameron rolled her eyes, wondering why she had to explain the obvious to him. "If we jettison the pod, we stop the burn *before* the roll becomes unrecoverable." She was abnormally calm, talking as if she were reading from a manual.

"What about the fuel flow?"

"The unrestricted flow will be sensed by the line pressure monitors, causing the fail-safes to trigger at the source end of the line."

Nathan had no idea what she was talking about. But it didn't matter as she wasn't waiting for him to agree with her.

"Pod is away," she announced confidently. "Now try and get us out of this roll."

Nathan grabbed the joystick, again pulling it to the left, but the Aurora handled differently than the Reliant had in simulations. The Reliant was a much older ship and was designed to fly on more gentle maneuvering curves. The Aurora was not as restricted in her movements and could assume almost any flight attitude the pilot desired. It was like comparing an airliner to a fighter jet, and Nathan had little experience in flying the latter.

"Our roll is starting to oscillate," Cameron warned as she watched the ship's attitude display. As the ship rolled on her longitudinal axis, the ends of that axis were starting to trace circles that were widening slightly with each revolution.

"Slave the bow docking thrusters on the port side to the stick to replace the missing pod," Nathan ordered.

"They're not going to be powerful enough," she warned as she followed his instructions.

"Override the safeties on the chamber pressure to get more power out of them."

"They'll blow," she warned. Cameron switched her comm-channel to send an urgent message ship-wide. "Attention, attention. Emergency evacuation. Sections twelve through fourteen. Decks C, D, and E. Seal off forward primary bulkheads."

Damn it. I should have thought of that.

"Overriding safeties. Maximum chamber pressure reset to twenty-five percent above normal."

Nathan again pulled the joystick to the left,

this time favoring the bow thrusters by angling the stick slightly forward as well. More alarms started sounding, and Nathan noticed a red warning light flashing on Cameron's console, increasing the size of the knot in his stomach. Suddenly, the flight console shook slightly and Nathan could feel his seat wobble, as a distant muffled explosion was heard.

"The chamber blew," Cameron said. "We've got a hull breach, deck D, section thirteen. Damage control teams responding."

"Casualties?"

"Unknown," she answered.

"Range to station?" The explosion in the docking port chamber had done exactly what Nathan suspected it might do, adding enough counter force to take the oscillation out of their roll and allow the remaining maneuvering thrusters to stop it altogether. Of course, Cameron didn't bother to acknowledge that he had successfully stopped the roll. But they were still closing on the station and would soon collide with it if he didn't stop their approach. Nathan knew that he couldn't use the forward braking thrusters, as there was only one left in working order on the right of the bow. That would put them into a slow flat spin instead of slowing their approach.

"Ten kilometers," Cameron updated.

The warbling collision alarm became more frequent as the computer voice upgraded the warning. *"Collision alert. Collision alert."* Nathan knew he had to do something fast before it was too late. He glanced over at Cameron, thinking he saw a momentary look of satisfaction on her face. She was sure it was about to be another failure with Nathan Scott at the helm.

"Warn the station to evacuate the decks facing us," he ordered as he pulled the stick back hard. "Pitching over."

"What?" She hadn't expected that.

"Do it!" Nathan watched the attitude indicator, stealing glances at the forward view screens. The view of the approaching station dropped quickly away, replaced by the black field of stars. He was flipping the ship end-over-end to point her tail at the station. "And bring the main drive online!"

"You're going to cook that station!" she argued as she sent out the warning message.

"I'm just gonna singe them a little," he muttered to himself.

He pushed the stick forward and held it steady just enough to stop the end-over-end flip. With the Aurora now coasting toward the station tail first, he gave the order. "Give me a one percent burn on the mains."

Nathan sensed Cameron's hesitation, sending her an insistent look.

"Firing the mains at one percent." She tapped a few buttons and brought the main propulsion system into play. "I hope they got out in time," she added, as if pointing out his mistake.

Although Nathan appeared confident, he felt like he was about to piss himself. Apparently, the captain hadn't been exaggerating when he bragged that his sim operators would make him cry.

"Collision alert. Collision alert."

"Range to station?"

"Five kilometers," she answered. "Closing at five hundred meters per second."

"Mains?"

"Burning at one percent."

"Any casualty reports yet?"

Cameron looked at the message board on her console. "Five injured, twelve missing."

"Damn it!" he muttered.

"Collision alert. Collision alert."

"Four kilometers, closing at three-seventy-five per second."

Nathan wanted to add more power to the mains, but he knew that if he wasn't already cooking the hull of the station, increasing his burn would.

"Three kilometers." Cameron reported calmly. "Two-fifty closure."

Nathan's pulse was racing and he felt his heart beating in his throat. He glanced over at Cameron. She was cool and calm, just like always. But then again, she wasn't the one who was going to have to explain to the captain why they barbequed the station.

"Two kilometers," Cameron updated. Nathan could sense the satisfaction in her statement.

"Collision alert. Collision alert."

Nathan's optimism was almost gone. *It's not going to work.*

"Message from the station," she reported. "Their hull temp is critical. They report structural failure in thirty seconds."

It felt to Nathan as if Cameron were saying, 'I told you so.'

"One kilometer, one hundred closure."

"All hands! Brace for impact!" Nathan said in resignation.

"Eight hundred meters, fifty closure," she updated.

Nathan expected the computer voice to remind him of the impending collision, but it did not. They *were* going to strike the station, but there was a *chance* it might only be a bump.

"Five hundred meters," Cameron announced, pausing for a moment before continuing. She couldn't believe what her instruments were showing her. "Zero closure," she added. She felt like she had been betrayed at the last second, just as she was about to witness another crushing blow to her adversary.

"Kill the mains!" he ordered. "All stop!"

"Mains are offline," she announced as she shut down all maneuvering and propulsion systems. "All systems reporting all stop."

Nathan breathed a sigh of relief. "Damn, that was close."

"Attention. All hands secure from collision alert," Cameron announced. "Repeat, secure from collision alert."

Nathan should have thought of that one too, but at the moment he didn't care. He was just relieved that he hadn't destroyed the station.

"We *are* still rolling slightly," she pointed out to him, making sure that he realized it was not a complete victory.

Suddenly, the lights in the room brightened, the projection screens surrounding them turned blue, and the back half of the room swung open.

Nathan nearly leapt from his seat as he left the simulator, not waiting for any critique.

"Fifteen minutes!" the sim controller called out to Nathan as he passed by.

Nathan waved acknowledgment as he exited the simulation center and headed down the corridor.

"You're at the helm on the next one, Ensign Taylor," the technician informed Cameron as she calmly got up and stretched her muscles. They had been sitting in the simulator for more than three hours.

"No problem," she said, smiling on her way out.

The sim controller, sitting behind his console above and behind the simulator bay, just shook his head in disbelief. "That is one icy bitch," he commented to the floor tech after Cameron had left the room.

Just then, the comm system buzzed. "Flight Simulations, Lieutenant Jacobs," the controller answered after pushing the speaker button to take the call.

"Work Taylor just as hard," the captain's voice announced.

"Yes, sir," the controller answered as the line went dead.

"Damn. He was watching that?" the floor tech asked.

"The old man sees everything."

* * *

Vladimir stood at the monitoring station in the reactor control room. Located just aft of amidships inside the forward edge of the propulsion section, it was directly aft of the ship's four antimatter reactor plants. From here, every detail of each of the Aurora's powerful antimatter reactors could be monitored and adjusted. Vladimir was busy taking readings and making adjustments to one of the reactor's electromagnetic containment bottles when the chief engineer, Lieutenant Commander Patel, entered the room and approached him.

The chief was an older man from India, in his

early fifties, with a deeply receding hairline. He was heavyset and, like Vladimir, had a passion for his work. He had quickly come to favor the Russian, taking him under his wing and bestowing more trust in him than any of the others on his team.

Accompanying the chief was a tall, distinguished, elderly gentleman with stark white hair and dark eyes. He was also a civilian, as evidenced by his lack of uniform as well as the way he carried himself. Vladimir instantly pegged him as a scientist, undoubtedly coming to admire the Aurora's advanced systems. There had been more than a few of them coming by lately.

"Vladimir," the chief greeted, gesturing him to step aside for a private conversation. "One moment, sir," the chief told the elderly visitor. He led Vladimir away from the elderly gentleman to speak privately. "I have a favor to ask of you," the chief said in hushed tones.

"Anything, sir." Vladimir had great respect for the chief. He had been a wealth of information and support as Vladimir learned his way around the Aurora's many systems.

"This man is from Special Projects. He has a team coming aboard as we speak. He has instructions to install and test some very important equipment on board this ship."

"What kind of equipment?"

"It's classified. All I know is that we are to give them everything they need, without question. These orders come directly from Fleet Command."

Vladimir looked puzzled. "What would you like me to do, sir?"

"I need someone to take care of this team, to be the liaison between them and the engineering department."

Vladimir did not like where this was going, as it sounded like he was going to be taken away from the work he loved in order to babysit a bunch of scientists. "You want *me* to do this?" Vladimir asked. He wasn't asking a question as much as he was pleading for a way out of the assignment.

"Please, Vladimir," the chief begged, "do it for me. I have so much to oversee already. I need someone I can trust to make decisions on their own."

"But sir..." Vladimir stopped mid-sentence as the rest of the Special Projects team entered the room, led by a stunning blond woman. Vladimir's concentration was suddenly lost.

"Don't make me order you, Ensign," the chief smiled, knowing full well that Vladimir would take the assignment willingly, especially after seeing the woman.

"Of course, sir. It would be my honor," Vladimir insisted, straightening his uniform.

"Good." The chief turned back toward the elderly gentleman as the rest of his team gathered beside him.

"I'd like you all to meet Ensign Kamenetskiy. He is my most trusted engineer. He knows almost as much about this ship as I do. I have given him orders to provide you with whatever you need. Vladimir, this is Doctor Karlsen, the project leader."

Vladimir immediately shook the elderly gentleman's hand. "It is a pleasure to meet you, sir."

"And this is his daughter, Doctor Sorenson," the chief continued.

Vladimir took the woman's hand, albeit with far more interest. "It is a pleasure to meet you, ma'am. If there is anything I can do for you, please, do not hesitate to ask."

Unimpressed by Vladimir's charm, Doctor Sorenson wasted no time getting started. "You have two unoccupied spaces on either side of the main engineering section, do you not?"

"Yes, ma'am. They are to hold the shield generators. They are due to be installed in a few days."

"Not any more, Ensign," she advised coldly. "There has been a change in plans. Loading ramps have already been attached to these compartments. Please unlock their exterior maintenance doors so that we may begin loading our equipment as soon as possible. And see to it that no one is allowed into either of these sections without clearance from us."

"Yes, ma'am," Vladimir relented, a bit confused.

"Also, we will need isolated and exclusive access to two of your reactors. The ones that were to power the shielding systems and energy weapons should work nicely."

Vladimir was shocked. She was asking to take half of the ship's power generation capacity offline to be used solely by their little project. He looked to the chief, who simply nodded his approval. "Is there anything else I can do for you?" he relented.

Doctor Sorenson looked at him for a moment before handing him a list. "This should cover it, Ensign."

Vladimir looked at the list, his eyes widening and his mouth agape. "May I ask what experiments you are doing that would require all of *this*?"

"You can ask," she responded as she turned and exited the room without answering.

Vladimir watched as Doctor Sorenson and the rest of her team exited the room, still in shock at her response.

"You'd better get started," the chief laughed, looking at the list in Vladimir's hand. "It looks like you've got a lot of work to do."

Vladimir turned and looked at the chief, a look of betrayal on his face.

"Oh, don't be that way, Vlad," the chief insisted. "Maybe you will learn something new. They are very smart people! This Doctor Karlsen has written many interesting papers on field generation!"

"Bah!" Vladimir exclaimed, wadding up the piece of paper and shoving it unceremoniously into his pocket. "Lucky for you, he has beautiful daughter!"

* * *

The thin blue beams of light dancing about Nathan's body flickered out, the hum of the machine fading along with them. With a slight jolt, the narrow platform Nathan was lying on started sliding out of the medical scanner and back into the empty room. As the platform came completely out of the tube, Nathan sat up and looked toward the control room window above.

"That's it. We're all done. You can get dressed now," the technician announced over the loud speaker.

Nathan hopped down off the platform. The scan was the last of a series of tests each of the crew had to go through as part of their preflight physical by the ship's chief medical officer. It had taken several hours to complete, requiring him to dress and undress several times. But it was a break from the back-to-back simulations that the captain had been putting them through for the last week.

The simulations had been brutal with every possible problem that the programmers could imagine being thrown at them. In fact, there had been a few that Nathan was pretty sure didn't even comply with the known laws of physics. The only saving grace had been that at least his arch nemesis, Ensign Taylor, was being put through just as much hell as he was. Only she seemed to be coping with it a lot better. Nathan was sure that when the time came for her physical, they would discover she was not entirely human.

Wearing nothing but his underwear, he made his way across the cold, bare floor to get to his pile of clothing sitting on one of the chairs. As he started to put on his pants, the door swung open and Ensign Nash walked in, fully clothed, a big smile spreading across her face when she saw Nathan standing there with a surprised look on his face, not yet half dressed.

"Well, well," she teased as she removed her shirt. "Doesn't this seem familiar?"

Nathan freaked, looking up to the control booth, sure that the technician overheard her remarks.

"Relax, Ensign. He can't hear us," she whispered as she tossed her shirt on one of the chairs and started removing her boots.

"Look, I've been meaning to talk to you," Nathan said, "you know, since we saw each other at orientation. But the training has been crazy and..."

"Don't sweat it," she smiled as she wiggled out of her pants, leaving nothing covering her but panties and a sports bra.

Nathan was suddenly reminded of that night, staring at her reflection in the mirrored tile on the wall of the anteroom in his father's home as she was pulling her skimpy evening dress back on.

"I got what I wanted," she told him, stepping toward the scanning platform. She hopped up on the platform and laid down, calling out to the control room above. "Let's get this over with! It's freezing in here!"

"All right, then," Nathan said. He pulled his shirt on, collected the rest of his things, and made a beeline for the door, adding, "I guess I'll see you around, then."

Jessica just smiled a satisfied little smirk as the scanner platform began sliding her into the scanning tube.

* * *

Most, if not all, of the Aurora's skeleton crew took their meals at the same time while they were still in port. It was probably the only time they would ever be able to dine together in a large group once the ship was under way, and the captain thought it would promote bonding amongst the overworked crew. It had been something that his wife had insisted on when his children were growing up, and for the most part it had worked, as his family was still close despite the fact that they were always separated by vast distances. Nevertheless, most of the crew still broke up into groups of two, three, or four, as one might expect, sharing conversation with the few friends they had made in what little free time they had during this hectic period.

The galley itself was not yet completely operational. The hot and cold service lines were installed, as were most of the cooking appliances, but there were no cold storage units installed other than a few temporary refrigerators brought up from Earth to serve in the interim. Because of this, they couldn't keep much in the way of inventory on board. Most of their food had to be prepared planet-side and shuttled up to be reheated, which was another reason for everyone to eat at once.

"She is unbelievable!" Vladimir complained as he ate. "She is, how do you say, a real ball-buster, yes?"

"Yeah," Nathan laughed, "that's how you say it."

"*Ensign, I need this. Ensign, I need that!* She always needs something! And when she gets it, still it is not enough!" He paused to take another bite of food. "I spent three days waiting on this wretch of a woman."

"What are they doing?"

"I have no idea! Can you believe? All I know is they need tremendous amounts of energy. And they are doing something outside, on the hull, with the shield emitters, I think. I don't know. They don't tell me anything. All I know is that this woman is making me crazy!"

Nathan had not known Vladimir for very long, just over a week. But he had never seen him so worked up about anything. He was usually very easygoing, letting everything roll off of him. "If she bothers you that much, why don't you ask to be reassigned?"

"I cannot," Vladimir explained, shoveling more food into his mouth. "The chief chose me personally. Besides, this woman, she is beautiful!"

"Ah, now it makes more sense," Nathan exclaimed.

Vladimir looked at him funny. "No, you do not understand."

"Oh I understand, all right," Nathan laughed, as a message came through on his comm-set. "Hold on," he told Vladimir, keying his microphone. "Ensign Scott."

"Captain wants to see you in his ready room right after chow, sir."

"Understood." Nathan's expression suddenly soured.

"What is it?" Vladimir asked, seeing the change in his friend's mood.

"The captain wants to see me."

"This is bad?"

"I haven't been doing so well in the simulations," Nathan admitted. "I think I might be getting fired."

"Nathan," Vladimir explained, "in the military, they do not fire you; they reassign you. They could demote you as well, but you are already only ensign and that is lowest rank academy graduate can have, I'm afraid. So he cannot demote you. But he could give you really bad job, like maybe waste processing plant." Vladimir shuddered at the thought of the place.

"Thanks for the pep talk there, Vlad. You've really cheered me up."

"What are friends for?" he responded as he finished his meal.

"Well, I might as well get this over with," Nathan decided, rising from the table.

"Think positive thoughts," Vladimir advised him. "And keep chin up, always look strong and confident." Vladimir moved closer and lowered his voice. "That way no one knows you are scared like little bunny." Vladimir laughed and slapped Nathan on the back, sending him on his way.

* * *

"Ensign Scott, reporting as ordered, sir." Nathan stood straight as a board, eyes straight ahead. The one good thing about standing at attention was that it made it easier for him to hide how nervous he was.

"Ensign Scott," the captain began, "at ease."

Well at least he's still calling me Ensign. That's a good sign.

"How's the training going?"

"Sir?" Nathan wondered if it was a trick question.

"How are you doing in the simulations?" the captain asked more directly.

"There's definitely room for improvement, sir."

"Yes, Ensign. I'd have to agree with you on that." The captain leaned back in his chair, something he liked to do while considering his next statement. "And how would you say Ensign Taylor is doing?"

"Better than I am, sir." Nathan figured if he was going to be honest, he might as well be brutally honest.

"How so?"

"She knows her flight and navigation protocols better than I do, sir. And she stays more levelheaded under pressure."

"And you feel that's a good thing?"

"I would think so, sir."

"Why?"

"Sir?" Nathan was confused, unsure of what the captain was getting at.

"You seem to think that Ensign Taylor has an advantage over you at the helm because she is more levelheaded under pressure. I'd like to know *why* you think that's an advantage."

"I believe it allows her to think more clearly, weigh all her options, and choose the best course of action."

"And you don't think you're capable of doing that?"

"I didn't say that, sir."

The captain leaned forward on his desk again. "But you do think it gives her an advantage. What are *you* doing that *she* is not?"

Nathan stumbled for a moment, trying to figure out what to say. "Sir, I believe that I get too emotionally involved in the situation."

"You mean you take it more personally?"

"Yes, I believe so, sir." The captain was looking at Nathan, like he was waiting for him to elaborate further. "It's... it's like I'm fighting a battle, sir, like it's me against the scenario, and I don't want to lose."

"And you don't think Ensign Taylor has this same problem?"

"No, sir, she doesn't. She just looks at the problem and calculates the safest solution."

The captain leaned back once more, taking in a deep breath. "If you don't bet big, you don't win big," he mumbled.

"Sir?"

The captain rose from his chair and started making his way around to the front of his desk as he spoke. "Ensign Scott, there are two kinds of officers: those that follow the book and those that use it as a general guideline." The captain sat down on the front of his desk, facing Nathan. "Are you following me so far?"

"I'm guessing that Ensign Taylor's the first kind of officer, and I'm the second."

"Actually, Ensign Taylor probably has the damned book memorized." The captain chuckled. "Hell, she probably sent the brass a list of grammatical errors."

The captain's joke raised a smile on Nathan's face. For the first time since he came into the ready room, he didn't feel like he was in trouble.

"You, on the other hand, you're the one saying, 'There's a book?'"

Suddenly, Nathan became nervous again. Captain Roberts could see the uncertainty in Nathan's eyes and decided to cut to the chase.

"Piloting a ship, that's a monkey skill. I can teach anybody to fly this ship. Hell, I can just tell the computer where I want to go and the ship will go there. 'Flying' on the other hand, well, that's a feeling, an instinct. And you can't teach instinct. You're either born with it, or you're not. I can sharpen it for you, but first you've got to have it."

Nathan looked at the captain, not sure if he was understanding him correctly.

"That's right, Ensign Scott, *you* have it. Hell, you've got it in spades. But, either you don't *realize* you have it, or you don't *believe* you have it. I haven't figured that out yet." The captain rose, walked back around, and returned to his seat. "Now Ensign Taylor, she doesn't have it. She's a skilled pilot, to be sure. And she's definitely as cool as they come under pressure. In fact, she's the perfect type for a navigator, and a top-notch one at that. But the helm is *not* where she belongs."

Suddenly it dawned on Nathan. "Are you saying..."

"That you're my new helmsman, Ensign Scott."

Nathan couldn't believe what he was hearing. "But sir, don't you think that..."

"A simple 'Thank you, sir' would be the correct response."

"Of course. Thank you, sir. It's just that Ensign Taylor has been doing so much better in the sims than I have. Hell, I crashed and burned most of them!"

"But not all of them, Ensign. You even managed to pull through a few that there wasn't supposed to be a way out of!"

"But I don't see how..."

"You need to give yourself a little credit, son," the captain said. "Do you really think Fleet just tossed me whatever graduates nobody else wanted? Hell, I handpicked every last one of you."

Nathan was taken aback. Up until now, he had been sure that getting assigned to the Aurora had been either some cosmic joke or the result of his father's influence.

"I picked *you* to be my helmsman and Ensign Taylor to be my navigator. You wanna know why? Two reasons. First, 'cause you're both perfect for the job, and second, 'cause you're polar opposites. You two fit the bill perfectly. Now all I've got to do is get the two of you to stop arguing like an old married couple and start working together."

Nathan's head was reeling from his sudden change of fortune. Ten minutes ago, he was sure he was about to get thrown off the ship. And now he was being offered the job of lead pilot, which also meant he was about to be promoted.

"Sir," Nathan said, "may I ask a question?"

"Please do."

"If you knew what positions you were going to assign when you picked us, why did you put us through all this cross-training, this competition?"

"That is an excellent question," the captain admitted, seeming quite pleased that Nathan was finally thinking instead of reacting. "I needed a way to make you *want* the position, a way to make you realize what you were capable of in the helmsman's chair. And of course a little cross-training never hurts."

Nathan stood silently for a moment, thinking about everything the captain had said over the last few minutes.

Captain Roberts opened his desk drawer and pulled out a small black box, tossing it to Nathan. "You might want to put those on, Lieutenant Scott."

Nathan opened up the box to see a pair of lieutenant's bars inside.

"I've given you both the afternoon off, so get some rest. You'll both be back at it at 0800 tomorrow."

"Yes, sir!" Nathan snapped to attention and saluted.

"Dismissed, Lieutenant."

Nathan turned to exit but paused before leaving, turning back to the captain. "Thank you, sir."

* * *

The first thing that Nathan wanted to do was share his good news with the only friend he had on board, Vladimir. But having never gone as far aft as the hangar bay, he was finding himself a little lost wandering the corridors of the lower aft decks where the engineering spaces were located. He was almost about to give up when he heard someone arguing nearby. Nathan followed the sound of their voices, realizing it was Vladimir. When he turned the corner, he found himself in the corridor outside the starboard shield generator compartment, one of the two spaces being used by the Special Projects team.

"I cannot give you so much power," Vladimir was

telling Doctor Sorenson firmly.

"Cannot or will not?" she challenged, only a few inches from his face. It was an unusual sight, being that his mighty Russian friend had a good thirty centimeters on her.

"I cannot give you that much power at once," he argued. "It is too much. The lines will overheat."

"They will not!"

"Protocols state that I cannot exceed maximum energy transfer rating for that line. I would have to install additional lines from reactor all the way to you."

"Then do it. What's the problem?"

"What's the problem? Do you realize how much work that would be? It would take days!" Vladimir noticed Nathan approaching, welcoming the interruption. "Oh, hello, Nathan," Vladimir greeted, shifting his focus away from the irritating woman. "I see you did not get fired," he joked, noticing the lieutenant's bars on his collar. "I hope you do not think I am going to salute you now," he added, shaking his hand.

"Excuse me," Doctor Sorenson interrupted, refusing to be put off by Nathan's intrusion. "We weren't finished..."

"Oh, where are my manners?" Vladimir apologized mockingly. "Nathan, this is Doctor Sorenson, the irritating woman I told you about. Doctor Sorenson, this is Lieutenant Scott. He is pilot, you know."

Nathan started to offer his hand in greeting, but thought twice about it when she started in on Vladimir again.

"Listen, don't think that you can just brush me off like this..."

"Please, Doctor," Vladimir objected, having

finally had enough, "will you stop talking for just one minute? I'm trying to congratulate my friend on his promotion. Do you have no manners?"

"Are you going to give me that power or not?" she demanded.

"Not," he answered calmly, knowing full well that the calmer he got the madder it made her.

"You leave me no choice but to go over your head," she threatened.

Vladimir wasn't affected by her threats. "Be my guest."

"Fine! I'm going straight to Commander Patel." she announced, as she stormed off in a huff.

"He is not commander!" Vladimir yelled as she walked away, not wanting to let her get the last word. "He is lieutenant commander!" Vladimir watched her go, hoping to get one more reaction from her, but got nothing. "Bah." He turned to Nathan, "Do you see what I have to put up with?"

"Vlad, do you really think you should piss her off that way? I mean, she seemed really mad."

"Not to worry," Vladimir assured him.

"Yeah, but she's going to your chief."

"She will not find him. He hates her more than I do. So then she will go to XO, who will tell her that such decision must be made by chief. Eventually she will come back to me. But by this time, she will be more reasonable."

"And then you'll give her what she wants?"

"Of course."

"Then why not just give her what she wants in the first place?"

"It is not so simple."

"You mean what she wants is not simple?" Nathan was getting more confused by the moment.

"That? No, it is easy! One day, at most." Vladimir could see that Nathan was not following him. "If I always run when she calls, then I am running, running, running, all the time. This way, we fight, she gets mad, and she leaves me alone for at least an hour, maybe two. This way I get work done. And she thinks twice before asking me for something else." Vladimir smiled, sure that he was making perfect sense.

"Okay." Nathan was still confused, but he was pretty sure that Vladimir had things well in hand. "You were right about one thing, though," Nathan agreed. "She is hot."

"Yes! I told you this!" he exclaimed as they started walking down the corridor towards engineering. "You know, I was not kidding before; I will not salute you."

* * *

"Calculating new course," Cameron said. "Transferring course to helm."

Nathan watched as the new plot drew itself out on his navigation display. He was about to change course when he realized she wasn't sending him in the direction he had asked. "Wait, that'll take us around the debris field. I wanted to go through it."

"It's safer to go around," she argued, confident she was correct.

Nathan couldn't believe she was doing this to him again. Ever since the captain had made him the helmsman, she had taken every opportunity to get in his way. "We don't have the time to go around. Besides, the sensors show most of them are no bigger than a meter, and the shields can handle that."

"If we go around, or more precisely up and over, we can skim through the less dense edge of the field, thereby reducing the risk to the ship. Once we come out above the field, we can punch it up to twice light and then drop out again a few minutes later on the far side of the gas giant. At most, we'll lose five minutes."

"But that'll put us in the wrong tactical position," he insisted. "If we plow straight through, the debris will scatter their sensors and they'll never see us coming. And when we come out, the star will mask our sensor signature and obscure a visual track. We'll have a clear shot!" Nathan was beginning to lose patience with her.

"Don't you think that's a bit obvious?"

"It's obvious 'cause it works, Cam! Now plot the course I asked for!"

"Fine, if you want to take unnecessary risks, just remember I'm on record as being against it."

"The course?" he pleaded.

"It's coming." Cameron began plotting the course but in no particular hurry.

But it was too late, as the ship was already entering the debris field. And with the radioactivity from the debris scattering their sensors, Cameron wouldn't be able to plot a course with any degree of accuracy.

"Well, great," Nathan exclaimed in frustration. "Forget it, Cam. You're too late."

"What the hell are you doing?" she asked as she realized they had already entered the debris field. "I didn't get the course plotted yet!"

"No kidding," Nathan said. It was the third time today he had been forced to 'wing it' because Cameron was too busy arguing with him to do her job in a timely fashion. And each time the scenario had ended poorly. It had been much the same way for the last few days. Every time he asked for a course, she objected. Every time he tried to deviate the slightest bit from flight protocols, she would quote the manual, chapter and verse. A few times she had been right, and Nathan had been the first to admit it, even if it had been after the fact on a few occasions. But most of the time, he had good reason to stray from protocol, and to make matters worse, he knew damned well that she was aware of it, despite her usual objections.

"You're too far below your proposed route," she insisted.

"How do you know?"

"We've been on this course for two minutes. You changed your angle slightly on the way in to avoid that large piece of debris in our path, and you didn't compensate with a course correction afterward."

"Probably because my navigator didn't give me a course to begin with," Nathan mumbled.

"You still need to come up at least two degrees."

Nathan was getting tired of her games. "You know what? Thanks, but no thanks. If I'm gonna screw up, I'd rather do it on my own."

Cameron said nothing. And a few minutes later they exited the debris field, out of position. The sensors immediately triggered a contact alarm. Nathan could feel his heart sink as the inevitable downward spiral that had recently ended so many of their simulations was about to begin.

"I've got four Jung ships closing fast dead ahead," Cameron announced, satisfaction evident in her voice.

"Like we didn't see that coming."

"They're firing missiles. Tracking twelve inbound. Impact in three seconds."

For a split second, Nathan contemplated maneuvering to avoid the incoming ordnance. But with the missiles only three seconds away, there wasn't much use and the simulation ended poorly, yet again.

Cameron felt a slight bit of guilt as Nathan resigned to inevitable failure. But as far as she was concerned, it was his fault for not listening to her in the first place.

The lights came up and the screens again switched back to pale blue as the back half of the room swung slowly open.

"Scott and Taylor, you're ordered to take a fifteen minute break, and then report to the captain's ready room," the sim controller announced over the comms. It had been entertaining to the sim technicians at first. They all knew there was going to be friction between the two of them after the captain had promoted Nathan. But after three days of the same old arguments, it was beginning to look like they were never going to get past their differences. And apparently, the captain had grown tired of it.

"You know, if you're gonna keep sabotaging me at every opportunity, we're never going to get out of this simulator and onto the bridge," Nathan said.

"Don't try to blame me because your crazy ideas never work."

"They never work because I never have any solid navigation behind them! And whose fault might that be? Oh, I don't know, the navigator, maybe?"

"You just want me to sit idly by and watch while you fly us into who knows what? Well that's not the way my job works, mister."

"That's Lieutenant to you, Ensign!" Nathan knew that pulling rank on her was not the best strategy. But of course, that hadn't stopped him from saying it.

"I believe, sir," she responded, emphasizing the word 'sir', "that it's my *job* to point out available alternatives, sir."

"Point out, yes! But you argue with me until my only choice is to do it your way or fly by the seat of my pants! I'm pretty sure that's *not* in your job description, Cam. But I'm sure you'll check the book and let me know if I'm wrong." Nathan got up and left the simulator. He needed to be as far away from Cameron as possible right now, even if only for a few minutes.

* * *

Cameron topped the ramp leading to the command deck and turned toward the bridge. It had not really come as a surprise when the simulation control officer told them to report to the captain. She knew that she and Nathan were not meshing as a team, but she was equally sure that she had been correct to point out the flaws in his unorthodox solutions. It wasn't her fault if he couldn't admit when he was wrong. If he would just heed her advice more often, she was sure that they would be doing a lot better in the simulations.

The more she thought about it, the more she felt like he was out to get her, to make her look bad. But surely the captain would see through his little charade. Surely the captain would recognize that Nathan had no discipline and no respect for procedure. The guy just jumped in and made things up as he went, with no planning or foresight. That was probably just fine for him before, when his daddy's money and power could pull his butt out of whatever fire he inadvertently jumped into, but this was different. He might be taking the entire ship into the fire with him.

Cameron tried to calm herself. After all, he was just the helmsman. It was the captain that would be making such decisions, not Nathan Scott. And the captain *knew* what he was doing. He had an exemplary record; she had checked. He had demonstrated the ability to innovate *while* respecting established protocols and procedures. If the captain veered away from policy, it was for good reason and with the full understanding of, not only what, but why he was doing so. The captain would never 'wing it' as Nathan had so frequently done.

Cameron turned the last corner before arriving at the bridge. She was mentally preparing to defend herself in front of the captain against any unjustified attacks that Nathan might launch at her. She would make sure that any decision the captain made was based on the truth and not on the wild accusations of Lieutenant Nathan Scott.

Cameron's determined pace suddenly slowed as she saw Nathan standing outside the entrance to the bridge. She was instantly curious as to why he was standing there, apparently waiting for her. But all she could bring herself to say was, "Lieutenant."

"I thought we should enter together," Nathan said. "We *are* supposed to be a team, after all."

The gesture surprised Cameron, but she wouldn't let it show. "As you wish."

They entered the captain's ready room together. Only this time, as the senior officer, Nathan would announce their presence.

"Lieutenant Scott and Ensign Taylor, reporting as ordered, sir."

Both Nathan and Cameron raised their hands in salute.

"At ease," the captain instructed, adding, "Close the door please, Ensign." He waited a moment for Cameron to close the door and return to stand at ease next to Nathan before he began. This time, his tone was far more formal than it had been in previous meetings.

"It has come to my attention that your performance in the flight training simulator has fallen far below acceptable levels. The report states that on multiple occasions you failed to act as a team; you let personal differences interfere with the timely performance of your duties, and you failed to achieve the goals of the given scenario on at least thirty percent of your simulations." Captain Roberts leaned back in his chair. "Thirty percent? Hell, I should've canned you both at five percent."

"Sir, I take full responsibility for our poor performance," Nathan said.

"Well that's certainly admirable, Lieutenant, but I don't remember asking for your opinion just yet." The captain sat there staring at Nathan, waiting for him to say something else, but Nathan only swallowed, hard. He looked at Cameron next, but her eyes were staring straight ahead, and as usual, her expression was cold and emotionless.

"I spent the majority of what should've been my rack time last night reviewing the video logs of your simulations. And I have to say that I am appalled. In fact, I'm not really sure which one of you I should be chewing out. Hell, if you two were married I'd be advising you both to seek divorce lawyers."

Captain Roberts got up and walked around to the front of his desk, just as he usually did when he was trying to make a point, only this time, he stood in front of his desk instead of sitting. He folded his arms in front of his chest, looking long and hard at each of them.

"Normally, I'd send you both packing and call up any cadets that have passed their sim qualifiers to replace you. But since we're due to start trials in a few days, I don't have that luxury. I know the two of you can *fly* this ship. And since I'm going to be on that bridge *telling* you what to do, all *you* have to do is execute my orders," he said. "And you will do so without hesitation. Is that clear?"

"Yes, sir," they responded in unison.

"And just in case, by some horrifying twist of fate, you should have to take action without orders, I'm going to give you some right now, so there will not be any confusion." The captain turned to Nathan, speaking to him directly. "Lieutenant, you shall follow standard flight operational protocols, without deviation, unless you are one hundred—no, make that one hundred and fifty percent sure that doing so would result in unacceptable risk to this ship or her crew. Is that understood?"

"Yes, sir!" Nathan answered.

The captain then turned his attention to Cameron. "Ensign Taylor, you are the ship's navigator. That means you plot her course. But it also means that you do *whatever* is necessary to help the helmsman fly this ship. Yes, it *is* your job to offer alternatives, but if the helmsman says he wants to fly this ship into the sun, you'd damned well better give him the course he asked for *before* you offer alternatives. Is that understood?"

"Yes, sir!" Cameron responded, swallowing hard.

"Dismissed, Ensign."

Cameron snapped a salute, turning and exiting in proper military fashion. Nathan continued to stand, frozen, wondering what would come next. Apparently, the captain had a bit more butt chewing specifically targeted at him.

The captain waited for Ensign Taylor to leave before continuing. "Lieutenant, I think we have a bit of a misunderstanding going on here. I'm pretty sure that when I made you helmsman, I put you in command of the flight team. Granted, at least for now that only means you're in command of Ensign Taylor, but you *are* in command. That's why I *made* you a lieutenant in the first place. But after watching you two love birds squabbling in my flight simulator for the last few days, I'm not so sure that was the right call." Something he had just said triggered a thought in Captain Roberts head. "Wait, you two aren't, I mean, you're not *together*, are you?"

"No, sir," Nathan protested.

"You don't *want* to be, do you?" The captain knew he was probably overstepping his bounds, as there were no set rules against such fraternization as long as it didn't interfere with one's duties. But it would've explained a lot.

"God no, sir," Nathan reassured him.

"Good." The captain breathed a sigh of relief, knowing that he had just dodged a bullet. "Just make sure you keep it that way."

"No problem, sir."

"Listen, Lieutenant, the most important part of being *in command* is being able to make the call when it needs to be made. Now there's nothing wrong with listening to the advice of your subordinates. And there's certainly nothing wrong with admitting that they're right and following that advice. But you do *not* debate the issue, Lieutenant. Not on the flight deck. That's what briefing rooms are for, son. Just remember, right or wrong, *any* decision made too late *is* a bad decision."

The captain rose from his desk and made his way back to his chair. "Now I suggest that you go and work things out with Ensign Taylor before you turn in for the night. I don't want to find you lying in medical later with a knife in your back."

"Yes, sir."

"Now fix this, Lieutenant, or I will."

"Yes, sir," he assured, snapping a salute.

* * *

The Aurora's hangar bay was only dimly lit, allowing just enough light so that a person could make their way through safely. Although the facility was finished and ready for operations, the Aurora's spacecraft and flight personnel were not due to arrive until well after the first shakedown cruise. For now, the massive space was being used as a staging area for components and supplies waiting to be installed or put into storage.

Nathan wandered between the stacks of boxes and equipment. "Taylor!" he called out. "I know you're in here!" He was lying, as he wasn't really sure she was there. He had gone to her quarters after leaving the captain's ready room, looking to make peace with her. He nearly had to order her roommate to divulge her location. Even then, she was only guessing that Cameron had come here, as it was one of the few places still left on the ship where she could be alone with her thoughts.

"Come on, Cameron! We need to talk!"

"What the hell do you want?" she finally answered.

Nathan spun around, trying to locate where her voice had come from. "Where are you?"

"Back here."

Nathan looked toward her voice. She was sitting on one of the rolling step ladders normally used for accessing the cockpit of fighters. There was a row of twelve of them neatly arranged against the far wall of the hangar. She was sitting at the top of one of the middle ones.

"What are you doing in here?" he asked as he approached.

"This is where I come to think." Her voice had a melancholy he hadn't heard from her before. "But you must've talked to my roommate to find me, so you already know that." She was being logical, as usual.

"Why here?" Nathan asked as he reached the row of step ladders. He was trying to establish some sort of rapport with her before hashing out their differences.

"I don't know. I guess it's because it's the largest open space on the ship. I mean, everywhere else is so cramped. Well, not cramped really, just no wasted space, you know? It kind of boxes you in, compartmentalizes your thinking. Here, everything is wide open." She looked down at him, standing at the bottom of the step ladder next to the one she was sitting on. "I know it sounds stupid."

"Actually, it sort of makes sense when you think about it."

"So, what do you want, Nathan?"

"We've got to figure out how to make this work."

"That's easy," she quipped. "Resign your commission."

Nathan was pretty sure she was joking but decided not to test her.

"You know," he began as he started up the step ladder, "the captain asked me if you and I were together."

"Oh, God," she exclaimed, realizing what he meant. "I hope you set him straight!"

"Of course I did," he assured. "I mean, come on, you and I?"

"Please, you are *so* not my type," she insisted.

"Me neither," he agreed as he sat down at the top of the step ladder next to hers. "I mean, nothing personal," he added, realizing he might have offended her. "I mean, you're really cute and all but..."

"You can shut up now, Lieutenant."

"Okay, then. Moving on." There was an uncomfortable moment of silence, as Nathan tried to figure out what to say. "Listen, I know you hate me, but we have to find a way to work together."

"You're right," she agreed. "I do hate you."

Nathan didn't know how to react to that. Finally, he turned towards her to say something and noticed a big grin on her face. "Oh, that was really funny," he admitted, a bit relieved.

"And it felt really good, too," she laughed.

"Let's be honest with each other," Nathan suggested. "Let's get everything out in the open."

"I thought that's what I was doing," she added. He was making it too easy for her.

"Enough, already," Nathan objected. "Okay, fine. Tell me what you hate about me."

"You sure you're ready? I mean, we could be here

a while."

"Okay, let's make it easier. Just give me your top three reasons."

"You're a cocky, arrogant, pretty little rich boy, and you've probably always gotten by on your charm, your good looks, and your daddy's money. And I highly doubt that you've ever taken anything seriously your whole life."

Nathan paused for a moment, a little taken aback. "Well, I'm pretty sure that was more than three reasons. But, I will admit that there is probably a little truth to *some* of that."

"Some?"

"Okay, most."

"Most?"

"Don't push it, Ensign." Nathan took a deep breath before continuing. "You're right... about all of it, actually. But that was *before* I enlisted. Since I got into the academy, I've actually been *trying* to do my best. For the first time that I can remember, I actually *believe* in something; I actually *care* about something." He paused to look at her. "Something other than myself, I mean."

"And I'm just supposed to believe you?"

"Well, I guess you don't have to, but it is the truth."

"Okay. Fair enough, I guess." Cameron wasn't quite sure what to believe. Nathan was opening up to her, which was something that she wasn't used to, at least not from men, and certainly not from Nathan. Most guys had found her too cold and calculating to ever get close to her in any real sense of the word.

"So," Nathan said, breaking another uncomfortable silence. "My turn?"

"Fair is fair."

Nathan began an exaggerated ritual, rubbing his hands together and pretending like he was loosening up for something really big.

"All right already! Out with it!"

"You're cold and dispassionate. You refuse to admit when you're wrong, and you're always trying to prove to everyone that you're better than me."

They sat there for a few moments, each thinking about what the other had said, trying to decide what was true and to come to terms with it.

"Well, you make me sound like a real bitch," Cameron mumbled.

"I wouldn't say that. I may have overheard others toss that word around, but..."

Cameron cut him off with a slap of the back of her hand against his shoulder.

"I am not dispassionate," she objected.

"Maybe that was the wrong word."

"So what do we do?"

"I don't know. Call a truce maybe?"

"I guess I can live with that," she resigned.

Nathan held out his hand, which Cameron reluctantly shook. "All right then."

Cameron rose from her perch and made her way down the step ladder. Once back on the deck, she turned back to Nathan. "You know, I wasn't *trying* to prove that I'm better than you," she explained as she turned to walk away. "I already *know* that I am."

Nathan just smiled and watched her walk away, thinking, *she really is a bitch.*

* * *

It had been a long walk back to his quarters from

the hangar bay, and all Nathan wanted to do was climb into his bunk and stay there. The day had been long and exhausting, at least emotionally if not physically. And he suspected that, despite their truce, the next few days were not likely to be any easier.

Nathan was sure that he had done everything possible to try to work with Cameron. In fact, he had purposely avoided giving her a direct order whenever possible so as not to make her feel like anything other than an equal partner. But after listening to the captain, he was starting to wonder if that had been a mistake. Nathan had never cared much about rank. He followed and respected it. After all, the fleet was a military organization and, like any other, it depended on rank and discipline in order to function, which he understood fully. But *having* rank had never meant much to him, personally. Of course, that could've been because until now he had always been pretty much at the bottom of the totem pole. Nathan liked his job. He loved piloting the ship, but as far as being in charge was concerned, it was starting to feel more like a punishment than a privilege.

"There you are!" Vladimir declared from his bunk as Nathan entered their quarters. "I was starting to wonder if you had fallen asleep in simulator!"

"I've spent the last couple of hours being verbally assaulted," Nathan explained as he took off his uniform shirt.

"What are you talking about?"

Nathan kicked off his shoes and fell onto his bunk, rolling over onto his back before continuing. "First, I was getting chewed out by the captain. Then I got an earful from Cameron's roommate."

"The little redhead?" Vladimir inquired. "She is full of fire, that one."

"Yeah, tell me about it. Then, I had to do a little verbal jousting with Cameron in the hangar bay."

"This does not sound like good time," Vladimir sympathized. "What did the captain want?"

"Let's just say that if Cam and I don't get our act together and start playing nice over the next few days, you're gonna have a new roommate."

"Bah! It will never happen, my friend. You will do fine. You will see."

"I wouldn't be so sure, Vlad. We've been screwing up the simulations left and right! If I was the captain, I wouldn't let us fly a cargo shuttle, let alone a starship."

"Nathan, you worry too much. These simulations they put you through, they are crazy! They could never happen! These people who make them, they are reading too much science fiction. Trust me on this. Such things do not happen to people such as us."

"I don't know," Nathan objected.

"Listen, when they give you normal stuff, you know, flying around, dock with this, dock with that—this you do okay, yes?"

"Sure, but..."

"The captain, he knows this. Trust me."

"Maybe, but it's not about flying the ship. It's about Cam and I not getting along."

"Yes, of this I have heard."

"What?"

"Everyone knows this," Vladimir explained. "They say you are like old married couple," he laughed. "Hey, maybe you should sleep with her!"

"Oh, that would really help!" Nathan protested.

"Okay, then maybe I should sleep with her?"

"Get serious."

"It is big sacrifice, yes. But for you, I am willing to do this," Vladimir joked.

"No thanks," Nathan chuckled. "That won't be necessary."

"Are you sure? I can go right now. I am always ready to serve."

"Enough, already!"

They both had a good laugh over the idea, after which Nathan decided to change the subject. "So, speaking of woman problems, how are things going in your part of the ship?"

"Better," Vladimir said. "She is not as bad as before. She is still a pain. But at least not as often."

"What happened? Did you sleep with her?"

"No, of course not," Vladimir protested. "Not that I wouldn't, because of course I would if necessary."

"For the good of the ship?" Nathan joked.

"Yes, for the good of the ship!" Vladimir announced proudly. "For the Aurora!"

"For the Aurora!" Nathan laughed.

* * *

Captain Roberts entered the briefing room at exactly zero eight hundred hours, his data pad in one hand and his coffee mug in the other. "Good morning, gentlemen," he greeted, as he made his way to the head of the table and sat down. Commander Montero, his executive officer, and Lieutenant Commander Patel, his chief engineer, were already seated at the table. "Thank you for coming. I know you all have more than enough work to do since we're still so shorthanded, so I'll try to keep this meeting as brief as possible."

The captain took another sip of coffee before continuing, calling up his notes on his data pad as usual to ensure that any pertinent information he might need would be at his fingertips. He was a man who believed in being well prepared whenever possible.

"The reason for this meeting is that Fleet Command is anxious for us to get under way on a limited test run of our primary propulsion systems. It seems that there is some concern over the efficacy of their design, as well as their projected performance capabilities. If that turns out to be the case, Command would like to be able to address these problems before the Celestia is fitted with the same propulsion systems."

"Captain," Lieutenant Commander Patel interrupted, "I am not aware of any of these concerns you speak of. In fact, our simulations predict that we should be able to reach eighty percent the speed of light, instead of the original projections of seventy-five."

"I'm not disagreeing with you at all, Chief," the captain assured him. "I'm quite sure you're correct. All I know is that Command wants us to be ready to depart for a basic lap around the block in twenty-four hours. If there's some other reason for these orders, they've decided that I don't need to know. What I do need to know is whether or not we are ready for a basic test cruise."

"All flight systems are online and ready, sir," the chief assured him. "And main propulsion has been ready for several days now. However, we do not have all of our weaponry installed, and we have no energy shielding installed, as the team from Special

Projects is still using those spaces."

"Well, do we have any weaponry?"

"Yes, sir. We have most of the forward rail gun turrets installed and ready, but all guns aft of amidships have yet to be hooked into main power. We also have the forward torpedo tubes ready to go, but the aft tubes still need to have their loading systems installed. All of those components are still sitting in the main hangar bay."

"That reminds me," the captain interrupted, turning to his XO. "We need to move as much of that stuff as we can into the cargo holds for the time being. We're going to need room for shuttle craft to operate out of the flight deck if anything goes wrong during our first sail."

"Sure, Captain," the XO promised. "But some of that stuff is pretty big."

"Well, move the smaller stuff out, and slide the bigger stuff off to the sides and out of the way. We don't need the whole bay clear, just enough room for five or six shuttles."

"Yes, sir."

"I've also insisted that we at least get a dozen torpedoes and ammunition for our rail guns, just in case. Something about sailing out in a warship without any bullets just doesn't sit right with me, even if it is just a few laps around the block."

"Captain," the chief said, "I just want to remind you that we'll be operating with only half our designed reactor capacity, since the Special Projects people hijacked the other half."

"Really?" the captain asked, somewhat surprised. "That's a lot of power. What the hell are they doing with it?"

"I really do not know, sir. They aren't talking.

Best I can tell is that it involves the shield emitters, since they've hijacked them as well."

"Maybe a new type of energy shielding?" the XO theorized.

"That's what I was thinking."

"Any idea when they'll be finished?" the captain asked.

"Not really. But they haven't been asking for as much lately, so maybe that means they've completed their work."

"Let's hope so," the XO added. "Those people make me nervous."

"Well, will two reactors be sufficient?" the captain asked Chief Patel.

"Yes, sir. More than enough for a little trip around the neighborhood. But we won't be able to use our FTL field emitters until after we get our other two reactors back."

"Understood. Okay, so that brings us to the crew," the captain said, turning toward Commander Montero.

"We've got one full skeleton shift trained and ready, Captain," the commander responded. "I wouldn't want to go into battle with them, but they should be able to handle a basic test sail without screwing anything up too badly."

"Very well."

"That reminds me," the commander added. "How's your little training project going?"

"Lieutenant Scott and Ensign Taylor are at least *trying* to work together. They still have a long way to go, but I think it might do them some good to get out of the simulator and into real space."

"I hope you're right," the commander cautioned. "I've seen some of their training tapes, and I've gotta tell ya, Skipper, those two scare me."

"Okay, so I guess I can tell Command that we're ready enough, then." The captain leaned back in his chair for a moment before continuing. "There's going to be an inspection tomorrow morning by Admiral Yamori. Let's make sure we're ready for it."

* * *

As the fleet was only about thirty years old and still relatively small, there were only four admirals in its ranks. Admiral Yamori was in charge of fleet development, which included the Special Projects division as well as the design and construction of new ships to fill out the Earth's burgeoning space defense force. Prior to his service in the fleet, he had commanded several sea-going warships in the Eurasian Navy. Once the Data Ark had been discovered, he had retired from the navy to study physics and advanced spacecraft design at the European campus of the Ark Institute. He was the only admiral in the fleet who had never actually commanded a space vessel. But then, his position was about building them, not operating them.

"You've made remarkable progress, Bill," the admiral praised, as they strolled the corridors of the engineering section, "especially considering how understaffed you've been."

"Thank you, sir," the captain responded. "We've been working around the clock to try and get her ready. But a lot of the credit goes to the station crews, sir. They've been working their tails off, every minute of every day. We couldn't have gotten this far without them."

"Yes, I'm sure."

"It also was a big help to have most of the components available in our hangar bay, sir," Commander Montero added. "We never had to wait for anything to be shuttled up to us."

The admiral had started his tour at the bridge, worked his way aft, and had just finished up in engineering when they had met up with Doctors Karlsen and Sorenson in the corridor.

"Ah, Doctor Karlsen," the admiral greeted. "And Doctor Sorenson. A pleasure to see you, as always. I hope everything is going well for you."

"If you'd like to take a look for yourself, Admiral, we are ready."

"Excellent." The admiral turned to the captain and the XO. "If you'll excuse me, gentlemen. I'll meet up with you later on the bridge."

"Yes, sir," the captain agreed. The captain and the commander snapped to attention, saluting the admiral as he departed.

The admiral followed the two doctors past the armed guards that had been at the entrances to both the port and starboard shield generator bays since the special projects team had come aboard.

"I'd love to be a fly on that wall right about now," the XO commented as they headed for the bridge.

"I have a feeling we're going to know all about it soon enough," the captain assured him.

CHAPTER FOUR

The day had started off like any other, up at six in the morning and breakfast at seven. Only today Nathan felt far more optimistic than he could remember being since coming aboard. It might have been the time spent on the bridge the day before, where the simulations that he and Cameron had run seemed to have gone more smoothly than usual. He didn't know if they were finally developing a working rapport, or if it was just that on the bridge, there were far more eyes on them.

But his good mood could also have been the result of a shorter than usual work day. Because of the inspection, the captain had given the entire crew the evening off, with none of the usual after dinner training or work teams that usually lasted right up until bedtime.

But most likely, Nathan's, as well as everyone else's, better than usual mood was probably due to the knowledge that today was a 'training free' day. In addition, scuttlebutt had it that they were going to take the ship out for a quick 'lap around the block' as the XO had referred to it. After weeks of intense training and late night work details, the crew was itching to show what they could do.

Of course, every section chief had objected to the idea of starting the Aurora's trials earlier than originally scheduled. There were still dozens of systems that were not completely installed. The galley, for example, still did not have functioning cold storage and the crew was still being fed by the mess halls down on Earth. More than half of the ship's weaponry was still incomplete. Her FTL fields were inoperative, as were the shields. But until the Special Projects team concluded their experiments and returned the emitters and the last two reactors to them, there was nothing that could be done about those systems.

But with the focus of the cruise being a test of the main propulsion system's sub-light capabilities, both the captain and Admiral Yamori were convinced that an eight-hour trip around the system would be safe enough. And the Reliant, which was currently conducting training exercises within the inner system, could provide assistance if something were to go wrong.

So with the rumor being that they would depart just after lunch, Nathan had taken a chance and was sitting down to a larger than normal breakfast with Vladimir. They had been a little late in arriving, thanks to his roommate's inability to get from quarters to the galley without stopping to strike up a conversation with at least one member of the opposite sex.

"I am so excited," Vladimir exclaimed as he sat down to eat. "I will finally get to see the engines in action. No more simulations."

"I second that last part," Nathan agreed as he started eating.

"And the best part is, while we are under way, that woman will not be bothering me."

"I hear ya." It suddenly occurred to Nathan that the reason he was in such good spirits this morning was simply because he knew that today he would be free of the usual tension between himself and Cameron, which in itself had turned out to be mentally exhausting. While actually under way, the captain or XO would be giving the orders. Although Cameron still had no problem 'offering alternatives' to Nathan, he had no doubt that she would not be offering them in the presence of command staff.

"I really hope that we get the chance to bring the engines to full power today. I believe we can get to at least eighty percent light, maybe eighty-five."

He watched in amazement as Vladimir shoveled food into his mouth. Nathan had been raised in a very proper family, where they had been taught to put down their eating utensils in between bites in order to ensure the slow, methodical chewing and swallowing of their food. Not that Nathan ate abnormally slowly; he had abandoned such rituals out of necessity over the years. But Vladimir was shoveling the food in before he had swallowed the previous bite, and he was still able to talk relatively clearly while he was eating. Nathan had dined with Vladimir nearly every day for the last two weeks and had yet to get used to his style of inhaling his meals.

"Are you in a hurry or something?" Nathan chuckled. "Why do you eat so fast? Slow down and enjoy your food."

"I know, I know... is bad habit. I get this from old job. I worked my way through school on rescue squad. It was very busy station. When you got chance to eat, you ate quickly or not at all."

"Now hear this!" the comm-system blared through the loudspeakers. *"All hands report to stations and prepare to get under way. Repeat, all hands report to stations and prepare to get under way. Departure in five minutes. That is all."*

"You see," Vladimir said, as he stuffed the last sausage into his mouth and then displayed his empty plate, comparing it to Nathan's full plate. "Just like on the rescue squad!"

Nathan began shoveling food into his mouth as Vladimir left the table, his engorged mouth still chewing away. After shoveling in several heaping spoonfuls, Nathan doubted he could fit much more into his mouth, so he grabbed the four sausages from his plate and headed out of the galley in a hurry.

The bridge was bustling with activity as the crew prepared to get under way. Technicians were performing last-minute checks on critical systems, and the communications officer was busily confirming the readiness of each department to get under way.

Captain Roberts sat in his command chair in the middle of the bridge, pretending to review some notes on the data pad that he carried with him everywhere. He very much liked having information at his fingertips, and as far as he was concerned, it was the best piece of lost technology yet recovered from the Data Ark.

The captain was listening intently to the sounds of his bridge staff as they prepared for their first real voyage. It would be a brief journey, only about eight hours round-trip, but for his crew of fresh graduates, or 'kids' as his XO liked to call them, it would be their first voyage and, therefore, always one to remember.

He could've waited until later in the day before setting out, giving them all a chance to mentally prepare before getting under way, but that would've been too easy. When faced with a short amount of time to train a new crew, it made sense to use every opportunity to test them. And this sudden call to set sail was the perfect chance to do just that. How quickly one could drop what they were doing and jump into action was a good indicator of how one would perform under pressure. It was something that he had learned from his first captain more than twenty years ago.

In a way, he felt a little guilty, like he had cheated. Unlike the rest of the crew, he did have a chance to mentally prepare. Not that he needed it, but he did take the time to visit with his family by vid-comm this morning. He had been unable to reach either of his sons, who were both serving in the fleet and were unavailable, but he had spoken at length with his daughter and even gotten to speak with his grandchildren. He had shared breakfast with his wife, also by vid-comm, just like he had done every morning since he reported for duty on the Aurora over a month ago.

The captain looked up from his data pad, scanning the eleven stations located around the perimeter of the bridge. They were all manned and ready, with the notable exception of a helmsman, who still had not arrived despite the fact that they were set to depart in under two minutes. He turned to face the tactical station located directly behind him, which was currently being manned by his XO. He had insisted on an experienced officer at tactical and Fleet Command had agreed to transfer one from the Intrepid when she returned to port in another week. "Any sign of our helmsman?" the captain asked Commander Montero.

As if on cue, Nathan came charging onto the bridge at a fast walk, still chewing his breakfast. "Sorry, sir," he apologized with a mouth full of sausage. "Got a late start," he added as he passed by and took his seat at the helm, directly in front of and slightly to the right of the command chair.

"Wipe your hands before you touch that console, Lieutenant," the captain warned, a touch of amusement in his voice.

"Yes, sir."

Nathan quickly wiped his hands on his pant legs, casting a guilty expression toward Cameron who sat at the navigation console to his left. Cameron looked away, still not able to understand how he had been promoted over her.

"Now that we're all here," the captain said. "XO, ship's status?"

"All departments have reported in, and all stations are manned and ready, Captain," Commander Montero reported from the tactical station. "We're ready to get under way, sir."

"Very well. Comm, contact the platform's control center and Fleet Command. Let them know the Aurora is leaving port."

"Yes, sir," the comm officer acknowledged.

"Lieutenant Scott, check that all boarding ramps have been detached and retracted, and release all mooring clamps."

Nathan checked the status display that sent a constant telemetry of mooring data from the platform's control systems. "All boarding ramps have been retracted and secured, releasing all mooring clamps." Nathan pressed a button on his side console to release the mooring clamps that held the ship in place.

Outside, more than twenty clamps located on the ends of long pneumatic arms simultaneously released their grip on the Aurora's mooring points. The sudden release allowed the negatively pressurized mooring arms to quickly pull away from the ship and back against the assembly platform.

Inside, there was a muffled *clunk* as the clamps released, and the ship seemed to dip slightly to port. It was only a slight sensation, one that might have gone unnoticed had they not seen the slight change in the ship's angle in relation to the assembly frame that surrounded them through the main view screen.

"Ship is free floating, sir." Nathan immediately compensated for the slight change in attitude with his docking thrusters, tapping his joystick ever so slightly, bringing the ship back into perfect alignment.

"Very, well, Lieutenant. Take us out."

"Thrusting forward." Nathan applied gentle forward pressure on the joystick. He held the pressure for only a second, maybe less—just enough for the ship to start inching forward.

The Aurora began to slowly slide out of the long octagonally shaped trusswork that had been her home since her construction had begun over two years ago. Every single work light was shining on her as she inched away from her berth.

The main view screen was a massive quarter-sphere display that encompassed the front third of the bridge. Starting at the floor and flowing up smoothly onto the ceiling, it gave the flight crew, the two most forward stations, and the command chair a onehundred and eighty degree view laterally, and nearly as much vertically. It was as if you were sitting in a bubble atop the ship herself, looking out into space. Despite the knowledge that it was only a projection, and that they were sitting in one of the most protected compartments within the ship, one couldn't help but feel exposed when surround by the amazing view.

From his position at the helm, Nathan could easily see that every viewport on their side of the assembly platform's main structure was packed full of faces, all there to witness this historic moment. For them, it was the culmination of years of hard work and long hours, and they had every reason to be proud of their accomplishment as they watched her go.

"Message from Fleet Command, sir," the comm officer reported.

"Go ahead," the captain answered, already anticipating the content of the message.

"Message reads, '*Bon voyage, and good luck to the crew of the fleet's newest vessel, the Aurora.*' End message."

"Thank you, Ensign. Pass it on; ship-wide, please."

Nathan continued to add velocity with each tap of the joystick until they were moving out of the berth at a respectable rate. He didn't want to seem too cautious or they might realize how nervous he actually was. Only a few short weeks ago, Nathan was about to serve as a third-string backup pilot on the oldest ship in the fleet. Now, by some twist of fate, he was the lead pilot of the newest and fastest ship the Earth had ever put into space. He had never aspired to such accomplishments. In fact, he had never been as patriotic as most of his classmates. His only ambition had been to get away from his father and lead his own life. But now, after all he had been through over the last two weeks, he was starting to feel the same as everyone else. He *believed* in something greater than himself.

Cameron watched as the opening to the end of the assembly berth passed them by, their bow breaking into open space high above the Earth. Despite her calm exterior, Cameron could feel her pulse racing with excitement at the sight of it all, even though it looked exactly the same as it had in the countless simulations they had run.

She too had joined the fleet to get away from her old life, and she had also lacked the patriotic feeling shared by most of her class. But ambition had never been something that she had lacked. For her, it was all-consuming. It drove her day in and day out and made her cold and competitive.

But she was okay with it, figuring that the sacrifice now while she was young would pay off later. She had no interest in becoming a baby factory like so many of her friends back home. She agreed with those who felt the Earth's population was being refilled at an acceptable rate, making such efforts not only unnecessary, but unwise.

And so she had committed herself to a life in the fleet, hoping to make captain someday. It had required her to forego any romantic entanglements, not wanting to deal with the additional distractions. Not that she didn't date on occasion. After all, a girl did have needs. But she had always been upfront with anyone of interest, which probably explained why she had few second dates.

"Clear of the platform, sir," Nathan announced.

So far so good.

"Very well, take us to departure altitude and prepare a course for Jupiter."

"Climbing to departure altitude," Nathan acknowledged. Nathan fired up the main engines at only a few percent of their overall thrust capacity in order to increase their velocity and climb to a higher orbit. A low, almost inaudible rumble began emanating from the stern of the ship as her massive engines began their low-intensity burn.

"Calculating course for Jupiter," Cameron reported. "Velocity, sir?" she asked the captain.

The captain thought about it for a moment before responding, a smile coming across his face. "Flight's discretion," he offered.

Cameron and Nathan looked at each other. Nathan's face was like a mischievous little boy who suddenly had a great idea. But Cameron's was a look of concern, probably due to her helmsman's expression.

"Within reason, of course," the captain added.

Nathan silently mouthed 'half light' to Cameron, who nodded grudging agreement.

"Recommend half light, sir," Cameron advised. "At Jupiter's current position, that will get us there in approximately eighty-seven minutes."

"A bit much for our first time out," the captain speculated as he shifted nervously in his seat. "But they did want us to test our new engines, so half light it is. But do us all a favor and take it up slowly. Remember, we've got untested inertial dampeners and a ship full of newbies who don't have their space legs yet."

"Yes, sir," Nathan assured him. "I'll bring her up nice and easy."

"Departure altitude in one minute," Cameron reported.

Captain Roberts pressed a button on the comm-panel on the arm of his command chair to address the entire ship. "All hands, this is the captain, prepare for acceleration in one minute." Without skipping a beat, the captain switched his comm to engineering. "Chief, we're going to take her up to half light. I trust you'll let us know if there are any problems down there?"

"Yes, sir, but I don't anticipate any," the chief engineer's voice crackled over the comm.

Nathan could imagine the excited look on Vladimir's face down in engineering as he programmed in a five-minute acceleration curve that would get them to half the speed of light in just under fifteen minutes. It was a very slow rate of acceleration considering what he knew the ship was designed to do, but the captain's earlier point had been a valid one, which Nathan had not even considered.

"Departure altitude achieved. Ready to break orbit," Cameron announced.

"Very well. Take us out of orbit, and make way for Jupiter. Half light, Lieutenant."

Cameron pressed a button on her console that changed the ship's condition to yellow.

Throughout the ship, the condition lights located along every corridor and every compartment suddenly changed from green to yellow as she announced the last acceleration warning to the crew. All at once, anyone standing immediately sat down and faced forward. If they weren't able to sit, they stood leaning against a wall that faced aft. If they couldn't do that, they grabbed onto something. The inertial dampeners were a new feature in fleet vessels and no one was quite sure how well they were going to work. And the last thing that a new crewman wanted was to fall on their ass during their first acceleration.

"Breaking orbit," Nathan announced as Cameron finished her ship-wide warning. He activated the acceleration sequence he had programmed moments ago as he changed the ship's heading. "On course for Jupiter. Beginning acceleration sequence."

All the bridge staff who were not facing forward suddenly stopped what they were doing and turned their seats toward the main view screen as the ship began to accelerate. The sliver of the Earth that had been decorating the bottom edge of the main view screen suddenly fell away from view as the ship pulled out of orbit and headed for Jupiter.

Nathan wasn't sure if it was his gentle acceleration curve or the new inertial dampeners, but the sensation was almost unnoticeable. In fact, it was even a bit disappointing, and he wondered how much the dampeners would help if he really had to punch it.

Fifteen minutes later they were traveling at half the speed of light, and Nathan had discontinued his burn. In about an hour, he would have to start a gradual deceleration burn so that they would settle into a comfortable orbit around Jupiter. Of course Cameron would let him know when and at what thrust to burn, but he was pretty sure that the rest of the crew would never feel a thing.

"Traveling at half light, Captain. On course for Jupiter," Nathan reported.

"Very well," the captain answered as he rose from his chair. "XO, you're with me," he added as he headed for his ready room door at the aft end of the bridge. "You have the conn, Lieutenant."

Cameron rolled her eyes as she noticed the big

toothy grin forming on Nathan's face.

* * *

Deceleration on approach to Jupiter had gone as planned, thanks to Cameron's precise navigational calculations. In only a few minutes, the Aurora would be captured by Jupiter's gravity well and fall into a stable orbit high above her equator. The eighty-seven minute trip had been uneventful thus far, a welcome change for Nathan from the gut-wrenching simulations they had endured previously. It had made him realize that perhaps Vladimir had been correct, that all he had to do was fly the ship wherever the captain told him. And that was fine with him.

He was just a bit surprised and more than curious when Doctor Karlsen and his daughter entered the bridge and went directly to the starboard auxiliary station. Located at the aft end of each side of the bridge just forward of the exits, these stations could be reprogrammed to act as monitoring and control stations for just about any of the ship's systems.

"What are they doing here?" Nathan whispered to Cameron as he tilted his head back toward the two physicists. Cameron just shrugged her shoulders, indicating she had no idea.

Immediately, everything that Vladimir had ever said about the irritating blond woman and the work they had been doing flashed through Nathan's mind. If they *were* on board to test some top-secret project, then the far side of Jupiter seemed a likely spot. He tried to hear what the two of them were talking about as they worked back in the corner, but they were speaking what Nathan assumed was Danish.

"Stand by to end deceleration burn," Cameron announced, drawing Nathan's attention back to his job.

"Standing by."

On Cameron's command, he cut the main engines, ending the deceleration burn, immediately after which the low rumble of the main engines subsided.

"Approach velocity and vector are perfect," Cameron announced proudly, despite the fact that Nathan was the only one listening. "We should settle into orbit in four minutes." Cameron switched her comm channel to hail the captain. "Navigation, sir. Jupiter orbit in four minutes."

"Very well, Ensign. Go ahead and pitch over. We'll be there momentarily," the captain instructed over the comm.

"Yes, sir," she said, before ending the connection. "You're clear to pitch over," she told Nathan.

"Pitching over."

Nathan pushed the joystick forward slightly, holding it there for several seconds. Although a smaller ship, the Aurora still had plenty of mass and it took more than just a small puff of attitude thrusters to get her to flip over in a timely fashion. The inertial dampening systems appeared to be doing their job, which allowed him to handle the massive ship more like a large fighter-bomber than a carrier vessel.

The Aurora had been approaching Jupiter tail first, using her massive main engines to decelerate. Most interplanetary trips were made at less than ten percent of light, from which the ship's braking thrusters were capable of slowing her down to orbital velocities. But since the purpose of their mission had been to test main propulsion, a more aggressive flight profile had seemed appropriate.

Now that the burn had completed, the ship was flipping end over end, her nose coming up to point in the direction of the gas giant. Everyone on the bridge watched in amazement as the planet seemingly rose from under the deck into view. It stopped its ascent to settle in the center of the view screen as Nathan applied counter-thrust to stop their pitch-over. The planet quickly grew as they approached until it filled the view screen's bottom quarter from side to side. As it grew closer, they could see the bands of brown, red, and orange clouds as they rotated in opposing directions around the surface of the planet. No one on the bridge had ever seen any planet other than the Earth in this way until now, and it held them all transfixed.

Except, Nathan noticed, the two scientists still working away in the back corner. Either they had seen such things before, or their work was so all-consuming that they didn't even notice.

They did notice when Commander Montero returned to the bridge and stepped up to the tactical station. Two armed marines had followed him, taking positions on either side of the port exit. A moment later, another pair of marines took a similar post at the starboard exit.

Nathan and Cameron exchanged concerned glances at the presence of the guards, unsure of what was happening.

"Captain on the bridge!" one of the marines guarding the port exit announced as Captain Roberts exited his ready room and entered the bridge. Although no one was expected to abandon their duties to stand and salute, all casual conversations ceased, and everyone instantly became more alert and focused.

The captain entered the bridge with a more serious expression than usual. "XO, lock down the bridge," he ordered as he passed by the tactical station and made his way forward to his command chair.

Commander Montero turned and motioned to the marines on the port exit, who immediately locked their hatch, the marines on the starboard exit following suit.

"Comm," the XO said, "lock out all internal communications except for tactical, the command chair, and those between the starboard auxiliary station and the shield generation compartments."

"Yes, sir," the communications officer answered.

"And take the deep space communications array offline until further notice."

"Yes, sir." The communications officer acted quickly to fulfill the commander's orders. "Deep space array is offline. Internal communications are locked out except for those specified, sir."

"Jupiter orbit achieved, Captain," Nathan announced. He didn't know what was going on, but he was sure it had something to do with their being in orbit over Jupiter. He glanced over at Cameron who, for the first time that he could remember, looked worried.

"May I have your attention," the captain announced.

His look was stern, his demeanor serious, and it made Nathan wonder what had happened to suddenly change his persona so drastically over the last ninety minutes.

"What I'm about to tell you is classified as top

secret, need to know only, and all of *you* need to know. The rest of the crew, however, does not, at least not yet. Before I begin, I would like you all to know that neither myself nor Commander Montero were aware of any of this until we opened an encrypted, position-locked file given to us by Admiral Yamori during yesterday's inspection."

Nathan and Cameron exchanged concerned glances at the captain's opening statement, as did many others on the bridge.

"Eighteen months ago, the Centauri system was invaded by the Jung Dynasty. Centauri forces were quickly overwhelmed, resulting in a total loss of her entire defensive force. At that point we lost our source of intelligence in Centauri space, so we must assume that the entire system is now controlled by the Jung. That leaves Sol as the last free system in the core."

A dead silence fell across the room, punctuated only by the occasional sounds of various systems giving faint tones to alert their users. Everyone in the room understood the gravity of the information. It was, after all, the reason most of them had joined the fleet in the first place.

For Nathan, it meant something more. He had spent endless hours arguing with his father about the importance of the fleet. And he had never been able to understand how his father, a man who had once believed wholeheartedly in the existence of the fleet, could've suddenly changed his mind. And now, with what everyone feared the most coming to be, he could finally convince his father how unequivocally wrong he had been. And while this should have pleased him, none of it seemed to matter now.

"Fleet intelligence assessments predict that an

invasion of Sol should be expected within a year, two at the most. The invasion of the Alpha Centauri system cost the Jung more than a few ships, and intel suggests that it will take them a while to reinforce their forces enough to be able to mount an overwhelming invasion of Earth. As you know, the Jung rule with fear more than anything else. And overwhelming victory in any campaign is of paramount importance to them."

Questions began to pop into the minds of the bridge staff. What were they going to do? What about their families? They had all heard rumors about what the Jung did to those they ruled. But why had they left port so early, before they were even fully armed?

The captain expected such concerns from his crew and intended on answering them as best he could. "We have been sent here, to the orbit of Jupiter, to test an experimental drive system that Fleet Command hopes will give us a significant tactical advantage over the Jung. If this prototype proves successful and we are able to install it into the rest of the ships in time, we might stand a real chance of saving the Earth."

The captain now had everyone's undivided attention, as their hope hung on his every word. "Doctors Karlsen and Sorenson from Special Projects are in charge of this test, so I will let them explain further." The captain motioned to Doctor Karlsen to take over as he stepped aside.

The tall, heavyset, elderly man moved from the back of the room to stand on the command platform. Nathan had only heard of the man until now and had not even seen his face. Rumor had it that he had lived, eaten, and slept in the shield generator compartments over the last two weeks. And after seeing the tired look on the man's face, Nathan believed the rumors to be true.

"Many years ago, during testing of a new, multi-layered energy shielding system, we accidentally discovered a new method of superluminal space travel. This system is capable of relocating a vessel to a distant point in space, many light years away, in the blink of an eye."

The doctor's Danish accent was heavy, making it difficult to understand, but the implications of what he was saying were quite clear to Nathan, as they were to everyone else as evidenced by the murmurs of response to the unbelievable news.

"Are you saying we could *jump* back to Earth, instantly?" Nathan couldn't help interrupting.

"Oh, much farther than that, Lieutenant," the elderly physicist assured him. "With this prototype, we can travel at least ten light years in a single transition event," he proudly proclaimed.

That statement caused the room to become even noisier. "Settle down, people!" the captain ordered.

"The only limitations we currently have are power, of which enormous amounts are required, and of course the risk of navigational inaccuracies, even the slightest of which could have catastrophic results."

That got the captain's attention. "What kind of results?"

The doctor looked perplexed as he tried to come up with an example. He was a man accustomed to speaking with other physicists, not with laymen.

"Well, there are so many. Space is not empty, you know. If your transition is not calculated exactly, you could end up appearing inside a planet or a star—or even worse!"

Even worse? Nathan thought. *What could be worse than jumping into a star?* He looked over at Cameron. He was sure that she understood what the doctor was talking about, as she had a far better understanding of the complexities of interstellar navigation.

"Thank you, Doctor," the captain said, taking charge of the room once more. "As you can all imagine, the ability to travel great distances so quickly would provide an enormous tactical advantage. Our orders are to help the doctor and his team test this new system. Using Jupiter to mask the test from any observers on Earth, we will attempt to transition to a point just outside the Oort cloud, approximately one light year away. If successful, we will transition back to our orbit around Jupiter and then return to Earth, so that the good doctor and his team may continue their work at what I expect will be an even more accelerated pace."

The captain looked about the room once more, noticing the looks of shock, concern, and amazement on the faces of his young crew. "Now I know this seems like a big risk, and that you probably feel like Fleet Command is using us all like guinea pigs—and you're probably right. But considering the severity of our situation, we're going to have to take some additional risks if we hope to prevent an invasion of our world. I don't see this being any more risky than facing down a fleet of Jung warships. And you all knew that you might have to do that someday." The captain looked around the room again. "Any questions?" He turned towards his flight crew, knowing full well that they would have a few.

"Sir," Nathan said, "what do we have to do during

this test?"

"Apparently nothing, Lieutenant," the captain answered. "From what I've read in the briefing file, and correct me, Doctor, if I'm wrong, the ship's velocity and course will remain unaffected by the transition event. So the direction and speed that we're traveling at departure will be what we're traveling upon arrival. Just be prepared to maneuver quickly should something suddenly be in our way," he added with a wink.

The captain's sense of humor was not serving to comfort his nervous crew, and he could tell. "Look people, this will all be over in a few blinks. After that, you'll all be in the history books and we'll be on our way back to Earth. It doesn't appear that the transition events will have any effect on the rest of the ship's systems, so for most of you things will go on as normal. This entire test will take about thirty minutes, after which we'll resume normal operations."

The captain scanned the faces of his crew, trying to make eye contact with each of them. "Now, I have to remind you that this is highly classified, and you are not to discuss it with anyone, not even with each other. Needless to say, if the Jung ever learned of this technology, they would attack immediately, destroying everything and everyone that stood between them and this technology. It is undoubtedly the biggest genie to be let out of its bottle since the invention of the hydrogen bomb." He paused one last time to let his words sink in and take their desired effect. "Now double-check all systems and stand ready. The test will begin just after we enter comm blackout with Earth as we pass behind Jupiter."

Nathan knew the captain was right. Space flight as they knew it, along with everything it provided, was about to change drastically.

"Five minutes to the far side of the planet, sir," Cameron reported.

"Lieutenant," the captain said, "when we come out of the transition, if you see anything in our path, don't wait for anyone to tell you to take evasive action. Understood?"

"Yes, sir," Nathan answered. He was starting to wonder if Vladimir had been wrong. Perhaps there *was* more to being the helmsman than just flying the ship wherever the captain told him.

"Ensign Taylor, the faster you can get a fix on our location after the transition, the happier I'll be."

"Yes, sir."

"XO, bring the ship to yellow alert, please."

"Yellow alert, yes, sir." The commander changed the ship's readiness status to yellow, again changing all the light bars throughout the ship and sounding the condition change alert. "All hands, yellow alert! Set ship's condition to yellow!" the commander announced ship-wide.

All over the ship, the crew rushed to make sure that everything was properly stowed away, every system was checked and ready, all nonessential systems were shut down, and all bulkhead hatches were closed.

A few minutes later, the last of the green condition lights on his tactical display changed to yellow. "Ship is set at condition yellow, sir," Commander Montero reported.

"Very well. Time to threshold?"

"One minute, sir," Cameron responded.

Down in engineering, Vladimir was getting nervous. The two reactors used by the Special Projects team had been running at one hundred percent for over four hours, long before he had come on duty, and he did not understand how they were using so much power. No one had informed him of what was about to happen, but he knew that the moment of truth for the Special Projects team was at hand. He only hoped it didn't result in damage to his reactors.

"Crossing threshold, sir," Cameron reported. "We are now on the far side of Jupiter from the Earth."

"Doctor Karlsen," the captain announced, "whenever you're ready."

Doctor Karlsen watched over his daughter's shoulder as she worked the console at the auxiliary station, making comments to her in Danish as she worked.

"Transition systems are ready," she announced. "Energy banks at forty percent capacity."

"Is that enough?" the captain asked.

"More than enough for transitions both there and back, Captain," she answered calmly, trying to hide her annoyance at the question during so critical a time.

"You think we'll feel anything?" Nathan whispered to Cameron, but got no response.

"Transition parameters locked into auto-sequencer. The system is ready for initiation."

Doctor Sorenson looked at the captain, who was

looking back at her over his shoulder. It was a polite gesture, as it was his ship to command.

"Let her rip," he ordered.

"Initiating transition in five..."

Despite the fact that they had been told there would be no sensation, and no change in ship's velocity momentum, everyone on the bridge turned their chairs to face forward.

"Four..."

The captain wondered what his wife was doing at the moment.

"Three..."

Nathan rested both hands on his console, as if to brace himself.

"Two..."

For some reason, Cameron did the same.

"One..."

Nathan held his breath.

"Initiating..."

Outside of the ship, a pale blue wave of light washed out from shield emitters that were scattered strategically about the hull of the ship. In a split second, the bluish light grew into a glowing ball that encompassed the entire ship. Suddenly, the light turned white as it fell back into the ship, erasing her from view. It all happened in an instant. One moment the Aurora was orbiting Jupiter; the next she was gone.

Inside the bridge, the main view screen showed the blue-white flash, flooding the entire bridge with a ghostly flash of light. It was like being caught unexpectedly by a really bright camera flash, causing spots in front of the eyes of all those unfortunate enough to be looking forward during the event.

"Transition complete," Doctor Sorenson announced. "Verifying position."

Despite the big blue-white blotch floating in his field of vision, Nathan frantically scanned the view screen for any signs of obstacles directly in their path.

"Position?" the captain asked.

"We are exactly two meters off our projected arrival point," Doctor Sorenson announced. "The transition was successful," she added with pride.

A man who cared little for emotional outbursts in such a professional situation, Doctor Karlsen simply put his hand on his daughter's shoulder and gave it a loving squeeze. She knew that, coming from him in their current setting, it carried far more meaning than anyone around them could understand. Inside, they were both beaming with pride as the culmination of ten years of work on what had started out as an energy shield project was now about to change the course of humanity.

"She's right, sir," Cameron assured the captain. "We're at the designated position, on the outer edge of the Oort cloud."

"My God," the captain exclaimed. "Sensor contacts?"

"The board shows clear, Captain," Commander Montero reported.

"Sensors may be inaccurate, sir," the officer operating the long-range sensor station advised. "I suggest we run a full diagnostic to make sure that they were not affected by the transition."

"I know I was," Nathan mumbled, still blinking repeatedly as he tried to make the big blue splotches leave his field of vision.

"Very, well. Get on it," the captain ordered as he turned to face Doctor Karlsen. "Congratulations, Doctors. You may have just saved the Earth," he added with a smile.

"Contact!" the sensor operator announced. "Just came on the screen. Transferring plot to tactical!"

Nathan felt a cold shiver pass over him.

"I've got it, Captain," the commander announced from the tactical station. "Running ID check against the intel database."

"Helm," the captain began in a low and controlled tone, "slow and easy, turn into the contact's bearing. And keep your thrust low to avoid detection, just in case they haven't spotted us yet."

"Aye, sir," Nathan responded. "Coming to port, slow and easy, minimal thrust."

"I've got a probable match," the commander reported. "Jung patrol ship, smaller than us, lightly armored, missiles, rail guns and shields—no energy weapons. Not much firepower really."

"Maybe, but in our current state, without any shields and limited firepower of our own? I'd say we're evenly matched," the captain observed. The commander nodded in agreement.

"We're pointed toward the contact, sir," Nathan reported.

"Very well." The captain turned his attention back to the commander. "Have they spotted us?"

"Not sure. But if we flashed outside like we did inside, our arrival would've been kind of hard to miss, don't you think?"

"Maybe, but we did come in behind them. If we're lucky, they're doing directional sweeps forward."

Commander Montero grimaced suddenly as the

information on his contact track changed. "No such luck, they're changing course and accelerating. They're headed our way."

"Comm, unlock all internal communications and sound battle stations! And get the deep space comm array back online! I wanna know if that Jung ship tries to send out a message!" The captain spun back around as the battle stations alarm sounded and the condition lights on the bridge changed to red, casting an eerie, faint, red tinge on everything in the room.

"Helm, full speed ahead. Bring her up to quarter light fast! I wanna be in close weapons range before she has a chance to take action!"

"Aye, full speed ahead. Coming up to one quarter light." Nathan brought the ship's main engines up to full power, instantly feeling the acceleration push him back in his seat despite the attempts by the inertial dampening systems to compensate.

All about the bridge, the crew struggled to maintain their balance as they worked under the force of sudden acceleration. Doctor Karlsen, who had been standing behind his daughter at the auxiliary station, nearly fell over but was caught by one of the marines guarding the starboard exit.

"Her shields are up, Captain!" the commander announced from tactical. "And she's deploying her missile batteries!"

"ECO, start jamming her, full frequency spread. Don't let her missiles lock on to us!" The captain turned back to tactical. "Load all forward torpedo bays and prepare to fire! Let me know when you have a solution."

"Captain, she's transmitting!" the comm officer reported. "Tight beam, aimed for Centauri space."

"How long?" the captain asked.

"Three point five years, assuming nobody intercepts it along the way and relays!"

"I have a firing solution, Captain!" the commander reported. "Tubes two and four are ready to fire."

"Fire two and four!" the captain ordered.

"But sir," the commander reminded, "they haven't fired on us yet. They'll see it as an act of aggression and use it as an excuse to…"

"If they get away and FTL it back to Alpha Centauri, they'll be invading us in months, Commander, not years!"

"Aye, sir, firing two and four," the XO responded, feeling guilty for questioning his captain's judgment.

Along the forward, starboard edge of the Aurora's massive propulsion section, two small doors slid open to reveal a pair of tubes. A second later a torpedo leapt out of the uppermost tube, followed a moment later by a second from the lower. Riding on massive tails of white hot thrust, the torpedoes sped away at fifty percent the speed of light, helped by the fact that the Aurora herself was already at nearly a quarter light.

"Torpedoes away! She's launching counter-measures!"

"They're not stupid," the captain observed.

"Velocity at one quarter light," Nathan reported. His head was spinning as he tried to keep track of everything that was going on. It was nothing like the simulations, which of course had seemed so real at the time. Now, there was so much more happening, so much more to think about. He couldn't understand how the captain was able to keep track of it all so easily. Nathan tried to concentrate on just his job and shut everything else out but could not.

"They've launched missiles!" the commander reported. "Six inbound. ETA thirty seconds!"

"Are we jamming?!" the captain yelled.

"Yes, sir! On all frequencies!" the electronic countermeasures officer reported.

"Torpedo impact in fifteen seconds!" the commander reported.

"Time to gun range?"

"One minute," Cameron reported.

Nathan looked over at Cameron to his left. She was still so calm with no hint of stress in her voice.

"Bring the rail guns online, point-defense mode! Knock those incoming missiles down!"

"Rail guns coming online!"

Outside, at a dozen different locations about the forward half of the ship, doors slid open and rail gun turrets quickly popped up into place, spinning around to come to bear on the inbound missiles. Not more than a few seconds after they deployed, they opened up in auto-fire mode, sending point-defense rounds out along their launch rails in a bright sparkle of blue current that leapt from their rails. The rounds were designed to break apart into hundreds of smaller explosive charges that would spread out and detonate, creating a wall of explosive kinetic energy designed to obliterate the incoming ordnance before it could reach the ship.

"Second contact! Down range of the first!" the sensor operator announced. "Transferring track to tactical!"

The commander examined the second track, comparing it against the first to save time, a trick he had learned on his previous assignment. "Same type of ship, Captain. Torpedo impact in five seconds."

"Helm, new course. Bring us onto the second

contact!"

"Aye, sir!" Within seconds Cameron had fed him a new course as Nathan raised the nose of the ship slightly and to the right to head toward the second contact.

"Torpedo impact!" the commander reported.

Everyone held their breath as they waited for the impact assessment.

"Contact one lost!" the commander announced happily. It was the Aurora's first shot fired in anger, and it was also her first kill.

"Can you retarget the second torpedo?" the captain asked, hoping to send it after the second contact to save time and ordnance. After all, he only had so many torpedoes in the forward bay. The rest were still in storage down in the hangar deck.

"Negative. Second torpedo was destroyed by their point-defense turrets!" The commander glanced back down at his tactical display, realizing that two of the six missiles launched by the first patrol ship had made it past their defense screen and were about to strike the Aurora. "Incoming ordnance!"

The first missile struck the bow, slightly port of her centerline. They were not big missiles, but without any shielding, they were big enough to take out one of their rail gun emplacements. And with less than half of them operational, they needed every one.

The ship rocked from the explosion, which could be seen on the main view screen, the glare bathing the bridge in yellow-orange light that faded quickly. The second missile could be seen streaking overhead on the view screen, striking aft of the camera emplacements against the elevated drive section at the stern of the ship. The second explosion could not be seen from the bridge, but they could definitely feel it.

"Deep space comms are down!" the comm officer reported. "That last missile must've taken out the array!"

"The second contact is making a run for it, Captain!" the commander exclaimed.

"Get a solution for one and three on that contact!"

"She's still out of range, sir."

"Ensign, how quickly can we get in range at full thrust?"

"Two minutes," Cameron reported.

"Full power, Lieutenant!"

Nathan brought the main engines back up to full power, pushing everyone back in their seats once more. Only this time, they were expecting it and were better prepared for the sensation.

"Torpedo range in a minute forty," Cameron reported calmly.

"Will we catch her before she can get up to light speed?" the captain asked the commander. Their FTL system was offline since the emitter systems were being used by the Special Projects team.

"I guess we'll see," the commander shrugged.

It seemed like it took forever for them to close the gap. The little ship could outrun them, but the Aurora could accelerate faster. But without the emitters, she could not generate the field that negated her mass and allowed for the transition into FTL velocities.

"We're passing through the first contact's debris field," the sensor officer announced. All along the ship, the sounds of debris striking the hull could be heard as pieces of the destroyed enemy ship of varying sizes struck the exterior of the ship. Most of it sounded like rain, although a few were loud enough to cause Nathan to flinch.

"Torpedo range in sixty seconds," Cameron reported.

"Firing solutions locked and ready," the commander announced.

"She's got an antimatter reactor on board, Captain!" the sensor officer reported.

"A patrol ship with an antimatter reactor?" the captain asked the commander. "You ever hear of that?"

"No, sir. But our intel on their ships is still limited."

"I wonder what else she's got." The captain thought for a moment. "Can you retarget the torpedoes to take out her engines without destroying her?"

"I can try, but I'm not making any promises." The commander looked at his captain, as if reading his mind. "Are you thinking what I'm thinking?"

"One ship is a coincidence..." Captain Roberts turned to look at his executive officer.

"Two is a trap," the commander finished for him. "Retargeting."

* * *

In the special operations section just forward of the Aurora's flight deck, Jessica and her teammates sat waiting for something to do. They were all highly trained in the art of specialized combat and covert operations, and they could handle just about anything. But during a yellow alert, all they could do was sit in their ready room and wait.

Being assigned to the Aurora was about the last thing that Jessica had wanted upon graduation.

She had hoped to get assigned to a deep cover intelligence gathering team that would be smuggled onto one of the core system worlds occupied by the Jung in order to collect intelligence to forward back to Earth. Such assignments were the dream of every spec-ops officer, since due to the difficulty of getting info back to Earth, they were authorized to take whatever actions they felt necessary to protect the interests of their homeworld. It was a life of excitement and danger, where your fate was in your own hands and not the hands of some brass hat sitting behind a desk somewhere back on Earth.

But instead, she had been assigned here. She understood why every ship needed its own spec-ops team. This ship, with its FTL capabilities, at least had the ability to get her somewhere interesting. So in that sense, it was better than getting assigned to one of the older sub-light ships.

When battle stations had been called, she had been sure it was a drill, despite the fact that it had not been announced as such. Even when the ship started maneuvering hard and accelerating sporadically, she still had her doubts. But then they heard, and felt, torpedoes being fired. And then the constant pounding of the rail gun cannons as they laid down point-defense flak. While they might fire the cannons in a drill, there was no way they were going to waste a couple of torpedoes. Those things were like small spaceships and were armed with small tactical nukes.

The final evidence had been the explosions, the first of which struck very close, above and forward of them, knocking them out of their seats. A few minutes after that, two more torpedoes were launched. Either they were fighting multiple ships or one really big one. But in the orbit of Jupiter? It just didn't make any sense.

After the last batch of torpedoes had been launched, it had suddenly gotten quiet. The main engines, which had been running at full thrust, had also quieted. And she was sure that she felt deceleration, though sometimes it was hard to tell with the inertial dampeners in play.

Suddenly the room turned red and the action alarm squawked a single blast. The master chief in charge of the unit picked up the comm handset and took the call.

"Spec-ops," he announced. The master chief listened intently for a few moments. "Yes, sir!" The master chief hung up the handset and turned to face his people. "All right, listen up! Suit up for an EVA boarding action! Two insertion teams, four elements in each team! You move out in ten minutes!"

"Holy shit!" Jessica exclaimed. *Maybe this ain't such a bad assignment after all!*

"Her main drive is definitely wiped out," the commander proclaimed. We nailed her square in the ass with both shots. Just about blew her tail off."

"What are you seeing over there?" the captain asked his sensor officer.

"She looks pretty dark, sir. I'm pretty sure she's running on emergency power. Her shields and weapons are down, but her antimatter reactor is still online. She's probably blown her power distribution system."

The captain turned to his comm officer. "Any signals coming out of her?"

"No, sir, not a peep. But I've only got the local

array to work with, so I'm not a hundred percent sure about that. If they used a tight beam, I doubt I'd see it."

"Could she be playing possum, luring us into a trap?" This time his question was directed back to Commander Montero.

"It is possible, but doubtful. She's pretty busted up. Most of her aft section is open to space."

"He's right, sir," the sensor operator added. "In fact, the only pressurized compartments I'm seeing are engineering and her bridge. Pretty much everything else is in vacuum."

The captain thought about it for a moment. His first instinct was to stand off and pulverize her with his eleven remaining rail guns. But there was a good chance that there was some valuable intelligence on that ship, maybe even some technology that might come in useful. No one had ever captured a Jung ship before.

"It is a risk," the captain admitted to his XO, "but I think it's worth it." He looked to his second in command for confirmation.

"Agreed," the commander said.

"Very well." The captain sat back down in his command chair. "Take us in, Lieutenant, slow and easy. Roll us over and park us directly above her topsides, roof-to-roof. Since we don't have any shuttles, they'll have to do this the hard way."

"Yes, sir," Nathan answered as he began rolling the ship. They had already decelerated and had been slowly coasting towards the disabled ship for the last few minutes.

"XO, let's keep all guns trained on her, just in case."

"Already done, sir."

The two boarding teams walked out onto the flight deck. Wearing armored combat EVA suits, each of them carried a small close-quarters weapon attached with quick-connect fittings to the chest plates of their suits. The flight deck's gravity plating was only a quarter of Earth norm, so carrying their transfer packs out across the deck onto the open landing apron was easy.

Jessica looked up as she stepped onto the apron. Directly above her was the crippled Jung patrol ship. It was only about half as big as the Aurora. It was badly damaged and she could see several openings in her hull through which they could probably gain access. The ship's rail gun turrets still looked operable, which made Jessica a little nervous.

"This is so cool!" her partner, Ensign Enrique Mendez, exclaimed.

"You can say that again," she agreed. Jessica knelt down and secured a heavy transfer line to the deck, setting the carefully coiled cable neatly down next to her.

"I sure don't remember this scenario in training, huh, Jess?"

"Me neither."

"Cut the chatter," her team leader ordered. "Mount up and let's get this show on the road. We go across as one, then split up after we reach the target vessel. Alpha goes forward and Bravo goes aft."

Each group lined up in pairs. One of them held the transfer pack in front of them, the other latched onto the first one's back. With a blast of the maneuvering jets in the transfer pack, each pair lifted off the landing apron of the Aurora and began their ascent to the roof of the Jung ship. It was slow going, as they didn't want to slam into the other ship at breakneck speeds.

Jessica and Enrique were the last to leave. Enrique operated the transfer pack with Jessica attached to his back—one hand on her weapon with it pointed straight ahead, and the other hand on the free end of the transfer line she had attached to the deck. The transfer packs had just enough thrust to get them over to the enemy ship, so the transfer line would be their only way back to the Aurora.

Jessica kept her eyes forward, looking for any signs of a hostile threat as they coasted toward the Jung ship. It was a rather ugly looking vessel, dirty and not well maintained, she thought. It looked more like what she thought a space pirates' ship might look like, if such a thing actually existed.

"Approaching the vessel now, sir," the report came over the comm.

The main screen was displaying the view from a camera built into the top of the Aurora just forward of her flight deck. It gave them a clear view of the boarding team as they made their way across the void between the two ships.

Nathan was amazed as he watched the spec-ops teams floating across in pairs, not understanding how anyone could do something like that, let alone *want* to do it. Spec-ops had a reputation back on Earth. 'Anything, anytime, anywhere.' Apparently they had meant it.

"Any change in that ship's status?" the captain asked.

"No, sir," the sensor operator assured him. "She's still at minimal power."

The inside of the Jung ship was dark, with only dim emergency lighting in operation. There appeared to be only a single battery-powered light in each section, which seemed hardly enough for the job. It seemed a little odd to Jessica, since you could read in the emergency lighting in the Aurora.

Jessica's team had gone aft toward engineering while Alpha team headed forward to capture the bridge. There was no gravity functioning onboard, although she could tell by the design of the ship and the floating debris that the ship was equipped with artificial gravity; it just wasn't working right now.

As they floated through the corridors, the closest thing they found to a crew was dead bodies floating about. But there were very few of them, and Jessica surmised that the sudden decompression probably sucked many of the ship's crew out into space. That was fine with her, as it meant fewer Jungs with guns.

They were forced to use the maneuvering jets built into their suits, as there was little to grab onto and the deck didn't seem to have enough metal in it to use the magnets built into their boots. Jessica tried to use her hands when she could, hoping to save as much of her limited suit thrusters as possible in case she needed them later.

Luckily, it had not been far from their entry point to the engineering section of the smaller ship, and a few minutes later they reached the access hatch to engineering.

"*We're taking fire!*" came a voice over her comm-set. *"Repeat, Alpha team is taking fire!"*

Jessica looked to her team leader for orders.

"You know the rules, Nash," he warned. "They have their job; we have ours."

She watched as her partner placed the demo charges on the hatch, taking a safe position just around the corner. After he finished placing the charges, he moved around the corner with her before reporting.

"Charges are set, L-T."

"Blow it."

"Fire in the hole," he announced.

There was a flash of light but no sound since they were in a vacuum. Hundreds of pieces of metal shrapnel flew past them. After waiting a moment, Enrique peeked around the corner to take a look. The corridor was full of smoke, but there was light shining through the smoke that he was sure was coming from the open hatchway into engineering.

"We've got a hole," Enrique reported.

The team leader and his partner took up positions on either side of the door. They each had to keep one hand on the hatch ring in order to keep from floating freely in the zero gravity of the hallway.

The lieutenant took a small marker stick from his utility pouch and tossed it through the hatch. As it floated across the threshold, it suddenly dropped to the floor.

"There's gravity in there," he reported. He pulled out his fiber optic camera and carefully snaked the lens around the edge of the hatch to look inside. On the far side of the room, he could see a man in a pressure suit frantically doing something at a control console. He couldn't see a weapon on him.

"I've got one bad guy, in a pressure suit, doing

something at a console on the left. I can't tell if he's armed."

Suddenly, his partner stuck his weapon through the hatchway and opened fire. Immediately, two blue-white blasts of energy were fired at the hatch from inside. The first one bounced off the wall inside, but the second one came through the hatch, catching the over enthusiastic ensign in the shoulder, instantly burning a hole through his armor, suit, and shoulder. He screamed in pain as the upper half of his suit suddenly depressurized, killing him a moment later.

"Shit!" the lieutenant screamed. "Mendez! Nash! Get ready! I'm tossing flash-bangs in five!"

Jessica and Enrique took up positions across the corridor from the hatch, ready to push against the opposite wall to propel themselves through the hatchway and into the room. A moment later, the lieutenant tossed a flash-bang grenade into the defended compartment. The grenade flashed silently on the other side of the wall, lighting up the corridor for a brief moment. Enrique launched himself off the wall, flying across the weightless hallway and into the next room. As he flew across the threshold, the artificial gravity in the compartment pulled him down harder than expected, knocking his weapon from his hand.

More blasts of blue-white light sprayed across the room, one grazing his left thigh.

Jessica had launched herself only a moment later, flying deeper into the compartment and landing just past Enrique, spraying fire in the direction of the enemy. The lieutenant jumped through the hatchway next, landing on his feet and scurrying along the wall toward the now silent enemy. He moved swiftly around the console and found the enemy lying on the floor, bullet wounds riddling his torso and face.

"Clear!" the lieutenant announced.

Jessica scrambled back to Enrique, quickly pulling out an emergency wound dressing.

"What the fuck is wrong with you, dropping your weapon like that?!" she scolded. "You weren't supposed to get shot, dumbass!"

"Sorry, Jess," he apologized, wincing through the pain. "I didn't know you cared."

"I don't," she corrected, as she applied the bandage. "I just don't wanna have to break in a new dumbass," she added with a grin.

"How is he?" the lieutenant inquired from behind the console.

"He'll live!" Jessica responded. "Lucky for you these suits are compartmentalized. Otherwise you would've decompressed and you'd be dead by now."

She quickly wrapped over the top of the bandage with a sealing wrap, and then pressed some buttons on his wrist mounted suit control to repressurize the damaged section of his suit. "You lost a lot of your air through that hole. You'd better head back now."

Jessica helped Enrique to his feet and got him through the hatchway and back into the corridor where he could float in zero gravity. "Use your suit jets and haul ass back to the ship!" She gave him a shove down the corridor to get him on his way. A second later his maneuvering jets fired and he picked up speed, disappearing around the corner.

Jessica leaned back into the engineering compartment and made her way over to the lieutenant. He was pushing buttons and looking at displays, trying to figure out what was going on.

"Shit! This is all in Jung!" he complained, obviously frustrated. "Do you read Jung?"

"Nobody reads Jung, L-T!" she defended. "Hell, I didn't even know they had their own language!"

There were several indicators on a section of the console that looked like it controlled the antimatter reactor. They were blinking red and their indicators were rising.

"I don't like this," Jessica grumbled. "Is that what I think it is?"

"Yeah, I think so."

"Captain, I'm not picking up any bio-signals from Alpha team," the XO reported, "and there's no more comm-chatter."

"*Aurora, Bravo Leader! We've got a problem!*"

"Go ahead, Bravo," the commander answered. As the acting tactical officer, it was his job to manage the boarding action.

"*Aurora, it looks like they've initiated an overload of their antimatter reactor! I'm not sure! It's all in Jung! But I'm pretty sure it's gonna blow in five minutes!*"

"Pull them out, now!" the captain ordered.

"Bravo, fall back! Repeat! Fall back! Return to the ship!"

"*Copy that!*"

"How long will it take us to get to minimum safe distance at full thrust?" the captain demanded.

Cameron punched in a string of calculations at lightning speed. "Estimate eight minutes, sir."

"What are you doing?" Jessica said. "You heard

him; we've gotta go!"

"I think I can buy you some time!" the lieutenant explained. "When I press this button, it makes the temp on the reactor drop a few degrees! It won't stop it, but I might be able to buy the Aurora a few more minutes to get clear."

"Are you crazy? You'll be vaporized!"

"At least I won't feel anything," he joked.

She looked at him through his visor, the fear evident on his face as he repeatedly pressed the button in a losing battle to delay the inevitable.

"Move it, Ensign!" he ordered.

"L-T!"

"Look, it may not be enough even if I do stay!" He looked at her sternly. "Go, Jess, please?" he begged.

She took a hesitant step backwards, paused, and snapped a salute before turning and running, diving head first through the hatchway and into the weightless corridor where her momentum carried her rapidly down the hall.

"How much longer until we can get outta here?" the captain asked.

"Two of them are on the transfer line now," the commander answered. "But one of them is still in the engineering compartment."

"What the hell? Get him out of there!"

"Bravo Leader, you've got one still on board! Sit rep!" the commander ordered. A moment passed before the XO repeated the hail. "Bravo Leader, Aurora! Do you copy?!"

"Aurora, Ensign Nash! The lieutenant has probably switched off his comm-set!"

Nathan turned his head suddenly, realizing that

it was Jessica out there. It wasn't that he had any particular emotional attachment to her, at least not the he was consciously aware of, but he actually *knew* someone who was out there, putting their life on the line right now, and that sensation was new to him.

"Nash, Aurora! Explain!" the commander ordered.

"He stayed behind! He's manually stalling the overload! He's trying to buy us a few more minutes! He probably went dark so we couldn't talk him out of it!"

Commander Montero looked at the captain, who had a blank look in his eyes. This new crew might be fresh out of the academy and inexperienced, but they were not lacking in courage.

"Understood," the commander transmitted solemnly. "ETA to Aurora?"

"Two minutes, sir!"

"Copy."

Jessica continued pulling herself along the cable, hand over hand, as she made her way back to the ship. She was nearly halfway there when she looked up and saw Enrique settling in on the Aurora's landing apron next to the base of the transfer line.

"Shake a leg, Jess!" he called over the comm-set. *"We ain't got all day, you know!"*

"Quit your bitching. I'm coming!"

Suddenly, Enrique's eyes widened as he noticed movement on the surface of the Jung ship.

"Jess! One of the turrets!"

"Captain," the sensor officer called out, "the

Jung ship, sir! She's got one of her gun turrets back online!"

"What? I thought she had no power!" the captain barked.

"I don't know how, sir, but she's got a turret swinging over to take aim at the landing apron," the sensor officer explained urgently. "More turrets coming online as well! Two, three, four... they're all coming to life!"

Rail gun rounds flew all around Jessica as she rapidly ascended the transfer line, pulling herself towards the ship as fast as her hands could move. Out of the corner of her visor she could see multiple flashes as more of the Jung cannons began to open fire on the Aurora, sending chunks of the hull flying in all directions.

"Oh shit!" she exclaimed.

A split second later, the Aurora's cannons opened up on the Jung ship. Enrique watched in awe as the upper hull of the Jung ship was torn apart by the Aurora's rail gun fire.

"Detach the line!" she called out to Enrique. "Let's get the fuck out of here!"

Without hesitation, Enrique did as his partner asked. He reached down to the base of the transfer line where it connected to the deck. After opening up a small panel in the side of the connection collar, he pushed the button in and held it down.

At the far end of the cable, where it connected to the Jung ship, the line released its connection and began to float away freely.

"Transfer line disconnected!" he announced.

"Aurora, Nash! The line is free! Get us out of

139

here!"

"Nash! Aurora! Are you secure?!"

"I'm secure, damn it! Now go!"

"Aurora, Mendez! She's still on the line, about fifty meters away!"

"Goddamn it! Just go!" she demanded. "I'll make it!"

"Take us out," the captain ordered, "but not too fast yet. We don't want her slamming against the hull."

Nathan started with the docking thrusters only, burning them for a few seconds as he tried to imagine Jessica, out there in the vacuum of space as she clung onto the transfer line while it swung her down toward the hull of the ship. He knew that no matter how slow he went, she was still going to hit hard.

"Commander!" Nathan yelled, suddenly having an idea. "Tell her to call out just before she impacts the hull! A couple meters, maybe!"

The commander didn't bother to ask Nathan why, figuring it wouldn't hurt.

"Good thinking, Nathan," the captain said. He already knew what his helmsman was up to.

"Nash, Aurora! Call out a few meters before you hit the hull!"

Out on the landing apron, Enrique was protected against the motion of the ship by her inertial dampeners. But out on the end of the transfer line, Jessica was not. It was all she could do to just hang on. With her legs wrapped tightly around the line to help keep her from sliding farther down it, there was no way she would be able to continue her ascent until after she hit the hull. That is, if she survived the impact.

As she dangled around on the line, spinning back and forth, she could see the impacts of the Jung rail gun fire on the hull of the ship. It was an ugly thing to witness, but the damage didn't appear too serious. She was sure that the Jung were firing blindly out of desperation and not really aiming strategically.

While the Aurora continued to accelerate, she could tell she was getting closer to the hull as her body weight on the line resulted in a lazy arc toward the ship. By her best guess, she was going to hit about fifty meters aft of the landing apron. But the apron itself was at least ten meters higher than the hull behind her, and it was an overhang with no way up. Even if she did survive the impact, how was she going to get back into the ship? Even with the inertial dampeners, she doubted she could climb around on the outside of the ship during full acceleration.

As she spun around again, she was able to see something near the spot where she thought she was going to land, something round. *A hatch!*

"Aurora, Nash! Is that a hatch I see just aft of the landing apron?"

"Affirmative! We're on it!"

Within seconds, the spec-ops master chief was running through the corridors of the Aurora on his way to the airlock just aft of the landing apron.

"Time to overload?" the captain asked.

"Unknown," the commander said. "Based on the lieutenant's original report, it should have already happened."

"I guess whatever he's doing is working."

"Captain, we're starting to show them our hindquarters. If we take too many hits on the stern without shields we might lose main propulsion," the commander warned.

"Helm, come slowly to starboard. Try not to show them our ass too much."

"Yes, sir."

The ship started to roll to starboard slightly as she started a slow right turn. Jessica's descent arc started to slide to port slightly, which by her estimates would make her land even closer to the airlock hatch. *Damn, Nathan. I underestimated you.*

Inside the ship, the spec-ops master chief arrived at the airlock and began depressurizing the chamber.

"Three meters!" Jessica called out over comms.

Without being ordered, Nathan pitched the tail of the ship down slightly to reduce Jessica's rate of closure thereby lessening her impact velocity. It wasn't much, but he desperately hoped it would help.

Jessica's eyes widened as she rapidly fell toward the ship. But then, suddenly, her rate of closure changed, slowing considerably. She realized the ship was pitching her tail down, and she knew that Nathan was trying as best he could to give her a soft landing.

Despite his best efforts, she hit hard, knocking the air out of her lungs. She rebounded from the deck, floating back up slightly, but the ships acceleration forced her back down, striking a second time. As she rolled over onto her side, the hatch, located not more than a meter away, suddenly opened. *I may have to give you another quickie, Nathan,* she thought as she struggled to get through the airlock hatch.

"Bridge, airlock fourteen! Nash is in!"

"All ahead full!" the captain ordered.

Nathan immediately brought the mains up to full power, feeling the acceleration as it pushed him back into his chair. *Those dampeners are pretty damned good,* he thought.

"How long until we get clear?" the captain asked again.

"Five minutes, sir," Cameron responded.

Nathan wasn't sure, but he thought he heard a touch of fear in her voice. *Perhaps she's human after all?*

The rail gun fire continued to rock the ship, diminishing as their distance from the enemy increased. The captain's mind was racing furiously, searching for options. If he put a torpedo into her, it might stop the overload. But it might also kill the brave lieutenant that was sacrificing himself to buy them some time. It also might trigger the overload even sooner. If he had his FTL fields, he could

143

probably accelerate past light speed and get clear, but all the emitters were being used by the Special Projects team. That's when the idea struck him.

"Doctor Karlsen," the captain said, spinning around, "can we make another jump?"

"You cannot simply snap your fingers and *jump* as you say," he argued. "It takes time to recharge the energy banks..."

"How much time?"

"At least one hour for every light year traveled," the doctor explained. "But there are other considerations..."

"There *is* enough energy currently in the banks for a transition back to Earth, Captain," Doctor Sorenson interrupted. Public speaking was not her father's strength, nor was seeing the big picture quickly. For all his brilliance in physics, he tended to have tunnel vision in such matters. "But it takes time to calculate a transition sequence..."

"How long?"

"Too long, I'm afraid," she admitted.

"What about Earth? Didn't you already have a sequence programmed to return to Earth?"

"Yes, but we're not even headed in the right direction. And we're already a considerable distance from our original departure point. I would have to recalculate..."

The captain was getting tired of all the details. He just wanted to know if he could use the jump drive to get away. "Ensign, how long would it take to get back to our original arrival point?"

"Maybe three minutes," Cameron estimated. "But that's only if we take a direct route, which would take us back into their weapons range."

"Doctor, what would happen if we jumped using

the sequence calculated for a return to Earth on our present course?"

Doctor Karlsen was flabbergasted and began babbling in Danish at his daughter. His daughter just ignored him, focusing her attention on the captain, as she knew he was just trying to get them out of an impossible situation.

"Honestly, I do not know," she admitted. "The safety protocols may not even accept the execute command, since the ship's heading does not match the..."

"Can you override the safety protocols?"

"Yes, but..."

"Do it!" he commanded.

"Captain, this is not a good idea," Doctor Karlsen protested.

Doctor Sorenson spoke to her father in Danish, trying to calm him down as she frantically tried to override the safety protocols.

"Captain," the sensor operator exclaimed, "their reactor's about to go!"

"Doctor," the captain urged, "we're running outta time!"

"There she goes!" the sensor operator cried out.

"Now, Doctor! JUMP!"

Doctor Sorenson tapped a few more keys before hitting the execute button.

"Initiating transition sequence!" she announced.

The ship was struck hard by the shock wave of the antimatter explosion as it disappeared in a bright flash of blue-white light.

"Transition complete!" Doctor Sorenson announced, obvious relief in her voice.

Nathan lowered his hand from his eyes. This time, he had shielded his face from the bright flash of the jump as it was carried into the bridge by the forward view screen. As he looked over to Cameron, he could see that she had done the same. He looked to his right and saw the sensor operator picking himself up off the floor.

"Status!" the captain bellowed.

Nathan looked over his console, checking that everything was in order. He looked over at Cameron, who nodded that her systems were fine as well.

"Helm is oper..."

"Contacts!" the sensor operator yelled out. "Multiple contacts, all around us! Transferring tracks to tactical!"

"What the hell? Where are we?" the captain asked.

The ship suddenly began taking fire, with massive explosions rocking the ship violently. The force of the ordnance was far more severe than what they had experienced earlier with the two Jung patrol ships.

There was the smell of something burning, like an electrical fire, and Nathan could hear the sound of short circuits coming from behind him.

"Return fire, all batteries!" the captain ordered.

"Which ship do we shoot at, sir?" the commander asked.

"Target the biggest one that's shooting at us!" the captain ordered. "At least until we figure out who the hell we're fighting!"

"All the fire is coming from the biggest contact, sir!"

"Then that's your target, Commander."

"She's huge, Captain," the commander exclaimed. "Gotta be twice the size of our Defender-class ships!"

"What? The Jung don't have anything that big!"

"We'll never take her out with rail guns, sir. Suggest we give her a full spread of torpedoes!"

"Helm, hard to starboard! Bring us to bear on the biggest ship!"

Nathan quickly turned the ship hard to starboard until the biggest enemy ship came into the middle of his screen. They were coming in on the enemy ship's port side and would have a perfect shot with their torpedoes.

"Get a solution, tubes one through four, and prepare to fire!" the captain ordered.

"Sir, those smaller ships, the multi-colored ones," Nathan said, "they're fighting the big one just like us!"

"What the hell did we jump into?" the captain muttered.

Seeing the Aurora turn into her, the larger ship immediately trained all her guns on her new attacker, ignoring the smaller vessels.

"She's trying to stop us short!" the commander yelled as the ship shook even more from the intense barrage of enemy rounds.

All about the bridge, circuits were shorting out, pieces were falling off the walls and panels; even a beam fell across the port exit, killing one of the marine guards that had still been standing his post. Nathan found himself flinching repeatedly as rounds streaked towards them on the view screen, barely missing the cameras before striking nearby.

"Firing solution locked!" the XO announced.

"Fire all forward tubes!"

On either side of the Aurora's leading upper edge of the main propulsion section, doors again slid open to reveal the torpedo launch tubes. Nearly simultaneously, four torpedoes shot out, their thrust plumes burning brightly behind them as they streaked towards their target.

"One through four away!" the XO announced. "At this range, those nukes are gonna shake us good, Captain."

"I know," the captain mumbled.

"Missiles!" the sensor operator called out. "Eight inbound. Transferring tracks to tactical!"

"Damn!" the captain swore to himself. "Are we jamming?!" he barked, angry at himself for not giving the command earlier.

"I started jamming the moment the new contacts were announced, sir!" the ECO answered, proud of himself for having taken the initiative when he knew his captain had been too busy to remember.

"Good boy!"

"Switching rail guns to point-defense mode," the commander announced from tactical.

There were only eight rail gun batteries left, as three more had been taken out by enemy fire since they had arrived in this unknown region of space. They stopped firing for a moment while they switched ammo feeds and began firing point-defense rounds instead of the standard explosive penetration rounds they usually fired.

"It's not going to be enough, sir," the commander warned.

"Time to impact?"

"Twenty seconds."

"How long before our torpedoes hit?"

"Ten seconds."

The captain spun around to face the forward screen just in time to see the first torpedo detonate, blowing a hole in the massive ship, the image of which by now nearly filled their entire screen. A split second later, there were two more explosions, just aft of the first one, causing multiple secondary explosions.

"Yes!" the captain exclaimed.

"Incoming ordnance!" the commander called out.

Five of the eight missiles made it past the Aurora's point-defense fire. The first one struck the nose at an oblique angle and bounced off without exploding, sending it right toward the view screen camera and causing everyone on the bridge to duck instinctively. The second missile impacted the starboard side of the bow, blowing away a portion of their primary hull. The third and fourth missiles both struck on the underside of the bow, which was more heavily reinforced. The fifth missile struck the starboard side, just below the shield generation compartment.

Nathan wasn't sure which, but between the detonations of the missiles and the shock wave from the nuclear detonations of their own torpedoes, they had gotten the living hell knocked out of them.

"The enemy ship is no longer maneuvering sir! But she can still shoot!"

"Pull us up, Lieutenant!" the captain ordered. "Show them our belly as we pass! It's the strongest part of the hull!"

Nathan pulled the control yoke back, but the ship wasn't changing course. He quickly double checked his console, only to find that he had lost all control. "Captain! The helm's not responding!"

"Doctor, can we jump again?" the captain asked desperately.

"Not possible! The system is offline!" Doctor Sorenson reported.

"Emergency braking thrusters!" the captain ordered. "Sound collision alert!"

Nathan fired the emergency braking thrusters, relief pouring over him that at least they still worked.

On the sides of the bow, the emergency braking thrusters fired, burning at full power as they tried to slow the ship. But she was traveling way too fast for them to have much of an effect, as they were designed to be used in docking emergencies, not at combat velocities.

Throughout the ship, the collision alarm sounded, followed by the computerized voice, *"Collision alert. Collision alert."*

"Evacuate the forward sections!" the captain ordered.

Nathan's eyes ran wildly across his console, looking for something that worked, anything that he could use to steer the ship and avoid a head first dive into the enemy ship's port side. But there was nothing. The only other functioning system was the docking thrusters, which would not generate enough thrust to turn away in time.

He looked up at the main view screen. The image of the burning enemy ship filled the entire screen now. She had stopped firing, as they were now so close that most of her batteries couldn't get a decent angle to continue pounding them. There were three holes in her side. One where the first torpedo detonated, and a second, larger one just aft of the first, probably where the second and third torpedoes had done their damage. The third hole was much smaller and was back towards the aft end of the ship. It looked like a penetration of some sort.

Nathan looked at the middle hole, the larger one. It looked like they were going to strike just forward of it. Suddenly, he had an idea.

"Time to impact?" the captain asked.

"Five seconds," the XO answered.

Nathan grabbed the joystick for the docking thrusters and pushed it hard to starboard. It wasn't much, but the bow inched over just slightly, redirecting them towards the hole.

The captain saw what Nathan was doing and smiled as he put his hand on Nathan's shoulder. He knew he had picked the right man for the job.

CHAPTER FIVE

Nathan's head hurt, really badly. He couldn't remember it ever hurting this badly before. And his leg, something in his left leg also hurt. He started coughing, the smell of smoke wafting into his lungs as he tried to take in a breath. He tried opening his eyes, but everything started spinning.

Squeezing his eyes shut, he tried to concentrate and stop the spinning. There were noises all about him. Crackles, pops, and fizzles. And there were muffled explosions in the distance. And the moaning, someone was moaning. A woman suddenly screamed, causing Nathan's eyes to snap open. Again his head began spinning, but not as badly as before. The room was dark except for a faint glow from the back of the room and the occasional flashes of blue-white light that coincided with the crackles and pops.

He rolled onto his right side and found he wasn't lying flat. His feet were lower than his head. For a moment, he couldn't figure out where he was, until it all started flooding back to him through the pain, the spinning, and the coughing.

He looked around, realizing he was lying on the long, angled cowling between the backside of the helm console and the bottom of the main view screen, which was dark. *I must've been thrown over the console.*

He could hear the woman who had screamed sobbing and saying something unintelligible to him, something in another language. He managed to slide off the cowling onto the floor, and crawl between the edge of the helm and the sensor operator's console. After squeezing between the consoles, he looked to his left and found that the sensor operator was slumped forward, his head crushed by the side console that must've torn free and fallen during the collision. A pool was forming below the dead officer, as blood ran out of his head and down the console, finally spilling onto the floor below.

Nathan crawled out from between the consoles and onto the floor, coming face to face with Captain Roberts. He was lying on his back, and his right eye was bleeding. His shoulder looked odd, and his uniform was stained with blood on his abdomen. Nathan thought he was breathing but couldn't be sure in the poorly lit room.

There was another sound, one that Nathan couldn't quite identify at first. Then he realized it was the sound of screaming, yelling, and weapons fire coming across an open comm-line somewhere. It occurred to him that somebody ought to be looking into that sound, someone in command.

He grabbed hold of the seat back at the helm station, using it to pull himself up. He winced in pain as he first put pressure on his left leg. He looked down at his leg, bending over and grabbing his left calf; it was wet, bleeding. He wondered if it was broken.

He looked around through the smoke and haze, looking to see who was in command. The captain was unconscious, probably still alive but definitely in no condition to command. He looked about for the commander but could not find him.

Nathan made his way up the step onto the main

bridge level and limped around to the back side of the tactical station. Lying on the floor behind the console was Commander Montero. His back was severely burnt, and his head had taken a severe blow from a beam lying on the floor next to him. Nathan bent down and turned him over, but he was dead.

Nathan managed to get to his feet and looked around the bridge. The only steady lighting came from two emergency lights located over the exits in the back corners of the room. In the back starboard corner, Doctor Sorenson was sobbing uncontrollably over the mangled body of her dead father. One of the marines was starting to move behind her as he regained consciousness. In front of her, the ECO was dead, his console having exploded in his face.

Nathan looked to his left. The ensign at the science station was just waking up, and below her, Cameron was also starting to show signs of life.

The sounds of weapon fire and yelling again came across the open comm-line. It was coming from the tactical station directly in front of Nathan which, for all intents and purposes, appeared to still be functioning. Again, he knew something had to be done about the sounds. That's when he realized that *he* was the most senior officer on the bridge. And he suddenly knew that he had to take action.

Nathan stood at the tactical station and switched the comm to ship-wide. "All hands! Prepare to repel enemy boarding parties! Repeat! We are being boarded! Find a weapon and defend yourself!" Nathan looked over at the marine who had just woken up. "We've been boarded!" he barked. *Where?* he thought, *Where are they?* He looked down at the tactical display and saw that the open channel was in the forward section. "Forward Section! Repeat! Forward Section!" Nathan spun around to the face the marine. "Secure this bridge! No one in or out without my orders!" The marine said nothing, just nodded and checked his weapon to make sure he was locked and loaded before moving to check on his fellow marines. Nathan glanced over the tactical display, trying to assess the ship's condition. Their bow was rammed deep inside the enemy vessel, and there was a large hull breach on the port side about twenty meters back. He assumed that the enemy troops were entering through the hull breach.

Finally, Cameron began to open her eyes and cough.

"Cameron!" Nathan hollered. "Cameron! Wake up!"

Cameron rolled her head from side to side as she woke, trying to make sense of what was going on around her.

"Help her up!" Nathan ordered the ensign at the science station, who had only become conscious herself a moment ago.

The ensign stepped down and helped Cameron to her feet, holding her steady until she could focus and get her balance.

"Cameron, are you all right?" he asked.

"Yeah," she responded in between coughs, "I think so."

"Take the helm!" he ordered.

"What? Why? What's going on?" she asked, looking around. "Where's the captain?"

"He's injured." Nathan continued checking systems on the tactical display.

"What about the XO?"

"Dead." Nathan called up engineering.

"Engineering, bridge! Can you hear me?"

"Dead? Then who's in command?" she asked, still not fully coherent. Suddenly, she remembered the chain of command, and the impossible dawned on her. She looked around the room, seeing only two marines, Doctor Sorenson, herself, and the ensign at the science station. She turned her head back to look at Nathan in disbelief.

Nathan's voice came blaring through the ship's comm-system for all to hear. *"All hands! Prepare to repel enemy boarding parties! Repeat! We are being boarded! Find a weapon and defend yourself! Forward Section! Repeat! Forward Section!"*

Jessica and the master chief ran down the corridor, jumping through hatchways as they passed through each section. Jessica was still in her EVA suit but had dumped her life support pack, helmet, and chest piece. The suit was a bit on the heavy side, but she figured the extra armor it provided would be worth it in a firefight. She held her automatic close-quarters weapon in front of her as she ran behind the master chief, who carried one of his own and was wearing a flak vest.

"What the fuck is going on?!" she demanded after hearing Nathan's voice over the loud speakers. "First we're slugging it out with warships, then we're boarding them, then we're slugging it out again, and now *we're* being boarded? I mean, what the hell? Last I heard we were orbiting Jupiter!"

"You know what your problem is, Ensign?" the master chief said as they ran down the corridor.

"No, but I'm sure you're gonna tell me!"

"You talk too much!"

The master chief turned the corner and suddenly found himself face to face with the enemy. Having never seen the Jung before, he hadn't known what to expect, other than the fact that they were human.

"Whoa!" he cried, ducking as the enemy swung the butt of his rifle at the master chief's face. The master chief hit the enemy soldier low, right in the upper abdomen with his left shoulder, driving him back against his friends. With his gun hand, the master chief reached around the first soldier and sprayed the ones behind him with automatic fire, sending at least three of them to the floor in a bloody pile.

"Get down!" Jessica yelled as she brought her weapon to bear.

The master chief hit the deck as Jessica emptied her entire clip at the rest of the soldiers, killing not only the first one, but the remaining four as well.

"You okay?" she yelled, dropping her empty clip and slapping in a fresh one as she ran past him toward the sound of weapon fire.

"Fuck me!" the master chief exclaimed, stunned that, not only had they just taken down eight enemy combatants, but he had made it through the encounter without a scratch. He immediately started looking himself over for wounds, still in disbelief.

"Come on! It ain't over!" she hollered, her voice full of excitement as the adrenaline coursed through her veins. All that combat training she had been through was finally coming in handy.

At the next corner, she came to a group of three shipmates trying to hold the corridor with small arms. There had been five, but two of them were dead, holes burnt in their bodies by energy weapon fire.

"How are you guys doing?" Jessica asked as she knelt down beside them and began to return fire. The smell of the burnt bodies was nearly overpowering.

"Better than them!" the first one answered.

"I don't know what kind of guns they have, but they do some serious damage!" the second one exclaimed.

"Yeah, I can see that," she answered as the master chief dropped down behind her.

"Here!" the master chief told his shipmates, offering a few of the enemy's energy weapons. "Thought you could use these!"

The first crewman looked at the weapon in disbelief. "Where did you get these?"

"Took 'em off the fuckers we just wasted back there," the master chief bragged, pointing back down the corridor the way they had come. "Figured they didn't need them anymore!"

"From back there?" the crewman asked, turning slightly paler.

"Yeah, I figure they were tryin' to flank ya!"

"Shit! Thanks, Master Chief!" The crewman looked at the weapons. "How do they work?"

"Hadn't thought about that," he admitted. "Let me see it," he added, grabbing the weapon back from the crewman. The master chief looked at the weapon for a moment. It looked like an over-sized flare gun, with a longer barrel and a large battery looking object situated just forward of the trigger. The master chief pointed it down the corridor and pulled the trigger, but nothing happened. After looking at it again, he flipped a switch, pointed it down the corridor, and pulled the trigger once more. This time the weapon discharged and a bright red bolt of light shot down the corridor, striking one of the status lights along the ceiling and obliterating it into a mass of molten plastic and metal.

"Like that!" the master chief smiled, handing the weapon back.

The other two followed the master chief's example and joined their friend on the firing line.

"Me, Nash, and three crewmen are holding this corridor for now, sir!" the master chief's voice reported over the comm. *"But if they get reinforced, they'll mow us down right quick!"*

"Understood!" Nathan answered. "Stand by," Nathan turned to Cameron. "Cam, I need you to take the helm!"

"Sure," she answered, resigning herself to the situation. As unbelievable as it was, Nathan Scott was legally in command of the Aurora, at least until a more senior officer from elsewhere on the ship assumed the role. "What do you want me to do?"

"Can you back us away from them?"

"I don't know," she admitted as she started checking to see what was working.

"Engineering, bridge! Respond!" Nathan called.

"Da! Engineering here! Nathan, is that you?"

"Yeah, Vlad! It's me!" Nathan could hear all manner of commotion coming through the comm from engineering. People were yelling in the background, alarms were sounding, and he was pretty sure he heard the sound of portable fire suppression equipment being used. Above it all, Vladimir was yelling instructions to someone.

"What are you doing on the command channel, Nathan? You can get in big trouble for this!"

"I'm in command!"

"Shto?"

Nathan had learned a few words in Russian just from sharing a cabin with Vladimir for a few weeks, and he knew that 'shto' meant 'what'. He repeated, "I'm in command!"

"Oh, bozhe moi!"

Nathan knew what that meant too.

"Listen, Vlad, can you get maneuvering back online?"

"I don't know, Nathan! Everything is crazy here! Let me call you back!" Suddenly the line went dead.

"All I've got is braking thrusters, Nathan," Cameron announced, "and docking thrusters, but nothing else!"

"Master Chief!" Nathan called over the comm.

"Yeah, go ahead!"

"What side of the primary forward bulkhead are you on?"

"Aft side!"

"Damn it!" Nathan cursed.

"Can you drive them back behind the primary forward bulkheads?"

"With a few more guys, maybe!"

Nathan spun around to face the marine guarding the port exit. "You two go down and help. I need them pushed back behind the primary forward bulkheads. Then lock those hatches and I'll flush the bastards out into space!" he ordered.

"Yes, sir!" the marine acknowledged, stepping forward and handing Nathan his weapon. "You might need this, sir."

Nathan was a bit stunned, but he realized why the marine was offering it to him. "What about you?" he asked.

"There's a weapons locker at the bottom of the

ramp, sir. We'll load up there on our way."

"Very well. Good luck." Nathan watched them leave, the second marine handing him his weapon as well. For the second time in less than an hour, Nathan was amazed at the bravery of the people he served with, unsure if he was worthy of being in their company.

He looked over at Cameron and, after making eye contact, tossed her one of the weapons. "Just in case," he told her. He looked at the science officer to the left of the flight console. She was obviously shaken but looked like she could still function.

"Master Chief!" Nathan called out over the comm again. "Two marines are headed your way, and they're bringing an armory with them!"

"Yes, sir!" the master chief answered.

"What's your name, Ensign?" Nathan asked the woman at the science station. He felt a little embarrassed that, even after a full eight-hour bridge shift with her the day before, he had yet to learn her name.

"Yosef," she answered a bit shakily. "Ensign Yosef, sir."

"What's your first name?"

"Kaylah."

"Okay, Kaylah. Is it possible for you to take over the sensors from your station there?" He needed someone on sensors more than he needed a science officer right now, but the sensor station was covered with blood.

"Yes, sir," she answered, "but it will take a few minutes to reconfigure the console and displays."

"Great, because I need someone on sensors more than I do sciences right now."

"But I'm not a sensor operator, sir."

"But you're all I've got, Kaylah. Besides, you're a science officer, which means that you must be pretty smart. I'm sure you'll figure it out quickly enough," he assured her.

"Yes, sir," she answered, turning back to her console to begin reconfiguring it to control the sensors.

"Master Chief!" a heavy male voice bellowed from down the corridor behind him.

The master chief spun around, ready to fire at anyone coming up from behind their position.

"Check your fire! Two marines on your six!"

"Well come on up and join the party, boys!" the master chief called out.

The marines sprinted down the corridor, keeping low, falling in behind the master chief to take cover.

"Glad you could join us, fellas!" the master chief thanked them.

"Weatherly!" the first marine called out, identifying himself to the master chief.

"Holmes!" the second marine added.

"Pleasure to meet ya, I'm sure."

"The lieutenant said you needed help pushin' them back?" Weatherly asked.

"Yeah! We got about a dozen Jung bastards hunkered down just this side of the primary bulkhead!"

"Them ain't Jung, Master Chief!" Holmes corrected him.

"Of course they're Jung, dumbass! Who the hell else would they be?"

"I dunno, Master Chief, but I'm pretty sure they ain't Jung! They came from that big-ass warship we rammed! Through a breach in our bow!"

"What big-ass warship?" Jessica asked, overhearing the conversation.

"Orbiting Jupiter?" the master chief added, a bit baffled.

"We ain't orbiting Jupiter any more, Master Chief!"

"What the fuck are you talkin' about?"

"Shut your yap, Holmes!" Weatherly warned. "It's supposed to be classified, remember?"

"Doesn't matter much now, does it?" Holmes argued.

"One of you better tell me what the fuck is going on before I shoot you myself!" the master chief threatened.

Sergeant Weatherly knew that his fellow marine was probably right and decided that, given the circumstances, it was better to share what he knew with the master chief. "We've been on the bridge for the last hour, Master Chief, and some crazy shit has been going on! Shit you wouldn't believe!"

"Try me!" the master chief demanded, as an energy bolt bounced off the wall just above his head, causing him to duck reflexively.

"They've got some new kinda engine or something! Can jump the ship ten light years in the blink of an eye!" Weatherly explained.

"Bullshit!" The master chief didn't believe a word of it.

"No, Master Chief! He's tellin' ya straight! They've already jumped the ship twice! First out to the Oort! That's when we tangled with those two Jung patrol ships. Then they had to jump again really quickly to get away from that antimatter explosion!"

"No shit?" the master chief asked, turning to

look at Jessica. She nodded confirmation to him, since that last part she had seen for herself. She just hadn't been aware of their actual location until now. "Then where the fuck are we now?" the master chief asked.

"Dunno! Shit, I don't think anybody knows just yet. We came out in the middle of some big space battle somewhere! Got pounded by this huge warship! Twice the size of anything we've got! Put four torpedoes into her and she kept on firing at us! We ended up ramming her and now were stuck with our nose in her side! That's where those troops are comin' from, through a breach in the bow! The lieutenant wants to lock them out on the breach side of the bulkheads so he can back the ship out of her and flush those sons of bitches out into space!"

Jessica had been listening to the marines throughout the ongoing firefight. "You keep saying the lieutenant!" she yelled. "What lieutenant? Where's the captain?"

"Captain's injured, ma'am! And the XO is dead! Happened when we rammed her! Lieutenant Scott's in command!"

"Holy shit!" she replied.

"Well I guess we'd better get this party started!" the master chief declared.

"Engineering, Mechanic's Mate Stewart here!" the male voice answered shakily over the comm.

"Where's Vladimir?" Nathan asked.

"He's busy trying to restore maneuvering, sir!"

"Where's the chief engineer?"

"I don't know, sir. I think he's dead! Vladimir's been running everything since the collision! You want

me to get him?"

"No, just tell him to hurry it up!"

Nathan looked up from his console at Cameron. "I don't think he's gonna get maneuvering back up in time."

"What are you going to do?"

Nathan thought for a moment, but nothing came to him.

"Kaylah? You got sensors up yet?"

"Yes, sir."

"Great, can you tell me how many people are alive in the forward section, forward of the primary bulkheads?"

Kaylah worked her sensors for a moment, retraining them on the Aurora. "There's a lot of interference, sir. Either from malfunctioning systems or from the enemy ship, but it looks like eight, not counting the combatants."

"Damn," Nathan swore. "Hope they can make it to emergency shelters."

"It's not going to matter much, Nathan," Cameron interrupted, "not if we can't back out of here."

Four flash-bangs and four fragmentation grenades came bouncing down the corridor, coming to rest at the feet of the enemy. Realizing what they were, the enemy soldiers tried to duck for cover, but most were too late. The fragmentation grenades went off first, followed a split second later by the flash-bangs.

Jessica waited behind cover for a few seconds after the grenades went off, giving the shrapnel from the blast enough time to finish ricocheting off the corridor walls before they charged. The two marines went first, dressed in the heavy assault body armor they had picked up from the armory and blasting away at anything that moved with their close-quarters weapons set for a wide dispersal. As soon as they ran out of ammo, they stepped aside and let Jessica and the master chief pass between them as they opened up in similar fashion. As they blasted away, the two marines reloaded and came back up behind them. Repeating this cycle several times, they were able to keep the enemy's heads down long enough to get down the corridor, peeling off to the left and right to engage the combatants in hand-to-hand combat. Once they had stepped to either side and out of the line of fire, the remaining three crewmen blasted away at the open hatchway with their captured energy weapons, effectively keeping the reinforcements on the other side of the bulkhead from pouring into the corridor.

Jessica began flailing away on the first enemy soldier. She struck him about the face with her fists several times before pulling her combat knife and gutting him. Sergeant Weatherly cold-cocked the next one with the butt of his weapon, then looped the weapon's strap around the dazed soldiers neck and swung him around into the third soldier, knocking them both down. After pulling his side arm, he put several rounds into each of them before turning it on the fourth soldier that now had Jessica by the throat and was holding her up against the wall. Suddenly, a bolt of energy from an enemy weapon caught the sergeant in the side and spun him around, knocking him off his feet.

Jessica fell to the floor as her attacker went down after being shot by Sergeant Weatherly. Ducking to one side, she swept her leg and knocked the last enemy soldier off his feet. She rolled forward and used her knife again, slamming it into the soldier's chest before he could get back up and giving it a twist to finish him off.

On the other side of the hallway, the master chief's fighting style, while not as graceful, was just as effective. One, two, then three enemy soldiers were tossed by the master chief out into the energy weapons' fire being poured down the corridor by their shipmates at the other end. It wasn't pretty, but it effectively ended all three of them. The fourth and fifth enemy soldiers were handled by Sergeant Holmes, who seemed to prefer a rather long and over-sized knife for his close-quarters action.

Either way, their side of the bulkhead was clear. Jessica signaled for the others to cease fire, after which the master chief swung the hatch closed and locked it before any more enemy troops could come through.

"Bridge," the master chief's voice called over the comm, *"the forward section is secured!"*

"Good work, Master Chief! Stand by!" Nathan looked at Cameron. "Try and back us out."

"It won't be enough thrust to..."

"Just try!" he pleaded, cutting her off.

"Okay," she conceded, as she began to apply braking thrusters. "Firing braking thrusters at twenty-five percent."

The ship began to vibrate, shaking an already loosened panel off one of the side consoles.

"We're not moving!" Cameron reported.

"Bring it up to fifty percent."

"Increasing thrust to fifty percent."

The vibrations became louder and the ship shook even more. But still it did not back away from the enemy vessel.

"It's no use!" Cameron protested. "It's just not enough thrust!"

"One hundred percent!" he ordered. Cameron spun her head around, giving him a look of disapproval the likes of which he had not seen from her before. And for a moment, he didn't think she was going to follow his orders. Finally, being able to wait no longer, he barked at her, "DO IT!"

His tone was also something that she had never heard from him, and it startled her somewhat as she turned back to her console and brought the thrust up to one hundred percent.

"Braking thrusters at maximum!" she yelled over the sound of the ship as it bounced and rattled. Damaged consoles started sparking again as the vibrations caused their burnt circuits to short. A portion of an already weakened overhead beam fell behind Nathan. Bits and pieces began falling everywhere.

"Sir," Ensign Yosef shouted from her console, "we're stuck on something!"

Nathan ran the few steps from the tactical console to Ensign Yosef's side, struggling to keep his balance as the ship shook. He looked over her shoulder at the console.

"There!" she indicated, pointing at the image on the sensor display. It was a black and white image that looked much like a computer-enhanced x-ray, but with multiple colors outlining some of the objects in the image.

"What is that?"

"It looks like a beam or part of the enemy ship's

structural frame!" she reported. "It must have given way when we collided and impaled us causing the hull breach! That's where they came in!"

There was another object that Nathan couldn't identify at first, something large. It had several lines and tanks all clustered together along with some nozzles coming out of it.

"Is this in our ship or theirs?" he asked, pointing at the unidentified yet familiar looking object.

"Ours, sir. It's the..."

"Docking thrusters!" Nathan spun around to face Cameron, suddenly having an idea. "Cameron. Remember how we stopped the roll in the simulator?"

"You can't be serious!" she protested, remembering it clearly.

"It might break us free!"

"Nathan, there are still eight people in the forward section!"

"But they're all at the aft end of that section! In the simulation, it only damaged the forward part! And it's only a matter of time before they blast through that bulkhead and take the ship!"

"This isn't a simulation, Nathan!" she warned.

"You think I don't know that?" he argued, looking around the room. "Really?"

Cameron considered Nathan's idea. It was a hell of a gamble, but she had to admit that without the more powerful maneuvering thrusters there was no other way to break free from the enemy ship.

"You're in command," she agreed, turning to reprogram the maximum pressure limits on the docking thruster's reaction chambers. "Resetting max chamber pressures," she announced. "Which side would you like to blow up first?" she asked sarcastically.

"Port side!"

"Firing port docking thrusters at full power."

The ship slid slightly sideways to starboard, causing Nathan to stumble to his left. There was a loud *crack* as the cowling over the forward side of the flight console fractured, probably the result of the severe jostling they were taking.

Suddenly, there was an explosion. It came from forward of them, underneath and to port. It was much louder than in the simulation and the entire ship lifted slightly before suddenly dropping back down, nearly knocking Nathan off his feet.

Without warning and in a surprisingly fast motion, the ship slid quickly out of the hole it had made in the enemy ship. The force of the exploding docking thruster made the hole even bigger, severing the beam that had impaled them and allowing the ship to slip free. It was like someone suddenly pulling the rug out from under his feet, and the motion knocked Nathan to the floor. That's when he realized the inertial dampeners were probably offline.

"We're free!" Cameron exclaimed, not believing it herself.

"No kidding," Nathan said, grabbing the tactical console and pulling himself back to his feet.

The sudden separation from the enemy ship left the forward section open to space, and Nathan hoped the sudden decompression had sucked the intruders out into the void.

"Kaylah! How many intruders left in the forward section?"

"None, sir! They were either sucked out or died inside!"

"How many of our people?"

She paused for a moment before reporting. Nathan knew he wasn't going to like the answer. "Six, sir," she answered solemnly. "They're sealed up in their berths."

Nathan tried to brush their deaths away, like he figured a good leader was supposed to do. But all he could think was, *I just killed two people!* He knew that many others had probably died already today, but the deaths of these two were the direct result of a decision *he* had made with full knowledge that he was putting them in harm's way. He wasn't sure that he could ever forgive himself. But he had to find a way to live with it, at least for now.

The Aurora backed slowly away from the damaged enemy warship, leaving a gaping hole in her side. Debris and the bodies of dead enemy soldiers floated freely, leaving a ghastly trail that led from the bow of the Aurora back to the hole. But once the ship began to move away, the warship's guns again had a workable firing solution and immediately opened up on her as she tried to escape.

The first salvo struck them near the bridge, catching them off guard, nearly knocking Nathan off his feet again. *There should really be a chair, here!* he thought, tired of always having to fight to stay standing.

"Jesus!" he exclaimed. "How can they still be able to fire?" Every second of the last twenty minutes had been a constant struggle to survive. And just when he was starting to think they had a chance, fate would throw another obstacle in their way.

The rounds continued to land on the upper side of their bow, bouncing them around so violently that Nathan could barely hear himself think. He was scared out of his mind and felt like he would piss himself every time they took a hit. At the moment, following in his father's footsteps and going into politics didn't seem all that bad.

Without any shields, each strike was ripping chunks off of their exterior hull, exposing the subsequent layers underneath. Nathan knew that before long, there would be more hull breaches, and eventually their luck would run out. One of those shells would get deeper inside before it detonated, ripping them apart in the process.

A few of the lights on the bridge snapped back on, along with a few additional systems. The main view screen flickered a bit, but still did not come back to life.

"Maneuvering just came back online!" Cameron reported.

"Get us out of here!" he pleaded.

More explosions shook the ship, the last one causing the entire ship to slide sideways a bit, slamming the tactical console into Nathan's side and nearly knocking the wind out of him.

"Can't we move any faster?" he shouted.

"We're at full reverse thrust!" Cameron defended. "It's just not enough! This ship wasn't designed to go fast backwards!" Another red light on her console turned green. "Wait! The orbital maneuvering system just came back on! Maybe if I end over..."

"Not exactly by the book, Ensign!" Nathan interrupted, already liking the idea.

"Yeah, I wonder where I picked up that bad habit," she said.

"You're not waiting for me to give you permission, are you?" Nathan asked. The inertial dampeners were still offline, and Nathan could feel himself getting heavy as she pitched their nose up hard.

"Not a chance," she smiled.

About ten seconds later, Nathan went from feeling abnormally heavy on his feet to feeling abnormally light as Cameron ended their end-over-end flip in abrupt fashion. He grabbed hold of the console in front of him just in time to keep himself standing as she fired the orbital maneuvering system at full burn.

"OMS is burning!" She watched her flight display as their velocity steadily increased. The orbital maneuvering system was only designed to increase their orbital velocity, thereby increasing an orbital altitude. If they only had the main propulsion working, they could get out of there in seconds instead of agonizingly long minutes.

"Engineering, bridge!" Nathan called over the comm.

"*Yes! Nathan!*" It still sounded like all hell was breaking loose in the background.

"Vlad, we're getting pounded! Can you give me any weapons?"

"*I am sorry, Nathan, but we only have one reactor online, and only running at fifty percent! I could maybe connect rail guns to same reactor, but it might be too much for one. I don't know.*"

"What about torpedoes? Can you give me torpedoes?"

"*Torpedoes should work. If crew can load the tubes, torpedoes have their own power source. Just push button and they go. But Nathan, you should know this.*"

"Why would I know this? I'm a pilot!"

Cameron held her hand up in the air, without turning around.

"Oh, and I suppose you did?" he asked her. She

173

offered no verbal confirmation, just a self-righteous smile that Nathan couldn't see from behind her.

"Is there anything else I can do for you Nathan? I am very busy right now." Something exploded in the background, and Vladimir shouted some more directions at someone.

"No thanks. Do what you can. Bridge out."

Nathan looked at the torpedo bay status display. There were no torpedoes loaded in the forward tubes, and the aft tubes were not yet completely installed.

"Torpedo room, bridge!" he called over the comm. "Torpedo room! Do you copy?" No one answered. "Damn!" He looked at the status display again when he noticed something. One of the torpedoes that the captain had launched at the enemy warship had not detonated, and it was still active.

"Kaylah!" he shouted. "Scan that warship! One of our torpedoes didn't detonate! Can you tell me where it is? Is it still stuck in them?"

Kaylah worked her console for a few moments before responding, as more of the enemy rounds exploded against the hull, continually bouncing the ship.

"I've got it! It's stuck just aft of amidships!" She spun her head to look at Nathan. "It's right in front of their reactor plant!"

"What kind of reactor?" he asked. They were still awfully close to that ship, and if they were using antimatter, he doubted they would be far enough away to survive the blast.

"Scanning!" Another shell struck, sending sparks flying as the panel above the ECO console shorted out.

"Kaylah!" Nathan begged, not knowing if they could take another hit. "What kind of reactor?"

"Fusion!" she answered. "They're using simple fusion reactors! Six of them!"

"Nathan! What are you going..." She wasn't able to finish her sentence, as Nathan wasn't going to waste time debating this one with her.

"All hands, brace for impact!" he called out ship-wide as he detonated the last torpedo's warhead.

Outside, in the silent black void of space, the aft end of the crippled warship suddenly broke apart in a blinding flash, shredding her midsection until the entire back half simply broke free from her. Moments later, her six fusion reactors started exploding in rapid succession, causing her tail to split into several large chunks while most of her forward section broke apart into countless smaller pieces.

Seconds later, many of those pieces hit the Aurora. They hit hard, so hard that one of the larger pieces caused her tail to dip down by thirty degrees in the blink of an eye. Without the inertial dampeners, any of her crew that were in the back half of the ship suddenly found themselves tossed up head first into the ceiling, before falling back to the floor again. But that wasn't the end of it. Along with countless smaller bits of debris, six more considerably larger sized pieces also hit them, albeit with far less force.

Nathan shook his head, shaking the fallen dust and debris off of himself. He was on the floor yet again, behind the tactical station, facing Doctor Sorenson. She had been holding her dead father the entire time, up until the last shock wave tossed her and her father's body into the corner on top of the body of the dead marine by the starboard exit. Other than her initial screams of shock and the subsequent cries of grief, he had not heard a peep from her during the entire battle. He wondered if she was in some kind of shock. Of course, she had every right to be; they all did.

He looked at her, seeing the look of abject fear in her eyes. "Are you all right?" he asked. After a moment, she looked at him. "Doctor Sorenson, are you all right?" he repeated. She stared in his eyes for a moment, finally nodding slightly. "Don't worry," he promised her. "We're going to be all right." He didn't really believe it, at least not completely. But he felt she needed some hope in order to hold it together.

Nathan struggled back to his feet. He could see that Cameron had somehow managed to stay in her seat at the helm the entire time and was busy trying to see what was still working. He made his way over to Kaylah to see that she too was unharmed. She looked even more shaken, with a small gash on the side of her head from flying debris, but she was conscious and already trying to get back into her chair.

"I need to know what other ships are out there, Kaylah," he told her as he helped her into her chair. "Without the main view screen, you're the only eyes we've got."

"Yes, sir."

It was still pretty dark in the room, and there were fewer systems offering information to him through the tactical console than before. "Damn!" he swore. "Now just about everything is down!" He looked towards Cameron at the helm in front of him. "How's the helm?"

"I've got nothing. Everything is down: no propulsion, no maneuvering. Even the OMS is down now, and we're still only running on emergency power." She turned around to face him. "We're dead in the water, Nathan," she said, folding her arms across her chest.

For a moment, Nathan felt like she was accusing him of something. He had not given her a chance to disagree with his plan to detonate the last torpedo. There simply hadn't been time for discussion, not if they were going to survive.

"Sensors are down too, sir. Well, not completely down, but they keep flashing in and out. It's hard to get a decent image to build."

"Keep trying," Nathan instructed, most of the determination having left his voice.

"Engineering, bridge." Nathan looked at the comm controls, they appeared to be dead as well. "Great. No comms."

"What do we do now?" Cameron asked.

Nathan looked around the room, hoping another bright idea would pop into his head. But nothing did. He had been lucky so far, and he knew it. He might have made one or two good decisions along the way, but the fact that they were still breathing was due to dumb luck. He just wondered how much longer his luck would hold out.

"Any ideas?" he asked, admitting that he had none of his own.

Cameron looked at him, saying nothing, but he could see in her eyes that she had no ideas either.

Nathan took a deep breath and let it out slowly. "I guess all we can do is wait," he resigned, "and hope that Vlad is still with us."

It was their first opportunity to stop and look around the bridge, to witness the amount of damage they had sustained. The helm and navigation consoles appeared undamaged for the most part, which was a good thing. The sensor and electronic countermeasures stations were both fried. But the auxiliary console behind them that had been configured for the jump drive seemed relatively undamaged, which was surprising considering the exit directly behind it had practically collapsed.

The comm stations at the rear of the bridge had suffered some sort of an explosive short circuit, but the port side auxiliary station, as well as the engineering and science stations, were all intact. And of course, the tactical station that Nathan had been using was also relatively undamaged.

All in all, he figured it could've been much worse. They were, after all, still alive. And that meant there were still possibilities. He only hoped that, whatever those possibilities might be, they weren't too unpleasant.

Cameron had taken it upon herself to deal with the injured. She had first checked on the captain, who still lay bleeding and unconscious, but alive for now. She did what she could, breaking out an emergency medical kit from the cabinet near the exit. Other than the captain and the four of them, the rest were dead. Altogether, a total of seven people had died on that bridge half an hour ago. She just wondered how many more had died elsewhere on the ship. They had left Earth on a simple test cruise with a skeleton crew of one hundred, which was barely enough to run the ship. They couldn't afford to lose even those that had died on the bridge, let alone others, not if they were to have any hope of getting back to Earth.

Earth, she thought, wondering in what direction it might be.

"Have you thought about those smaller ships?" Cameron asked him.

"What?" He had been off in his own little world when she asked the question.

"The other ships out there, the smaller ones that were attacking the big one that nearly took us out."

"Oh yeah, I've thought about them." It was a lie; he hadn't. "Well, if any of them survived the shock wave, they've probably hightailed it out of here by now. I mean, a big ship like that has gotta have friends, right?"

"Maybe. But what if they're still out there?"

"What, you think they're gonna come after us?" he asked.

"Why not?"

"We didn't have a fight with them."

"We didn't have a fight with the big one either, but that didn't stop them."

"Maybe they thought we came to help the smaller ships."

"It's possible."

"Then shouldn't the smaller ships be thankful we helped them out?"

"Maybe. But what if they're pirates. They could be coming back to board us right now."

"Space pirates? Come on, Cam." It sounded too silly to him. But then, the more he thought about it... "Ya think?"

"I don't know what to think," she admitted with a sigh.

Nathan thought he saw a bit of desperation in Cameron's expression. And he knew how she felt. "Let's just think positive thoughts, okay?" he encouraged.

Suddenly, a crackly voice came across the comm at tactical, a crackly voice with a Russian accent. *"Nathan! Can you hear me?"*

Nathan jumped up and ran back to the tactical station. "Yes, Vlad! I can hear you! What's your status?"

"Well, I'm okay," he joked, causing Nathan to smile, *"but the ship, she is not so good."*

"Can you get power restored?" Nathan knew that they could only go for so long without power.

"Yes! Soon! We are working on it now! But Nathan, I had to hot-wire the comms to tell you something. There are ships approaching us from behind. I think they are going to land inside the hangar deck."

Nathan's mind began racing. Who were they? Was it the same ships that had been attacking the warship that nearly destroyed them? If so, why were they coming here? Were they coming to board them? If not, why else would they try to land? Maybe some of the smaller ships were from the bigger one. Maybe that's who was coming to land.

Nathan managed to break from his out-of-control thoughts for a moment. "How do you know?" he asked Vladimir.

"We have power here, and I have man on sensors. He saw them. He says if they are landing, it will be in few minutes."

Nathan knew one thing for sure; no matter who they were, he couldn't just let them walk onto the ship unescorted. And if they were another boarding party, which seemed the most likely scenario, they needed to be stopped at the flight deck, before they got deeper into the ship.

"I need to get someone to the hangar deck," Nathan said to himself. "Vlad, can any of you keep them from entering?"

"We don't have any weapons, Nathan!"

Nathan thought furiously for several seconds,

his eyes dancing around the room as if looking for inspiration. "Is the wireless working?"

"Yes! I tried calling you on it before, but you did not answer,"

"Sorry, I didn't have them on."

"What kind of commander doesn't wear wireless?" he said to someone near him.

"I gotta go, Vlad! Get power up as soon as you can!"

Nathan grabbed his headset and put it back on. "Master Chief, you still with me?" he inquired urgently through his headset. "Master Chief, bridge! Do you copy?!"

"Bridge, Ensign Nash here." There was a pause. *"The master chief is dead."*

Nathan had only met the man once, when he tricked Nathan into touching the outside of the ship as a joke, but for some reason, the news of his death startled Nathan, causing him to lose his train of thought.

"Jessica?"

"Yeah."

"How many of you survived the shock wave?"

"If you mean that last wild ride you gave us, then just me, Sergeant Weatherly, and two other tech specialists."

"You're still armed, right?"

"Uh, yes," she answered sarcastically.

"Get everyone you can to the hangar bay! We've got ships coming in with unknown intent!"

"What? Who the hell are they?"

"I don't know! Just get over there and don't let anyone from those ships leave the flight deck!" he ordered. "Now move it, Ensign!" He wasn't sure why he threw in that last part. Maybe it was because that's what he thought the captain would say. Maybe he was trying to act more like a leader. Or maybe he was getting tired of being questioned. He didn't want to be in charge, especially now. But command had fallen on his shoulders and he wasn't about to shirk away from his responsibilities, not this time.

"On our way," she replied, hearing both the urgency and the desperation in his voice.

"And stay on wireless. The hardlines aren't reliable right now!"

"Yes, sir!"

CHAPTER SIX

Jessica stepped carefully around the storage crates that had been repositioned at the forward end of the hangar bay. It had been slow going making her way from the entrance to her present location, about halfway into the massive compartment. More than half of the emergency lighting in the hangar had been knocked out during the battle, causing long shadows to be cast by the many crates still stored in the bay. In addition, many of the smaller containers had been knocked about by recent events, creating a maze composed of crates of varying sizes and shapes, strewn about in no discernible order. She had noticed, however, that they would make good cover in the event of another firefight, which is what she was expecting.

Following her were Sergeant Weatherly, the two surviving technicians that had fought off the first boarding party, and three other crewmen they had picked up and armed along the way. As they broke out into the open, she looked about, glancing up to either side of the bay. There were catwalks located about two decks up, running the entire length of the bay.

"Sergeant," she whispered as she stopped, "put two up on each side," she instructed, pointing to either side of the bay. "Tell them to open fire if our guests start shooting. You stay with me." The sergeant turned to deploy their remaining forces, sending the two that had fought with them earlier to the starboard side, while the two of the others that had just joined them were sent to the port side.

Jessica took up a position crouched on one knee behind a crate out in the middle of the bay. The sergeant joined her. About one meter high and three meters long, it would provide good cover for their confrontation.

"As good a spot as any," she whispered. "They'll have to come through that smaller personnel hatch built into the bay door," she explained, pointing at the large bay doors at the opposite end of the bay. She had been through this entire section only an hour ago on her way to board the Jung patrol ship back in the Oort cloud. "There's no decent cover between them and us, so they'll have no chance, as long as those guys on the cats can shoot straight," she added.

"Bridge," she whispered over her comm-set, "we've established a defensive position in the hangar bay. No one's getting through here without some serious firepower."

"Don't shoot first and ask questions later," Nathan warned over the comm-set.

"I know, sir. We could use some intel."

"Exactly. But don't take any unnecessary chances, either. We're running out of crew."

Just then, the hatch lock turned and the hatch swung open. She watched across her gun sights, waiting for someone to step through the hatch. It was at least ten seconds before a helmet leaned in and peeked through briefly before disappearing again.

They're not stupid, she thought. She tightened her grip on her weapon, her entire body tensing up in preparation to fire as the first visitor stepped cautiously through the hatch. It appeared to be a man, dressed in a pressure suit similar to their own. He was still wearing his helmet, the interior of which was lit, but from this distance she couldn't make out any facial features. He was, however, carrying a weapon that looked exactly like the ones carried by the enemy boarding party they had just defeated. And to her, that wasn't a good sign.

"You notice that weapon, ma'am?" the sergeant whispered in a barely audible fashion.

"Yeah," she whispered back. "Just hold. Let's wait for a few more to step through."

They watched as the first one took a few steps into the bay, after which he stopped and twisted his body about, scanning the dimly lit interior. He turned back toward the hatch as three more stepped through, two men and a woman. As they began to move forward, Jessica and the sergeant popped up from behind their cover, weapons held high in firing position. "That's far enough!" she shouted.

Two of the male visitors immediately raised their own weapons in preparation to defend themselves.

"DON'T DO IT!" Jessica insisted, leaning slightly forward to not only prepare herself for her weapon's recoil, but also to emphasize her point, the sergeant imitating her posture.

The man at the center of the group of visitors raised his hands up slowly, stopping about chest high. He turned his body right and left, leaning back slightly to see the four others, two on each side, their weapons also trained on them. Realizing Jessica and her team had the tactical advantage, he motioned for his men to lower their weapons.

"That's it!" Jessica instructed, as she watched

them stand down. "Put them on the deck!" she continued, sweeping her weapon in a downward fashion to indicate her meaning. The two armed men slowly placed their weapons on the deck before standing upright again, hands held out and up to communicate their cooperation.

The leader of the group slowly removed his helmet. He was a rugged-looking fellow, perhaps in his late forties to early fifties, with light brown hair and dark eyes that looked both sympathetic and fiercely determined at the same time. He looked at her for a moment, as well as at the others under her command, after which he said something unintelligible to Jessica, something in another language. He repeated himself one more time before realizing that she did not understand him. It was apparent by his expression that her lack of comprehension was a bit surprising to him.

The other two men removed their helmets next. Both were considerably younger than their leader, one with black hair and eyes, the other with similar features but of considerably darker complexion. Neither of them smiled, however, only glancing upwards out of the corner of their eyes to assess the guns trained on them from above.

The fourth one to remove her helmet was, as Jessica had observed, a woman, young enough to be the daughter of the leader, but not possessing any similar features. She was of similar complexion, with long straight black hair and green eyes that held the same determination as their leader's.

"Bridge, engineering," Vladimir's voice came across the internal comm-system. Nathan was

instantly encouraged by the improved clarity in the hardwired comms.

"Go ahead."

"Main internal communications are fully operational again," he announced proudly. *"We are working on getting full power restored to command decks."*

"Great..."

"Bridge, Nash," Jessica's voice interrupted over the wireless.

"Hold on, Vlad," Nathan told him, switching back to Jessica. "Go ahead."

"We've got four, uh, visitors in custody down here."

"Who are they?"

"No clue; they're not speaking English."

"What are they speaking?"

"No clue there either, sir. What do you want us to do with them?"

Nathan thought for a moment. Somehow, he needed to speak with these people, to find out who they were and what had just happened out there. More importantly, he needed to learn their intentions.

"Bring them to me, I guess," he said, not really knowing what else to do.

"To the bridge? I wouldn't advise that, sir," she warned. *"Too risky."*

He could tell she was trying to hide that last statement from their guests, even if they didn't appear to speak the same language. He didn't see what harm it could do, especially considering their current inoperable state. But he also knew that being a graduate from the spec-ops school meant that Jessica probably knew better about such matters.

"You're right," he admitted. "Bring them to the main briefing room on deck C. I'll meet you there."

"*Yes, sir.*"

"Vlad?" Nathan asked after he switched back.

"*Yes.*"

"How are you for crew down there?"

"*I'm not sure,*" he admitted. "*There are six of us, including myself. We have found four dead, two of them we cannot identify, and three more are missing.*"

"What about Chief Patel?" Nathan asked. At some point in time, he was going to have to figure out who should actually be in command. Surely, somewhere on the ship there was a higher ranking officer who was still alive and could relieve him.

"*He is still missing,*" Vladimir answered, a touch of sadness in his voice.

After a respectful pause, Nathan made his first battlefield promotion. "I guess that makes you chief engineer, Vlad."

"*Yes,*" he answered soberly. "*Then I guess I should be getting back to work,*" he added before clicking the line off. Nathan knew that Chief Patel had been important to Vladimir, as he had talked about him often and had been looking forward to learning from the chief. So he had to figure that the loss was difficult for his friend.

Nathan stood straight and straightened his uniform. "I'm going to the briefing room to meet our visitors," he announced as he turned to exit. "You have the bridge, Cam," he added.

"Me?" It caught her slightly off guard. "Why me?"

Nathan looked around the bridge. Other than Doctor Sorenson and Ensign Yosef, Cameron was the only other person in the room. "Why not?" It wasn't much of an answer. It was just the first thing that came out of his mouth.

Cameron had no response, her mouth just hanging slightly open in shock as she watched him exit. She couldn't see the smile on his face as he exited, as it was the first time he could remember that she had been left speechless.

* * *

Nathan entered the briefing room a few minutes after Jessica and their guests. The room was a bit large for such a small gathering. But considering how its contents had been tossed about recently, it probably was just as well. It had been easy for them to push the knocked over tables and chairs out of the way.

As he entered, he saw the four visitors sitting at the table that had been hastily set up. There were two younger men, an older man, and a young woman who had green eyes the likes of which Nathan had never seen. There was a strength and compassion behind them, and he found it difficult to look away.

The leader of the group rose as a sign of respect to Nathan, whom he considered to be the leader. The expression on the man's face seemed a bit off to Nathan, hinting that Nathan was not what the visitor had expected.

Jessica's reaction to the man's attempt to stand was more defensive, immediately raising her weapon, with the other two guards following suit. She saw in the man's eyes, as he froze half standing, that he was aware of the threat, just as she noticed how the other two men's bodies suddenly became taut, as if preparing to take action. This told her much of the experience and demeanor of these men, and she didn't much like what she saw.

"It's okay," Nathan immediately intervened, not wanting things to turn ugly. He watched as Jessica and the guards slowly lowered their weapons, allowing the man to finish standing. The man nodded at Jessica, as if to pay respect to her alertness, but she couldn't help but feel like he was silently conveying an open challenge to her. There was something in this man that she did not trust.

The leader of the group finished standing and began to speak in a strange language. Although Nathan did not understand him, it was obvious that he was trying to identify himself, by patting his chest and repeating the word 'Marak'. Within moments they had managed to learn each other's name, but that was all. But there was something about the language that he kept speaking to the woman sitting next to him. It sounded familiar to him. That's when he realized that it sounded a lot like Russian.

"Engineering, briefing room!"

"Yes, Nathan."

"Vlad, listen, I'm here with some visitors, from those ships you spotted approaching. They're speaking a language that sounds like Russian to me. Can you try to speak with them?"

"So I am translator now?"

"Just give it a try, Vlad. Say something to them in Russian." Nathan pointed at the comm-set, indicating to Marak that the voice on the other end would be speaking to him.

"Vui ponimayetye po Rooski?" Vladimir said through the comm. The leader of the group looked at the woman next to him, a puzzled look on his face.

"Vui po-ni-ma-ye-tye po Roos-ki?" Vladimir repeated a little more slowly, sounding a little impatient. The leader started speaking in his language again, this time into the comm-set as if he were expecting the man at the other end to understand him.

There was a moment of silence, broken only by Vladimir's voice. *"That is not Russian. May I go now?"*

"Sure, thanks." Nathan sat down, rubbing his face with his hands. It had been worth a try. The humans living on the core worlds were descendants of people from Earth. Fleet intelligence indicated that many of the primary languages spoken on Earth more than a thousand years ago when they first began to colonize other star systems were still being used out here, at least in some derived form. That was why all communications officers were usually fluent in at least half a dozen languages. But their only comm officer was dead, and even though they had translation software, with all the systems down, he wasn't able to utilize the programs. *This is not going to be easy,* he thought. *What should I try first?* After thinking for a moment, he looked at the man and started talking slowly and clearly to him. "Where-are-you-from?"

The man just looked at him. Nathan thought he saw a spark of understanding in his eyes, like he thought he understood what Nathan was trying to ask him but was afraid to answer incorrectly. The woman, she had the same look, but even more so than her leader. Nathan repeated himself, after which the two of them exchanged words in their own language. It sounded as if the woman was trying to explain something to her leader, maybe something she understood, or at least thought she understood.

"We-are-from-the-Sol-system," he began. Nathan frantically searched his mind for the right words, which was usually not a problem for him. But these people were from another world, another planet. *How do you communicate with someone from another planet?* "Sol? Have you heard of it?" he asked in frustration. Again, he thought he saw a glimmer of recognition from the woman. "Earth?" There were more unintelligible words exchanged between the woman and her leader, and Nathan got the feeling that the two of them were in disagreement about something. "Earth? Have-you-heard-of-Earth?"

The leader said something else to the woman in a stern voice, after which she spoke up. "I hear," she said, thinking for a moment before continuing, "I-hear-Earth."

"You have?" Nathan responded, shocked that he had actually made a connection, no matter how slight. "You've heard of Earth?"

"Yes," she answered, her pronunciation of the simple word slightly off. He could see she was struggling to try to use a language that she might once have learned but had long since forgotten. "I-have. I-heard-of-Earth."

"Then you speak English?"

"An-glees?" she mispronounced.

"Yes, Eng-lish."

She thought again then realized what he was saying. "Ah, Angla!" she exclaimed excitedly. Suddenly a flurry of communication erupted between her and her leader that seemed to last forever before she finally settled down to try to communicate with him.

"I-learn-Angla-much-young," she stated slowly, thinking about each word before speaking them.

"Please-slowly. I-to-understand-you-much."

He could see that she was struggling to remember the language that she had learned when she was young. "I-will-speak-slowly. My-name-is-Nathan." It was difficult for Nathan to control his excitement over his new found ability to communicate with her. And all manner of questions were popping into his mind, making it impossible to select which one to ask first.

"Me, Jalea."

"Jalea?" he grossly mispronounced.

"Jah-LEE-yah," she corrected.

"Jalea?" he tried again, getting a nod of approval from her.

"Ask her who was shooting at us," Jessica suggested. Nathan motioned with his hand for her to be patient.

"And he is Mah-rahk?" Nathan asked, pointing to her leader.

"Yes. Marak."

"Marak-is-your-leader?"

She thought a moment before responding. "Yes." Her tone of voice left Nathan less than convinced, and he wondered if he was their leader, or just the leader of this little group. But he figured he could unravel that mystery later.

"Where-are-you-from?" he asked next. "Your-world? Your-planet?"

"Bah-KAH-rah."

Nathan repeated the name of her planet to verify the pronunciation.

"The-big-ship. Was-it-from-Bakara?"

"No," she answered immediately. "Ship-from-Takara."

"Takara? And they are bad, these Takarans?"

"Yes. Takar, very bad."

"You fight them, yes?"

"Yes. Long time. Many years."

Jessica was growing impatient. "Ask them why they're here?"

Nathan knew she was right. He was letting himself get swept up in the situation and was not thinking of the big picture. They were still without main power, and the sensors were down. They didn't have maneuvering or main propulsion back online yet, let alone any weapons. And to top it all off, he had no idea what the tactical situation was in the immediate area. Hell, he didn't even know where the immediate area was.

"Okay. Why are you here?"

"To help," she answered instantly, and with a smile. "We call. You no answer. We come. You help us. Now we help you."

Nathan was a little surprised by the offer. He had no idea how they might help them given the circumstances, but the fact that they were offering seemed a positive step. "How can you help us?"

"Your ship, broken. We help fix," she explained, pointing at the other two men. Up until now, Nathan had thought of them as their personal security detail, but she seemed to be indicating that they were some kind of engineers or technicians.

"You can help us fix this ship? How?"

"These men, very smart, fix many things. Maybe they fix you."

Jessica did not like the idea and feared that Nathan was thinking of accepting the offer. "Lieutenant, I don't know about this. Maybe we should just say thanks, but no thanks, and try to fix it ourselves?"

"Soon, more will come," Jalea added. "Very soon,

maybe few, maybe many."

"Yeah, that's what I was afraid of," Nathan admitted, more to himself than to Jalea.

"Nathan," Jessica spoke up, pulling him aside and turning away from them, "four strangers, only one of which barely speaks our language, cannot be of enough help to justify the risk," she insisted.

"How do you know they're only talking about these four? They're only from one ship, and there were at least six of them out there before."

Jessica began to offer more reasons, but Nathan turned away from her to speak with Jalea again.

"How many people do you have that can help?" he asked slowly.

Jalea turned to Marak, undoubtedly asking him the same question. "Many," she answered.

That did sound like it might help, and Nathan's expression turned from one of skepticism to one of curiosity.

Marak noticed the change in Nathan's expression and said something else to Jalea.

"We have many more to help, but not here."

"Could turn into an ally." Nathan explained to Jessica. She still didn't look convinced. "I'll let you keep your big gun pointed at them the whole time," he promised, drawing a patronizing look from Jessica.

"You're in command," she said.

Nathan turned back to Jalea and Marak. "We accept your offer," he explained slowly, "but this nice lady and her friends will have to watch you. I apologize, but we do not yet know you very well. Is that all right?"

Jalea explained the terms offered by Nathan as best she could to Marak. The two of them seemed to debate the issue for a bit longer than Nathan would've thought necessary. But then again, sometimes he and Cameron probably debated things for a bit longer than normal as well. In fact, the captain had scolded him for allowing it to happen too often.

Finally, Jalea turned to him. "Yes, is good."

"Wonderful!" he exclaimed. "Now, these people will take you to where we need the most help." Nathan turned to Jessica. "Escort them to engineering, please."

"Yes, sir," she reluctantly agreed.

Before she could get away, Nathan grabbed Jessica by the arm and stepped in close to her ear and whispered, "I wasn't kidding before, Jess. Keep an eye on them at *all* times."

"I had planned on it," she assured him.

Nathan smiled at them as they filed out of the room, one of the armed crewmen leading the way with Jessica and the other crewmen following them out the door. After they had left, Nathan flopped back down in his chair, breathing out a sigh of relief. After a moment, he turned on the comm-set. "Engineering, briefing room."

"What is it now, Nathan?"

"Vladimir, I have a surprise for you."

* * *

As Nathan made his way forward from the briefing room, he noticed several people helping the injured get to medical. He realized that it only made sense that anyone not helping with damage control would be helping with the injured. It just hadn't occurred to him, like so many other things today.

"Help!"

Nathan spun around, the cry coming from somewhere behind him. He didn't see anyone. "Hello?" he called out.

"Help me!" the voice cried out again. It was a woman's voice, and it sounded like it was coming from around the corner farther down the corridor. Nathan broke into a jog in the direction the voice had come from, stopping at the corner to look down the corridor in search of the woman calling him.

About ten meters away was a young woman that Nathan recognized as one of the scientists working on the jump drive. Bloodied and disheveled herself, she was fighting a losing battle to get a seriously injured crewman to medical for treatment. The injured man was considerably larger than she, and she would've had difficulty handling him even in an uninjured state.

Nathan quickly ran over to help her with the injured crewman. "Here, let me take him," he offered.

"I can't make it," she pleaded. She looked like she was about to collapse herself, probably from the large gash on her forehead that was still actively bleeding. Nathan immediately stepped in between them, taking the injured man's arm and draping it over his right shoulder. Once he had the man securely in his right arm, he grabbed the woman with his left arm to provide assistance to her as well.

"Here," he told her. "Hold on to me."

"I don't think I can make it," she pleaded. "I just need to rest."

"Come on, it's just a little farther. You're almost there."

She continued to plod forward, her head hanging down low from fatigue.

"Your leg, it's bleeding," she pointed out to him,

noticing his blood-soaked left pant leg.

"Yeah, I know."

"Does it hurt?"

"Quite a lot actually," he chuckled, wincing in pain with each step. He had thought his leg was broken when he had first woken up back on the bridge. But the more he had gotten used to the discomfort, the more he was convinced that it was just a deep laceration at most. He had managed to ignore the pain up until now, with more important concerns to distract him. But now, with the additional burden of these two injured persons, each step was sending blinding pain shooting up his left leg into his hip. "I'll be all right."

The trip to medical felt like it took forever, despite the fact that it only took a few minutes. As he approached, he called for help and two more crewmen rushed to help.

Nathan followed them into medical, not realizing what he was walking into. There were at least twenty people with varying degrees of injuries. Some had obvious broken bones and severe lacerations that would probably only require some bone knitting and suturing. Others had far more serious injuries, including traumatic amputations, wide open abdominal wounds, and crushed torsos. And nearly everyone had some sort of burn, which explained the strange smell that hit him as he entered. Oddly though, the less seriously injured seemed to be in the most pain, while the more critically wounded seemed to be too far out of it to feel anything.

He watched in horror as those who could, helped care for those who couldn't. Most of them had little more than basic emergency medical training, and it was doubtful that any of them had practical experience. Yet they were all in here, doing the best that they could in unbelievably difficult circumstances. They were in a barely lit room full of the injured and dying, while drifting in a wrecked spaceship that was waiting to be picked off by the next enemy that came along. *How did we end up this way?* he wondered. *How did it get this bad?*

He had almost made it across the main treatment bay when he noticed an open door to an adjacent room. The room seemed oddly quiet, especially considering the limited space in the main treatment area. Nathan wondered what was in that room, and why it wasn't being used to treat the wounded. The room was unlit, except for the scant light spilling into it from the main treatment area. Perhaps it was the darkness that piqued his curiosity and drew him closer to the door to peer inside. He wished he hadn't. In the darkened room were the bodies of the dead, piled unceremoniously just to get them out of the way. The gruesome sight caused a wave of guilt to wash over him. *Did these people all die because of me? Because of the decisions I made?*

It was almost too much for him to bear, and he quickly made for the small utility room nearby, barely making it to the wash basin before heaving up his breakfast. His head spun and his skin became cold and clammy. Were it not for the counter, he probably couldn't have remained vertical. He stood there for several minutes, trying to pull himself together. But the guilt was still twisting his gut into knots and making him want to vomit again, despite the fact that his stomach was empty.

"Are you all right?" a female voice came from behind him. He turned his head slightly to look at her.

"I'm fine," he lied.

"Yeah? Well you don't look fine. How much blood did you lose?"

"Huh?" he asked, turning to face her. She was a petite Chinese woman, young, wearing a medical uniform that was stained with blood. Her long black hair was tied back in a pony tail that had also been pulled up into an additional knot, no doubt to keep it out of the open wounds of her patients. She wasn't even wearing the usual exam gloves that medical personnel always wore, having given up on changing them every few minutes as she jumped from patient to patient in rapid succession. She looked like she had been at it for days, even though it had been just over two hours since the first jump put them into harm's way. Despite it all, she was still observant enough to notice his discomfort.

"Your leg," she explained, "it's bleeding."

"Oh, that," he remembered, realizing it was still throbbing. "I can wait. Besides, you've got plenty of patients worse off than me."

"Are you sure?" She suddenly noticed that he outranked her, and added, "Sir." Then it dawned on her. "Are you here to talk to the captain?"

Hope suddenly sprang forth in Nathan's mind. *He's still alive? And he's conscious?* Suddenly, he thought that an end might come to this nightmare called command. If the captain survived, even if he was infirmed for a while, at least he might have someone to come to for advice in the interim.

Nathan looked at the woman, noticing her blood-smeared name tag for the first time. 'M. Chen M.D.' "He's alive?" he asked. "How is he, Doctor? Is he conscious? Can I speak to him?"

"Maybe. He's in and out," she warned. "He's

severely injured."

"Will he make it?"

"If we can get him back to Earth, maybe. He desperately needs surgery."

"Well, can't you do it?"

She looked at him a moment, puzzlement on her face. "I'm just a resident, not a surgeon. He needs to be taken to a properly-equipped facility with a good trauma surgeon, and soon."

Nathan's hopes suddenly began to fall again. "I don't think that's an option right now."

"Surely you sent out a distress call. It shouldn't take more than a few hours for help to arrive from Earth, right?"

"I'm afraid you're the only chance he's got right now, Doctor."

"But I'm *not* a surgeon. I've only assisted in a few minor surgical procedures so far," she protested. "Besides, we can't perform surgery as long as the power is out."

Nathan hadn't thought of that. "And if the power was restored?" he asked. "Could you operate then?"

Doctor Chen looked around, thinking of how she might pull that off. "Maybe, I guess. I could have someone call out the procedures to me from the medical database to help."

"How long has he got?"

"I don't know. Could be hours, or it could be minutes," she admitted. "But I still don't see why we can't just wait for a rescue ship to come. He'll have a much better chance if..."

"There is no rescue ship coming!" he interrupted, frustration getting the better of him. She could tell that he was upset by their current situation. And she saw by the insignia on his uniform that he was bridge staff, so he probably knew more about their situation than she did.

"Can I see him?" he asked.

"Yes, but keep it brief," she warned. "He's in the corner," she added, tilting her head to the right.

Nathan stood up straight, gathering his strength as he straightened his uniform. A few moments later, he was standing at the foot of the captain's bed. His head was wrapped with a bandage that was soaked with blood where it covered his right eye. His right shoulder still appeared odd, and Nathan realized it was probably worse than a simple dislocation. He had a large, wet bandage laid over the right side of his abdomen that was also stained with copious amounts of blood. He had several large bags of fluids hanging from the ceiling, all connected to an intravenous line that had been placed in his left arm. And there was a large bag of a synthetic blood replacement fluid connected to a tube leading to the one in his right arm. He was breathing on his own through an oxygen mask that fogged up slightly with each exhalation. His face was swollen and puffy, and at first Nathan wasn't even sure it *was* Captain Roberts.

Nathan stared at him for several minutes. He wondered what the captain would have done differently if he were still in command. Would he have killed two of his crew just to suck the boarders out into space? Would he have put the ship in further jeopardy by detonating that torpedo while they were still too close? Would he have allowed those strangers to come aboard and help repair the ship? But mostly, he wondered if the captain's injuries had somehow been his fault as well.

He was about to leave, as the guilt was starting to

make him nauseated once more, when the captain spoke.

"Lieutenant," he whispered from behind the oxygen mask.

Nathan tried to come to attention, fighting back the nausea that was still swelling up inside him. "Yes, sir!"

"How's my ship?" he managed to ask.

"She's busted up pretty bad, sir. But we're still here, and repairs are under way."

"How's the XO?"

Nathan was afraid to answer but knew that he had to be honest. "I'm afraid he's dead, sir."

The captain coughed several times, which appeared to cause him much discomfort.

"Chief Patel?"

"Missing."

"Who's in command?"

"I'm afraid I am, sir."

The captain flashed what looked like a smile to Nathan, but it was hard to tell with all the swelling. "Well, we're still alive, so I guess you're doing okay so far."

Nathan felt his guilt swelling up again. "I don't know about that, sir," he admitted. "I think I've just been lucky so far."

"Nonsense," the captain insisted. "You're a natural born leader, Nathan. Just like your old man."

The statement struck Nathan as odd. Although he was aware that the captain knew *of* his father, he *wasn't* aware that he knew anything *about* him.

"Sir, I don't know that I can do this," Nathan admitted. The thought had been running through his mind since the moment he had assumed command,

and it felt good to finally admit it to someone.

"Bullshit. Just remember, it's not about being right and knowing all the answers. It's about making the call." The statement had taken a lot out of the captain, who closed his eyes for a moment to rest. Nathan thought for a second that he might have slipped back into unconsciousness, but then his eyes opened again, slowly. "Nathan, take the bars from my uniform."

Nathan looked around, finally spotting the captain's cut-up uniform shirt lying on the counter behind him. He picked it up and carefully removed the blood stained bars. He was about to hand them to the captain, when he realized his intentions.

"Put them on," he ordered softly from behind the oxygen mask.

Nathan reluctantly replaced his lieutenant's bars with the captain's bars.

"I hereby order you to assume command of the Aurora, effective immediately."

Nathan looked down at the floor, unable to look the captain in the eye. He didn't want the captain to see the fear in his eyes: the fear for his captain's fate, the fear for his own fate, and most of all, his fear of command. After a few moments, he managed to raise his eyes to meet those of his dying captain, stiffening and offering a salute.

"I relieve you, sir," Nathan announced quietly, but with far more conviction than he expected.

The captain could not return his salute. "I stand relieved." A wave of calm seemed to wash over the captain at that moment, as he closed his eyes again. Nathan started to turn away to exit when he felt the captain's hand tug at Nathan's shirt, stopping him.

"Get them home," he stated emphatically as

Nathan turned back to him. "Get the jump drive home," he coughed. "It's their only hope."

Nathan watched as the captain's grip on his shirt loosened, his hand falling back to the bed as his eyes closed. Suddenly, an alarm on the bio-monitor started beeping rapidly, startling him. *Oh my God.*

Doctor Chen had been watching the entire exchange as she cared for a nearby patient. Hearing the alarm, she dropped what she was doing and came running over. "He's crashing! I need some help in here!"

Doctor Chen pushed Nathan aside as she rushed past, her eyes on the bio-monitor the entire time. "He's in V-Fib!" she declared.

Nathan backed away, making room for the few people available to help the doctor as she frantically tried to resuscitate the captain. But Nathan already knew it was too late. The captain had known it as well. That was why he had transferred command to him.

Nathan exited the sick bay and began wandering the corridor, his mind racked with an overpowering combination of guilt and grief. The medical bay was packed full of people with injuries he had probably caused, and there was a pile of bodies, bodies of men and women, all of whom had sworn to serve their world just as he had upon graduation only a few short weeks ago. *Is this what it's like to be in command?*

He wandered down the corridor, not really headed in any particular direction that he was aware of. He passed an ensign that was carrying supplies back to medical. Upon seeing the captain's bars on Nathan's collar, the crewman immediately stopped and snapped to attention, which was something that was only done for upper level command staff. At that moment, the lights in the corridor came back on, and suddenly, Nathan knew exactly where he was headed.

* * *

Minutes later, Nathan walked onto the bridge. A young marine armed with a close-quarters defense weapon snapped to attention as he passed.

"Captain on the bridge!" the marine announced. It was the first time Nathan had been referred to as captain, and it felt strange, but in a good way.

Cameron spun around from the tactical station, expecting to see Captain Roberts miraculously healed and returning to take command and get them safely home. But instead, she saw Nathan, wearing a pair of blood-smeared captain's bars.

"Sorry," Nathan apologized, seeing the disappointment in her eyes. "It's just me."

"I guess it's official, then," she admitted reluctantly. She also knew what it probably meant. "Is he..."

Nathan didn't answer. He didn't have to; she saw it in his eyes.

"You might want to clean the blood off of them," she whispered as they turned back to the tactical station.

"Maybe later."

"Main power just came back online a minute ago," she told him, noticing his attention to the tactical displays.

Nathan looked around the bridge, noticing that they had cleaned it up in his absence. "I see you tidied up the place a bit."

"Yeah, well, with everything down there wasn't much to do. And a few people showed up to help, so we moved out the bodies and as much debris as possible. We got a tech to shut down the damaged consoles so we won't have any more sparks or fires if you decide to bounce us around again."

"How many systems are back up?" he asked, ignoring her sarcasm.

"We've only just started assessing things since the power was restored a few minutes ago. We've got most of our local sensors back online, although Kaylah says that until she can run a full diagnostic on them, we shouldn't trust their accuracy out to more than a few million kilometers. She also reports that there are five more small ships out there that have taken up positions all around us. I can't tell if they're in position to attack us or defend us."

"Yeah, well, they said they were here to help."

"Really? You spoke to them?"

"Yeah, one of them speaks *Angla*."

"What?"

"Angla. I think it means *really bad English* in their language," he said. "They're down in engineering helping Vlad right now."

"You think that's wise?" she questioned.

"Don't worry. Jessica has orders to keep a close eye on them."

"Jessica?"

"Ensign Nash, from spec-ops? She's one tough nut. Kinda scary. You'd like her," he jabbed. It felt good to lighten the mood after what they had been through over the last couple of hours.

"I see. How many of these *helpers* are there?"

"Four, for now. If it works out, there's more available if needed."

"Four? How's she going to watch all four?"

"She's armed. And she's got help," he assured her. "Besides, they warned us that more of the enemy might return soon, so I figured we'd better accept their offer and get out of here as quickly as possible."

"And you just believed them?"

"For now, cautiously." Nathan stepped up to the tactical console and pressed the comm button. "Engineering, bridge!"

"Yes," Vladimir answered.

"How's it going down there?"

"I'm sorry, Nathan, but it will take longer than I thought to get maneuvering and propulsion systems back online. The damage is worse than I expected."

"Well, at least you got main power up; that's something."

"Thank you, Nathan, but it was not me. It was those people you sent down. They are pretty good engineers. Difficult to speak with, but they are very smart and learn quickly."

"Glad to hear it. Keep working on maneuvering and propulsion. Bridge out."

"Lieutenant!" Jessica called out as she entered the bridge with Jalea at her side. Nathan spun around, not expecting to see Jessica back on the bridge so soon. "Oh, excuse me, Captain," she corrected, after seeing the bloody bars on his collar. "We need to talk."

"I thought you were watching our guests." Nathan said, somewhat surprised.

"I've got Sergeant Weatherly and the rest watching them. Besides, this couldn't wait," she insisted.

"Jalea, this is Cameron," he introduced.

Jalea, still not terribly confident in her ability to

speak English, offered only a respectful nod, taking Cameron's handshake when offered.

"Listen, we've got problems," Jessica continued, interrupting the pleasantries. "According to Jalea, there are more Takaran ships on their way..."

"What? I hope you don't mean more like that last one, 'cause it nearly killed us." Nathan did not like where the conversation was going. He had just been officially placed in command, and he was hoping for a little more time to get used to the idea before the next crisis.

"No, smaller ones, she thinks..."

"Anything on sensors?" Cameron interrupted, turning towards Ensign Yosef.

"No, sir."

"I don't understand." Cameron said to Jessica. "How does she know they're coming?"

"Their ships reported it. They picked up the incoming vessels on their sensors a few minutes ago. I brought Jalea up here so she could translate between you and their ships."

"Good thinking," Nathan commended.

"Actually, it was Marak's idea," she admitted. "He thought it would be better for her to remain with you, as your translator, for now."

"But how are Marak and the others going to communicate with our people in engineering?"

"Vladimir figured out that their language is a mixture of Slavic and Germanic languages, with a little Arabic thrown in."

"Odd combination," Cameron observed.

"Yeah, well, Vladimir speaks German as well as Russian, and with Jalea's help he managed to fill in a few of the blanks, at least enough for now. He's pretty smart; I'll give him that."

"Captain," Ensign Yosef interrupted, "I've got them now! Transferring to tactical."

Cameron looked down at the tactical display. "Two of them, much smaller than the first one. They're moving fast, maybe twice light, so we can't outrun them."

"We can't outrun anything in our current state," Nathan added, the frustration obvious in his voice.

"How long until they reach weapons range?" he asked Cameron.

"Well, they'll reach us in about twenty minutes, assuming their weapons range is about the same as ours. Maybe fifteen?"

Nathan thought some more. No propulsion, no maneuvering, no weapons. To him it all equaled one thing—no options. He looked around the bridge. There were marines guarding both exits once more, and two more ensigns had come in and man the two auxiliary stations that had been reconfigured to manage both communications and electronic countermeasures.

"Can your ships stop them?" he asked Jalea.

"No, Takaran ships big, very strong."

"Can you call for help?" Jessica interjected.

"No, help too far. No time."

Nathan noticed that Doctor Sorenson was sitting quietly at her station, running systems checks to keep her mind off of her father's untimely demise. "Doctor Sorenson," he asked, "can we jump again?"

She stared at him coldly for a moment, finally answering. "I do not think you understand the complexity of this system, Captain," she warned. In her mind, she blamed the reckless manner in which Captain Roberts had used the system for the death of her father. The first transition algorithms had taken days to calculate and even longer to verify. And these people thought using it was like jumping over a puddle. "You can't just jump, jump, jump, whenever you like..."

"Doctor," he interrupted, trying to take a more gentle tact, "I understand what you're saying and, under normal circumstances, I wouldn't dream of using it in such a haphazard manner—but these are *not* normal circumstances. We've got more enemy ships on the way. We've got no weapons *and* we're adrift. I don't see any other options."

She looked at him again, realizing he was right. "Maybe. We just got power back minutes ago, and I haven't finished running diagnostics on the transition sequencer yet. But the field generators are okay, and there is still enough energy in the storage banks for a short jump, maybe two or three light years at the most. I do not know the state of all the field emitters on the outside of the hull. We took a lot of weapons fire, and if too many of the emitters are damaged, the fields may not initiate properly."

"What happens if they don't?" Cameron asked.

"I'm not sure."

Cameron could see in the doctor's eyes that she at least had a suspicion of what might happen. "What do you *think* could happen?"

"Part of the ship might not jump."

"*Part* of the ship? I don't think I like the sound of that," she insisted.

"Neither do I. Doctor, can't you check the emitters from here?"

"No. We did not have time to add hardwired sensor leads to all the emitters, so we used wireless ones on more than half. But the external comm array is damaged, so I am missing status information on at least half of the emitters."

"Well," Nathan said, "I guess the next question is, How do the Takarans treat prisoners?"

"No prisoners. Takar execute all rebels." Jalea answered solemnly.

"I don't like the sound of that either," Cameron added.

"Rebels?" Nathan asked.

"Yeah, I was getting to that," Jessica explained. "Seems these people are part of a rebellion against an oppressive regime. Nasty people, from what she tells me. They've been fighting them for decades and have nearly lost everything. I'm not sure, but it sounds to me like we arrived just in time to save their butts. They had lost twenty ships before we jumped into the middle of it and took out that warship."

"When did you..." Nathan began to ask.

"We talked on the way up," she interrupted.

"Well, that explains why they want to help us," Nathan realized.

"Yeah, they want our ship for their little war," Cameron said under her breath. She wasn't sure how well Jalea understood English and didn't want her to be aware of her suspicions.

"Or maybe they're just looking for an ally." Nathan offered.

"To be honest, sir," Jessica interrupted, "I don't think they knew what to expect when they came aboard. They tried to hail us first but got no answer."

"Comms were down," Cameron reminded him.

"Is there enough room in the hangar bay for the rest of the rebel ships?" he asked Cameron, an idea brewing in his head.

"Yeah, I think so, if we park them tight. They're a bit bigger than a fleet tactical shuttle, but they should fit."

"Doctor, will the additional mass of those ships affect your jump calculations?"

"Not at all. The transition system uses the same mass canceling technology as the FTL system."

"Jalea, have all your ships land in our hangar bay," Nathan told her.

"This is not a good idea," Cameron warned him. "You heard what she said—*part* of the ship might not jump."

"Better than *all* of us being executed," he argued.

"I'm with her, sir," Jessica agreed. "Besides, I don't like the idea of taking on who knows how many more rebels."

"How many people on your ships?" Nathan asked Jalea.

"Twenty, I think. But I not understand," she added.

"Twenty? I can't watch twenty of them. I've only got six guys right now, and four of them aren't even combat trained."

"Keep them in the hangar bay for now. I doubt they're going to want to keep all their ships bottled up for long after we jump anyway. I know I wouldn't," Cameron explained.

Nathan looked at Jessica, who finally resigned to the inevitable. "You're the boss."

"You can have my two marines, if it makes you feel better." Nathan offered.

"No, better you keep them, in case something goes horribly wrong," she advised.

"Why you want ships here?" Jalea asked again, confused.

"If you bring the ships here, I can get us all far away from the Takaran ships," Nathan explained.

"I must speak with Marak," she told him, pulling a small communication device from her pocket. Nathan indicated to her that it was all right, and she began explaining the situation as best she understood it to Marak. Although they could not understand what was being said, it was obvious that Marak was not enthusiastic about the idea.

"Marak, he not want do this. He not understand why," Jalea told him.

"Trust me, I can get us out of here, like that," he told her, snapping his fingers.

"How? Your ship not move," she insisted.

"It's complicated," he told her. "Hell, I don't even understand it myself," he mumbled. "You just need to trust me."

She said nothing. She only looked into Nathan's eyes.

"We're going, with or without your people," he warned, "in..." He paused, looking to Cameron for an answer.

"Thirteen minutes."

"Thirteen minutes," he finished. "So if you don't want to go, you and Marak better leave now, before it's too late."

After another pause, Jalea resumed her argument with Marak over her communicator. Only this time, she seemed to be arguing in support of Nathan's plan. Finally, after what seemed like an eternity, she switched channels on her communicator, apparently giving instructions to the rest of their ships.

"They will come," she assured him.

"Great!" Nathan exclaimed, happy to have a plan to act upon. "Jess, get some people down to the hangar bay to help get our guests situated. And keep everyone there, nobody leaves the hangar bay until further notice."

"Yes, sir," she acknowledged as she turned to head for the exit.

"Captain," Doctor Sorenson interrupted, "it might be safer if I actually had a destination this time."

"Can you plot a jump that quickly?"

"It's not really a plot," she explained. "I have to write an algorithm that will control the entire process so that our jump is for the correct distance. The course will have to be plotted by your navigator."

"I guess that would still be me," Cameron volunteered, knowing that there was no one else available.

"Well then, can you write the algorithm that quickly?" Nathan asked the doctor.

"I can write it, yes, but there will not be enough time to verify its accuracy."

"I can live with that," Nathan said. "Jalea, we need somewhere to go, a place to hide while we make repairs. Somewhere close. Do you know of such a place?"

"I think, yes. Korak," she told him.

"Korak?"

"KOO-rahk," she corrected.

"Great! Don't really care how you say it," he mumbled. "Show her," he told Jalea, pointing toward Doctor Sorenson. "Kaylah, can you help them figure it out?"

"It looks like we're currently in a system that's part of a five-star cluster," Cameron explained, pointing to a chart displayed on the tactical station in front of her and Nathan. It had taken a few minutes to figure out what Jalea had been describing. With

Kaylah's help, they were able to put together a rough plot. "It's pretty small, considering, only about eight light years in diameter. And if I'm understanding her correctly, there's gotta be at least a dozen inhabited worlds scattered throughout the entire cluster."

"I've never even heard of such a system," Nathan commented. "Where the hell are we?"

"Yeah, I was thinking the same thing," Cameron admitted. "I know one thing; we sure aren't in the core."

Nathan had come to the same conclusion the moment that Jessica had told them about the rebellion. That was surely something that Fleet Intelligence would've known about. And to their knowledge, the entire core and most of the fringe worlds were controlled by the Jung Dynasty. They would not have allowed someone like the Takarans to rule over such a system in their own backyard.

"Do we have a destination?" he asked.

"Well, we're currently in the primary component of a binary system," she explained, pointing at the display. "Over here is the secondary component, Korak, about one point five light years away. It's small, only one gas giant orbiting a red dwarf. Dozens of moons, one of them inhabited by some sort of mining colony. The system is mostly an asteroid field beyond that, and a pretty dense one so it's a good place to hide. She says that, if we're lucky, we can hide out there for at least a few days. There are one or two Takaran ships in that system, smaller ones, like the ones that are inbound now. But Jalea says that it would take at least a couple of days for word of us to reach them. I guess they have some kind of really fast comm relay probes that can go like a hundred times light or something.

But at least there won't be anyone looking for us for a few days. And since the asteroid field is so dense, unless they're watching for us, they're not likely to notice when we jump in."

"Yeah, they wouldn't be expecting that, would they?" he chuckled. "Then I guess that's our destination. At the least, it might give us enough time to get maneuvering and propulsion back online." Nathan turned his attention to Ensign Yosef, monitoring the sensors from her science station. "Ensign Yosef. How many rebel ships have landed so far?"

"Only two, sir."

"Two?" Nathan quickly activated the comm. "Jessica! What's taking so long down there?"

"These ships are bigger than we thought, Captain. I don't know if we're going to be able to fit them all in here!"

"Well, leave one in the airlock and one on the apron if you have to! Just get them on deck!" Turning to Cameron, he asked, "How long before they can fire on us?"

"Five minutes, maybe," Cameron answered. He knew she was guessing. They knew nothing about Takaran weapons and technology.

"Jalea," he said, drawing her away from Doctor Sorenson's side, "we need to get your ships on board more quickly. There's not enough time." She looked puzzled. "Not enough time," he repeated. "Go faster." Suddenly, she understood what he wanted and began communicating the problem with Marak. A moment later he heard Marak's voice giving a rather important sounding command over their communicators. He didn't understand what he was saying, but from the tone of Marak's voice he was pretty sure that if he had, he wouldn't have liked it.

"Nathan," Cameron called, "two of the rebel ships have reversed course!"

"What?"

"They're on an intercept vector for the incoming Takaran ships."

"What are they doing? They'll be destroyed!" Nathan spun back around to face Jalea. "What did he tell them to do?!"

"Need more time," she explained. "They give."

"They give? You mean they give their lives?" Nathan couldn't believe what he was hearing. "Do they know this?"

"They know," she answered, with no emotion showing in her voice.

"The rebel ships have fired on the Takarans, and they're changing course, heading away from us."

"Did their fire..."

"No effect," Cameron reported. Nathan was now standing next to her at the tactical display, watching the engagement. "The Takaran ships are changing course, pursuing." They watched for less than a minute, until the two Takaran ships caught up to the rebels and obliterated them. "The rebel ships are destroyed," Cameron reported. "They're resuming original course. ETA six minutes, weapons range in one."

"How many people were on those ships?" Nathan asked Jalea coldly.

"Six," she answered in much the same tone.

Nathan couldn't believe what he had just witnessed. Six people had just sacrificed themselves for nothing. At the most, it might have gained them an extra minute.

"They're firing!" Cameron reported. "Missiles

inbound, tracking four, all nukes! ETA thirty seconds!"

"Bridge, hangar bay! The last of the rebel ships are on deck!"

Nathan stood there staring intently into Jalea's eyes. She didn't blink, didn't look away. Where he had once seen strength and compassion, he now saw only a cold ruthlessness that he wasn't sure he could understand. And he knew he didn't like it.

"Captain!" Cameron begged.

"Kill the view screen," he ordered calmly. "Doctor Sorenson, it's time to go."

CHAPTER SEVEN

"Transition complete," Doctor Sorenson reported with just the slightest hint of relief in her voice.

Cameron immediately switched the view screen back on, revealing a sea of asteroids of varying sizes. Nathan couldn't help but marvel at the view. He had never seen an asteroid field, and by his understanding, this one was far more dense than most. The field of stars before them had an unusual twinkling quality, as the numerous asteroids too distant to see with the naked eye passed in front of stars, causing them to blink off and on. His gaze was fixed on the screen for at least a full minute, so long that Cameron was beginning to wonder what he was staring at.

"Anything on sensors?" he finally asked Ensign Yosef.

"No, sir, just rocks."

Nathan wasn't sure he could believe it, not after the previous two jumps. "What? No Jung patrols? No mammoth Takaran warships? No rebel hordes?"

Cameron just gave him a sideways glance, unimpressed by the timing of his sarcasm.

"I'm just checking," he defended.

Jalea exclaimed something in her native language, astonished at what she had just witnessed.

"How is this possible?" she finally asked in English, her eyes wide.

"I really don't know," Nathan admitted, "but

lucky for us, it is."

"Captain," Cameron said, "I suggest we start a plot of all the nearest asteroids, just to be on the safe side."

"Good idea."

"Just so you are aware, Captain," Doctor Sorenson interrupted, "the transition system's energy banks are now down to less than ten percent."

"And that's bad?" he asked. There was still so much he didn't know about this new system.

"It will take at least a few hours to charge the energy banks enough to execute even a short transition. That's assuming we're able to run our reactor at one hundred percent the entire time."

"Understood, Doctor. When time permits, I think we're going to need a full briefing on the capabilities and limitations of your... What did you call it?"

"Hyperluminal Transition System."

Nathan mumbled it to himself, giving up halfway through the name. "You know what? Let's keep calling it a jump drive for now."

"That's not exactly accurate," she protested.

"Maybe not, but it's a lot easier to say. Besides, that other one will never catch on," Nathan added as he opened a comm channel to engineering. "Engineering, bridge."

"Yes, go ahead," Vladimir responded, sounding more than a bit annoyed at being bothered again.

"Can you run the primary reactor for the jump drive at one hundred percent?"

"What is this jump drive?" he asked, having not heard of it before now.

"Doctor Sorenson's little project."

"Of course, I should have known." Nathan could hear the change in the tone of Vladimir's voice.

"*Yes, this I can do. But please, for no longer than is necessary.*"

"Understood," Nathan acknowledged, switching off the comm.

"Captain," Ensign Yosef warned, "if the Takarans come looking for us, that reactor is going to be like a big sign pointing out our location, regardless of all these asteroids."

"How long does it take to shut down an antimatter reactor?" he asked Cameron, embarrassed that he didn't know.

"Ten to fifteen minutes, I think."

"Actually," Doctor Sorenson interjected, "we rewrote the shutdown procedure to satisfy our abort protocols. We can have the reactor offline in about three minutes, and the core would no longer be emanating any discernible energy output within seconds of starting the abort process."

"Excellent. Problem solved then." He turned to Ensign Yosef, "If you pick up any signs of a Takaran ship, don't go through me. Just tell Doctor Sorenson and she'll shut down the reactor, okay?" Nathan looked at each of them to make sure everyone understood their part.

"Nathan," Cameron said in a hushed tone, "I think our jump drive has made quite an impression on the locals." Cameron looked toward Jalea, who was now standing by the port exit in the back corner of the bridge facing away from them as she excitedly conversed with Marak over her personal communicator. It was obvious that the jump had taken her completely by surprise. Nathan could understand how she felt, as a few short hours ago even he had not known such a thing existed.

"You think this is going to be a problem?" he

asked Cameron.

"I don't know, but I think it certainly has the potential to become one."

Nathan thought about it, wondering how it would affect their relationship with these people. Would they insist that they share the jump drive technology with them? Would they try to take it by force? How would they use it? If they were engaged in a rebellion against superior numbers, then this would certainly give them a tactical advantage. And how far would they be willing to go to obtain this advantage?

"Maybe we should make sure all of our weapons lockers are properly secured. And make sure the jump drive is still under guard as well."

Cameron nodded her agreement then walked over to the ensign handling communications, quietly passing the instructions to be put into motion.

"Captain," Ensign Yosef called, alarm in her voice, "I found one, an asteroid with a trajectory that shows a ninety-eight percent collision probability."

"How big?"

"Big enough, sir."

"You see? I knew it!" Nathan exclaimed, throwing his hands up in frustration. "I knew it was too good to be true!"

"How long do we have?" Cameron asked the ensign.

"Estimate impact in forty minutes."

Cameron turned to Nathan, who was looking like he had reached his limit in crisis management for the day. "Okay," she offered, trying to offer support. "Let's just work the problem."

Nathan looked back at Cameron. Although she had been as shaken as the rest of them after the encounter with the Takaran warship, she was back to her old self again—cold and calculating.

"You're right," he admitted. "Work the problem." Nathan raised his hands and locked his fingers behind his head, trying to think of a way to avoid the collision. "We can't jump, and we've got no maneuvering or propulsion." He looked at Ensign Yosef. "I'm assuming it's too big to blow apart with rail guns, correct?" Ensign Yosef simply nodded, saying nothing. "No matter; they're not working anyway," he reminded himself.

"Torpedo? Maybe one of the nuclear ones?" Cameron offered.

"We already shot all four forward tubes, and the auto-loaders aren't installed yet. I doubt we could get them loaded in time."

"I don't think a nuke would make much difference with this one, sir," Ensign Yosef reluctantly admitted.

"That big, huh?" Nathan asked rhetorically. He looked back to Cameron. "Got any ideas?"

Cameron simply shrugged. "Maybe you can blow something up again," she suggested, half-heartedly.

"Don't tempt me," he warned. "I haven't ruled that one out yet."

"Well, how far do we need to move to avoid the collision?" Cameron asked, making her way back to Ensign Yosef.

"One moment." Ensign Yosef began running the calculations. After a few moments, she answered. "Not that much. If we could just speed up or slow down by as little as a few hundred meters per second, we'd just miss it. But we would have to do it before we get too close to the asteroid, or its gravity will pull us in."

"Well how do we do that without propulsion?"

Nathan asked.

"Captain," Jalea interrupted, "you need to move ship?"

"Uh, yes. Why?"

"We can do this, I think."

"How?" Cameron inquired.

"With our ships. This we do, many times. When we capture ships, or to bring broken ships home."

"A tow?" Nathan wondered aloud. "But your ships are not that big."

"But they are very strong," she assured him. "Marak agrees; this can be done."

"Have you ever towed a ship this big before?"

"No," she admitted, "but a first time, there must be for everything."

"I don't know about this, Nathan," Cameron warned.

"Would you rather I blow up the stern docking thruster pods?"

Within minutes of receiving their orders from Marak, the four rebel ships had made their way out of the hangar bay and back into space. The Aurora, like any other ship in the fleet, had numerous hard points located on her hull. Normally used for mooring purposes, these points had direct attachment to the underlying frame of the ship and would be more than strong enough for the tow operation.

The rebel ships were equipped with powerful grappling claws designed to grab a ship and punch through her hull if necessary. In this case, the rebel ships simply grabbed hold of a mooring point, and then started standing off from the ship, reeling out their tow lines as they moved away.

Nathan stood behind his previous station at the helm, gazing out of the view screen that surrounded the front third of the bridge. By now, they could see the approaching asteroid. It had started out as no more than a speck against the blackness, but within minutes it had grown to fill half the screen. Three of the rebel ships were in position with their tow lines running from their top side down to the ship. Each ship was at least a few hundred meters away, angling out at about forty-five degrees from the Aurora, and they were keeping their tow lines taut with weak but steady thrust while they waited for the last ship to get into position.

"The last ship is moving into position now, sir," Ensign Yosef reported.

"How much time?" he asked.

"We've got five minutes to get up to speed before we're too close to escape its gravity well, sir."

Nathan turned to Jalea. "You know, they all have to burn in unison for this to work."

"Controls for one ship will control all ships," she explained.

Nathan understood what she meant. Fleet tugs used a similar method, slaving the flight controls for all tugs into the bridge of the ship being pulled, thereby using the tugs like they were external propulsion pods. It had been one of the simulations he had been required to pass during his flight training, and it had been a difficult one to master. Luckily, in this case, someone else would be doing the piloting.

"Prepare yourself," Jalea warned as the voice on her communicator completed what sounded like a countdown, albeit in another language. Nathan could hear the voices of the rebel pilots as they chattered back and forth over Jalea's communicator. The countdown ended with the last word being spoken louder and more urgently than the ones preceding it.

On the view screen, the main engines of the two visible rebel ships began to glow a faint amber. As he heard the voice of the lead rebel pilot over Jalea's communicator, he could tell that he was announcing his increases in thrust. They watched as the rebel engines' thrust ports faded from amber to yellow as their levels increased. As the thrust levels increased, so did the stress level in the lead pilot's voice.

"Three minutes," Ensign Yosef announced.

The main thrust ports on the rebel ships again changed, going from yellow to a brilliant bluish white. The lead pilot's voice was now yelling.

"They are at full power," Jalea announced.

"Jesus," Cameron exclaimed. "She wasn't kidding about those little buggers being strong. Look at the amount of thrust they're putting out."

"Two minutes to impact," Ensign Yosef updated.

The asteroid was now filling more than half the upper side of the main view screen, its horizon sinking farther and farther down the screen on its way to the floor. The lead pilot's voice yelled another announcement, and the rebels' engines became pure white, expanding their radius somewhat and taking on a blinding brilliance.

"What are they doing?" Nathan yelled.

"Their engines are burning much more than normal," Jalea exclaimed. There was more yelling over the communicator, but this time from some of the other pilots.

"What is it? What's wrong?"

"Engines very hot now," Jalea explained.

"They can't keep that burn rate up for long," Cameron warned.

"Sir," Ensign Yosef interrupted, "our velocity is climbing! It's working!"

Nathan could hear more excited voices over Jalea's communicator as the rebel pilots realized they were starting to move.

"Impact in...," Ensign Yosef suddenly stopped mid-sentence, watching her sensor display as it updated. "We're going to miss it, sir!" she announced, obvious relief in her voice.

"Tell them to reduce their engines before they rip themselves apart!" Nathan ordered.

Jalea began yelling instructions into her communicator. An inquiry came back from the lead pilot.

"Captain, the pilot wants to know if you would like them to go a little longer, maybe help you away from rocks."

"What do you think, Cam?" Nathan asked.

"This field is pretty big, sir. They'd have to get us a lot of velocity to clear it in anything less than a few days."

"That's okay, Jalea," Nathan apologized. "Please ask them to turn off their engines."

"As you wish."

Having avoided yet another catastrophe, Nathan hoped they might finally have a chance to regroup. It was the first time since they had left the orbit of Jupiter that there wasn't some immediate calamity about to befall them.

He had watched the entire towing operation standing behind the helm station. And now, with the immediate threat averted, he dropped into the captain's command chair without even realizing the significance of where he sat.

"Don't get too comfortable," Cameron warned, turning her chair to face him. "We still have a lot of work to do."

Nathan leaned forward in the command chair, his elbows resting on his knees. He couldn't help but feel that he should know what she was talking about, but at the moment, all he could think about was that he was incredibly thirsty.

"We're going to need to put together some sort of damage report, at least of the most critical stuff," she explained. She paused for a moment, her tone becoming more serious. "And we need to get an idea of how many people we lost today," she added, "or more importantly, who we've got left to run the ship."

Nathan thought about what she was saying. *How many people we lost today.* He wasn't sure he really wanted to know. Most of the crew had only been on board for a few weeks, himself included. He had only known a handful of them by name. The idea that now he never would know them just didn't seem possible. Every one of them knew that a life in the fleet came with risks, but he was quite sure that, like him, none of them had expected this much risk this soon.

"Yeah," he sighed, "I was in medical earlier." The memory of it was still fresh in his mind. "I was there, you know, when he died." It bothered Nathan to speak of it. He hadn't known Captain Roberts for very long, and what little interaction had occurred had been strictly professional. But Nathan couldn't help but feel that he had lost someone who would've been very important to him, had he survived.

"I kind of figured," she admitted.

"You know, right before he died, he said, 'Get the

ship home.' More specifically, to get the 'jump drive' home, that it was their 'only chance.'"

"By 'their' he meant 'Earth', right?" Although the captain's meaning had been obvious, Cameron didn't care for ambiguity.

"I'm pretty sure." Nathan looked down for a moment, thinking. He had a terrible feeling that there was something more going on than any of them realized, but he couldn't quite put his finger on it. Until he figured it all out, he wasn't sure who he could trust.

But he also knew that if he was going to get them home, he would need help. He had accepted the responsibility of command, passed to him by his captain. But inside, he knew he wasn't ready for it. There was so much he still didn't know, so he was going to have to trust someone. Other than Vladimir, Cameron was the only other person on board that he really knew. In fact, they had spent so much time together in the simulator over the past two weeks, he probably knew Cameron better than he knew Vladimir. So if he was going to trust anyone, he might as well start with her.

Nathan sat back up, recomposing himself before continuing. "Listen, if we're going to get through this and get home, we need to get organized. I'm going to need an executive officer."

"Who did you have in mind?"

Nathan raised his head to look at her, a slight smile forming at the corner of his mouth.

Cameron suddenly realized his intent, sitting up straight in shock. "Oh, get serious."

"You're the most qualified person I know, Cam."

"I'm the only person you know, except for Vladimir, and there's no way I'm letting him become

XO."

"Then you'll do it?"

"On one condition. I get to object whenever I want."

"Like I could stop you." He smiled.

Cameron smiled back. "Not in a million years," she laughed.

"Then it's a deal?" Nathan held out his hand to shake on it.

"Yeah," she reluctantly agreed, taking his hand. "It's a deal."

"Great. Besides, I need Vlad in engineering anyway."

"You're an ass," she exclaimed, tossing his hand aside.

"Well, since you're XO now, I guess it falls on you to determine the condition of our ship and her crew. Feel free to grab whomever you need to help."

"Yes, sir," she answered, mocking a salute.

"But don't be gone too long. I need to go down to medical and get my leg treated. And I want to go by engineering to see how Vlad is doing with our guests."

"I can pretty much do everything from here," she offered, feeling a bit guilty that she had forgotten that he was wounded and had probably been in pain the entire time. "If you prefer, you could go now."

"Thanks, no. I just want to rest for a few minutes first. Besides, maybe you should at least take a quick break, get off the bridge, stretch your legs a bit."

"I could use a trip to the head," she admitted. Nathan could tell that she too welcomed even a short respite. Cameron stood up to leave. "I think I'll do a quick walk around the main decks, get a feel for the general condition of things," she said. "I shouldn't be too long, maybe an hour."

"See if you can rustle me up some water, will ya?" he said, smiling.

"I'll see what I can find," she promised as she walked past. She felt herself instinctively about to place her hand on his shoulder, as a show of bonding and support as she passed, but stopped short of doing so. She still wasn't sure how all of this was going to play out, and she wasn't entirely comfortable giving him her full support just yet. Less than a week ago, they had been competing for the same spot at the helm. Had she gotten that position, it would've been her sitting in the command chair instead of Nathan Scott.

"Doctor Sorenson," Nathan asked as he rose and stepped over to her station, "I know you've had a difficult day, probably more so than the rest of us. I just want you to know that I am very sorry about your father."

"Thank you, Captain." In all the commotion over the last few hours, she had not been given any time to mourn his passing. "I appreciate your concern, but I'll be all right." She paused for a moment before continuing, gathering her thoughts. "You know, ever since my mother died, this project was all that he had."

"I'm sorry, Doctor. I didn't know."

"Please, call me Abigail," she insisted. "Anyway, that was more than ten years ago." She looked away from Nathan, her eyes welling up again despite her best efforts. "That's why I joined this project. If I hadn't, I probably would never have seen him. It consumed his every waking moment." She wiped her eyes, a smile breaking through the sorrow as she looked up at Nathan. "He said that this technology would 'change everything.'"

"At least he got to see it work for himself before he died," Nathan offered.

Abigail just nodded, still trying to keep her emotions under control. "Funny thing is, I knew this project would kill him. But I always assumed he would work himself to death in his lab."

Nathan felt guilty for imposing upon her during such a difficult time, but he needed the skills that only she could provide. "Listen, Abigail, I hate to ask you for anything else—I mean, you've already saved our butts twice today—but I need to know what kind of condition your systems are in. I need to know what I can count on this 'Hyperluminal Translator Thingy' to do for us." Nathan flashed the same smile that usually got him out of trouble with his mother.

"Just go ahead and call it a 'jump drive'," she conceded.

"You see? It is easier," he bragged. "Anyway, maybe later you could fill me in on how this thing works, and what we can, and more importantly cannot, do with it."

"Yes, of course," she agreed, nodding her head up and down several times as she sniffed. "Whatever needs to be done."

"Great. Thanks, Abigail." Nathan put a comforting hand on her shoulder as he turned toward the port entrance, where Jessica had just entered.

"Sir," Jessica greeted him as she approached, "now that all of the rebel ships have left, I have nothing left to guard. Marak and his two guys are still working in engineering, and I've got a couple guys watching Marak's ship. So I came up here to see what I could do."

Nathan had known that Jessica was strong the first night he had met her, but he had been more than impressed at how she had handled herself over the last few hours. More than anyone, she had met every challenge thrown at her head-on, without hesitation. More importantly, she had demonstrated excellent instincts. That was something that you were born with—a lesson he had learned from Captain Roberts. Nathan had always been good at sizing people up quickly. That was a talent he had inherited from his father. And he knew that Jessica was someone he needed in his corner.

"In special operations school, they not only teach you about specialized combat and tactics, right? They also teach you about things like intelligence gathering and security, stuff like that?"

"Yes, sir. Spec-ops are trained to go covert, to gather intel, hit hardened targets and the like, so it also requires a detailed understanding of security." Jessica could go on about her highly specialized training for hours, as it was a great source of pride for her. But it suddenly occurred to her that there was probably a reason for his question. "Why do you ask?"

"I'm going to need someone to handle the ship's security, at least temporarily. I've got enough to think about, and you seem to have a knack for this sort of thing."

"I appreciate the offer, sir, but I'm not sure I'm ready," she protested.

"More so than any of us," he pointed out. "So, you'll take the job?"

Jessica smiled at the idea of the extra responsibility. Even if it was only temporary, it would still look great on her service record.

"Yes, sir. Thank you, sir," she said as she snapped a salute.

"Great," he exclaimed, returning her salute half-heartedly. "Then I've got a job for you," he explained, gesturing to her to follow him.

They walked over to Jalea, who was helping Ensign Yosef try to figure out where they were in relation to Earth. It was turning out to be considerably more difficult than expected.

"Excuse me, Ensign," Nathan apologized, "but we need to borrow Jalea for a while." Ensign Yosef nodded and returned to her work as Nathan led Jalea away, heading toward the back of the room.

"What may I do for you, Captain?" Nathan noticed that Jalea's pronunciation was getting a little better, as was her syntax. He had a feeling that she had spoken the language quite well at some point in her life, and that it would not be long before she became fluent once again.

"Earlier, you said that it would take some time for a message to get here. What did you mean by that?"

"When you escaped, the Takarans would send message to all ships. All ships must look for you, near them."

"And it would take a couple of days for a message to reach the ships that are here, in this system."

"Yes," she confirmed, nodding.

"How the hell can they get messages between systems that fast?" Jessica was shocked at the news. If true, it created a new tactical twist that she would have to pay close attention to in the future.

"They have some sort of communications relay, a drone or a ship maybe. Apparently it can go over a hundred times the speed of light," Nathan explained.

"I was hoping you could learn a bit more about that, and anything else you can."

"When message arrives, ships will look here first," Jalea interrupted.

"Yeah, so would we," Jessica agreed.

"Listen, Jalea, would you mind if Jessica asked you some questions? We could really use more information about the Takarans, the rebellion, and this whole system," he explained. "It would really help us a lot."

"Please, I must check with Marak on this," she told him, pulling her communicator from her belt.

"Of course."

Nathan and Jessica took a few steps away, moving closer to the entrance of the captain's ready room to give Jalea a moment to confer with her commander.

"If they can get messages between systems within days instead of months or years, that gives them quite an advantage, especially if these people cannot," Jessica explained.

"Yeah, that's what I was thinking," he agreed.

"I wonder what else they have," Jessica added.

"Captain," Jalea had finished conferring with her commander, "Marak says I can do this, mostly. But some questions, maybe I cannot answer."

"I think she means there are some things she is not allowed to tell us," Jessica mumbled.

"Yeah, I got that," he answered. "That should be fine," he assured Jalea as he led her into the ready room. "I'm sure anything you can tell us will be very helpful. Let's go in here where we can talk more privately," he added, motioning her to follow Jessica into the ready room. "I'll join you in a moment."

Jalea followed Jessica into the captain's ready room as Nathan stepped over to the temporary communications station that had been configured at the port auxiliary station just in front of the port exit. "Ensign, connect me to engineering, please." A moment later, Vladimir's voice came bellowing across the comm speaker.

"Yes! Bridge, go ahead!"

"Vlad, I hate to tell you this, but you've only got twenty-four hours to get this ship ready for combat."

"I'll do my best, Nathan!" Whatever else Vladimir said after that was unintelligible to Nathan, as it was mostly in Russian. But Nathan was sure it wasn't for polite company.

"I don't think he's happy," Nathan decided.

"No, sir," the ensign handling the communications station agreed.

* * *

The first thing that Nathan noticed as he walked into medical was that it was less chaotic. It was still full of patients, and there were still at least a dozen non-medical personnel helping to care for the wounded, but everyone had a place to recuperate and all appeared to be receiving proper care.

There had only been two doctors, two nurses, and one medical technologist on staff when they had departed Earth. For a crew of only one hundred, it had been more than enough. And unlike many other parts of the ship, the Aurora's medical facility had been completed and fully stocked prior to departure.

Every member of the crew had basic emergency medical training while at the academy. Nathan himself had completed the course in his first year but had never cared much for the simulations. He had always felt the requirement unnecessary. Every ship in the fleet had top-notch medical facilities and staff, a necessary luxury for ships that routinely spent several years away from home.

Despite it being less chaotic, the main treatment room was still a mess. There were bloody bandages and linens piled in every corner, and the floors were stained nearly everywhere you looked. There were even blood splatters across some of the walls where some of the more serious injuries had probably been treated. But those that were not directly involved in patient care were trying to help out by cleaning up the room as best they could. Nathan even noticed one of the civilian scientists from Doctor Sorenson's team, the same one that he had helped in the corridor earlier, following people around with a data pad as she frantically tried to keep notes on every patient's treatment for their medical records. It made Nathan feel good about the people on this ship. When everything fell apart, they had all come together to try and pull through as a team. He couldn't help but wonder if all the people of Earth would behave in the same fashion, should the Jung invade their home.

As Nathan made his way across the main treatment area, he could feel the stares of his shipmates. At first, it made him uncomfortable, as he didn't understand why they were all looking at him. Then he realized that they were staring at *him* because he was wearing captain's bars on his collar, the very same bars that Captain Roberts had bestowed on him earlier in this very room, just before he surrendered to his injuries. These people were no longer his shipmates, Nathan realized. They were his crew. And they would be looking to him to get them out of this mess—to get them home.

A wave of nausea began to wash over him once more, and Nathan tried to quicken his pace without looking too obvious. Was it all the blood splattered about the room that was making him ill? Or was it simply the sudden realization of the enormity of his new responsibilities? Unable to think clearly, he headed for the same utility room where he had heaved up his breakfast an hour ago. At least in there, no one would be staring at him.

Nathan again found himself hunched over the sink. Luckily, he had nothing left in his stomach to expel, but he still felt dizzy, and he definitely did not want to go back out there and face all those stares again. He had only just graduated the academy three weeks ago. His command simulation scores had barely been passable. It had only been his natural instinct for flying that had landed him the helmsman position on the Aurora. And even then only by the grace of Captain Roberts, who for some strange reason saw potential in him. *But what if Captain Roberts was wrong?*

"Some captain," he mumbled to himself.

"What's that?"

Nathan turned to look behind him. Doctor Chen was sitting in the corner, just like the last time he had been in this room.

"Doctor Chen, we've got to stop meeting like this," Nathan joked. "People will start to talk." He flashed the same school boy smile again, only this time it was a little less charming and a bit more forced.

"You finally decide to let me take care of your leg?"

"Yeah, something like that."

"Hop up on the counter," she instructed, rising from her stool and coming toward him. "Let me take a look."

Nathan used his good leg and both arms to boost himself up to sit on the counter, turning slightly to give her a better angle to his injured left calf. Doctor Chen was a little cleaner than before. She had changed out of her blood stained uniform and was wearing surgical attire. But despite her clean outfit, she still appeared emotionally exhausted.

"I noticed there are fewer patients here now," Nathan commented as she began to examine his leg.

"Yeah, well some of them didn't make it." She looked up at him, realizing that he hadn't considered that possibility, as guilt washed over his face. "I'm sorry. That was rather insensitive of me." There was expediency in her manner as she cut away his torn pant leg in order to expose his wound. Nathan imagined that she had done this many times this morning. "Actually, a lot of them did make it," she continued. "I sent the walking wounded back to their quarters to recuperate. A couple of the marines that survived were rated as combat medics, so I've got them running around keeping an eye on the injured for me. They can contact me through the comms over the med channels if they need something."

"That's pretty good thinking, Doc."

"Not really," she admitted as she finished applying the bandages that would cover his wound while the bonding agents worked their magic. "It's standard disaster management. I learned it during my internship. Frees up beds for the more serious cases."

"Any word on Doctor Thomas?"

"Still missing," she told him as she finished his bandage.

"Well, I guess that makes you chief of medical for

now."

Doctor Chen said nothing in response as she finished bandaging his leg. Nathan could feel the tension and knew it had been brought on by his last statement.

"Doc, you okay?"

Doctor Chen just looked at him for a moment. "No, I'm not," she admitted. "I'm not okay. And I'm sure as hell not ready to be in charge. I'm only three weeks into my residency! I barely know what I'm doing half the time!"

"Hey, come on," he urged, trying to reassure her. "Look at me. I've only been at the helm for a little over a week! And I'm suddenly the captain?"

"You don't understand. All those people out there, they expect *me* to save them. *Me.*"

"Yeah, I saw those people out there, Doc. And you know what? *I'm* the one who got them injured in the first place! They're out *there* because of what *I* did, because of the decisions *I* made! You wanna trade places?"

She stared at him again for a moment before finally speaking. "Hand me the pneumo-ject from the cabinet behind you."

"The what?"

She shook her head, a slight chuckle in her voice as she reached behind him to get the device herself. "You wanna trade?" she mocked as she loaded the pneumatic syringe. "I'll do it but only on one condition."

"What's that?" he asked, cringing as she injected the medication into his leg.

"Promise me it's only temporary."

"No problem," he assured. "The minute we return, I'm sure they'll replace us all with more experienced officers."

"Good, because I don't want to be in charge any longer than I have to."

Nathan wanted to tell her that he felt exactly the same way, but he had no idea where they were or how long it would take them to get home. The last thing the crew needed was to know that their captain didn't *want* to be in command.

"Well, I think I should warn you that it might be a little longer than you think." Nathan braced himself for her reaction but got nothing more than a concerned look from her tired eyes.

"What are you talking about?"

"It may take some time for us to get back to Earth."

"But they'll come for us as soon as the fighting is over," she surmised. "I mean, Jupiter is only a few hours out, even by our slowest ships, right?"

"Well, we're not exactly orbiting Jupiter anymore," Nathan admitted as she finished bandaging his leg. "Maybe you'd better sit down."

Doctor Chen had taken the news of their situation, and the details of how they had gotten into trouble, better than Nathan had expected. In the end, she had realized that, despite her misgivings about her own abilities, she was the only person on board even remotely qualified to do the job. Nathan had thanked her for his treatment and left her to tend to her numerous patients. As he left medical, he had a feeling that the petite, soft-spoken doctor was far stronger than she realized.

* * *

Getting to engineering had been more challenging than Nathan had expected. Because of the size of the hangar bay, most of the corridors skirted around it, between the bay and the inner hull. Unlike medical, which had been located deeper inside the ship, these sections had taken a considerable beating. Most of them were still intact and passable. However, Nathan had been forced to make a few detours to get around some of the more severely damaged sections. He wished that he had thought to go *through* the hangar bay instead of around it. Not only would it have been easier, but he also would've gotten to see the rebel ship that was still parked inside.

Nathan worried about what he would find when he got to engineering. It was located at the uppermost edge of the amidships section, just forward of the massive propulsion section at their stern. The location had been chosen to facilitate quick changing of her reactor cores. But that left the area more vulnerable to attack. Captain Roberts had been aware of this weakness. During their battle with the Jung patrol ships, he had protected it by attacking head on, and later by rolling the ship to show their reinforced belly while passing over the enemy.

The smell of burnt electronics became noticeable as Nathan approached engineering. Once he stepped through the main hatch, it became almost overpowering. There were signs of burnt-out panels and exploded consoles everywhere. Several of the damaged consoles had multiple data pads wired into them to act as temporary interfaces until they could be properly repaired. There were several expended fire suppression bottles lying about, along with a few pieces of burnt clothing. In the corners were piles of circuit boards so badly burnt that they could not be repaired.

A half dozen crewmen, most of them engineers or technical specialists, were busy trying to repair the most urgent systems. In the middle of it all was Vladimir, bigger than life, barking out orders to at least three different work teams simultaneously. In contrast to Doctor Chen, Vladimir appeared to be enjoying the challenge.

"Vlad!" Nathan called out as he went toward his friend. Vladimir spun around to see Nathan limping slightly on a bandaged leg and sporting bloody captain's bars on his collar.

"Nathan!" he smiled. To Nathan's surprise, his energetic roommate gave him a big hug. "I'm so glad you survived, my friend." Before Nathan could speak, the Russian turned and barked more commands to a nearby work team before continuing. "And you are a captain now?!" he added, slapping Nathan on the back. "But still, I am not going to salute you."

Nathan noticed one of the rebels scurry past carrying some type of wiring harness. "How are they doing?" he asked Vladimir, tilting his head toward the passing man. "Are they much help?"

"Yes! They are very good! Not as good as me, of course, but they seem to know their way with such things. It makes me wonder what they have in their ships," he added under his breath.

"You think they might be more advanced than us?"

"Nathan, everyone is more advanced than us!" he exclaimed.

Nathan hadn't thought about it before, but now he realized that Vladimir might be right. The people of Earth had only started getting back into space about thirty years ago. There had been little research and development done beyond the technologies found in the Data Ark. With the threat of a Jung invasion looming over them, there hadn't been time. They had heard that a few of the fringe worlds had been less impacted by the plague, so it made sense that some of them could've developed more advanced technologies over the last millennia while the people of Earth were rebuilding from the ground up.

"But with these people, I think it is sometimes yes, sometimes no." Vladimir could see by Nathan's expression that he was confused. "At some things, they are amazed, like they cannot believe what they are seeing. At others, they cannot believe we are still using them!" he laughed.

"How are the repairs going?" Nathan asked, getting back to the reason for his visit.

"Oh, terrible! So many things not working! No engines, no maneuvering, only two good reactors. And as you can see, many consoles are badly damaged. It will take weeks to repair! But do not worry, Nathan. We will fix it. We will fix *everything*."

"How long until we have maneuvering again?"

"A few hours at most. Main propulsion, I do not yet know. But soon, we will have all four reactors online, so we will have full power once more."

"Then do we have weapons?"

"Soon, soon," Vladimir promised. "First rail guns, then torpedoes. Missile batteries, they must still be installed. But since we have no missiles to fire, it does not matter."

"Well, the sooner you can get us moving, the better. I have to tell you, being a sitting duck out here makes me nervous."

"Just try to keep us out of trouble for a while,

Nathan. That would be of great help."

"I'll do my best, but our intel says we've only got about a day at the outside."

"Intel? What intel?"

"Our guests. They tell us the Takarans will come looking for us soon."

"Who are these 'Takarans'?" Vladimir had spent the entire time in engineering, and still had no idea of what they had been through. All he knew was that he and his fellow engineers had been bounced around on three separate occasions. "What is going on, Nathan? Where are we?"

"I wish I knew. My best guess is somewhere out on the fringe."

Vladimir looked at Nathan like he was crazy. "The fringe?"

"I know it sounds crazy..."

"It is not possible!"

"It's complicated..."

"It's got something to do with evil doctor woman, yes?" Vladimir surmised.

Nathan again recounted the day's events for the benefit of his friend. Vladimir took the news far better than Doctor Chen had. In fact, he seemed more excited about the existence of the jump drive than anything else. And it appeared that his new chief engineer was looking forward to the challenges ahead with absolute glee. It had not been the reaction Nathan had expected, but it had been a refreshing one.

* * *

"So how bad off are we?" Nathan asked Cameron as she followed him into his ready room. As he entered, he was suddenly struck by the starkness of the now empty room. It had been at least sparsely decorated when it had been occupied by Captain Roberts, but now it had been stripped of even those few mementos.

"I took the liberty of clearing out the captain's belongings," she explained, noticing his reaction. "I hope you don't mind."

It had not occurred to Nathan that this task would need to be performed. And now that she had done it, he realized that it would not have been easy for him. For that small kindness, he was surprisingly grateful. "No, not at all," he answered softly. "Thank you."

"You're welcome."

"What did you do with..."

"I packed them safely away," she assured him. "I'll see that his family receives them when we get back."

Nathan nodded his approval as he made his way across the small room and around the desk. "You can skip the engineering stuff. I already got that from Vlad."

"Well, the bow took a beating. There are multiple hull breaches. Most are from weapons fire as we backed away from that Takaran warship. The biggest breach of course is from ramming them."

"Not my fault," he defended. "We were pretty much dead stick at the time."

"Yes, I *was* there," she reminded him before continuing. "The forward section is going to be uninhabitable until the breaches are sealed and the hull is repaired. In port, that would take a few days. Out here..." she shrugged, indicating she had no idea.

"Maybe never," Nathan admitted.

"Of course, most of the forward section is housing, and some recreational areas. But since we're shorthanded, there should still be plenty of housing available aft of the forward bulkheads."

"And what about crew?" he asked hesitantly. He knew he wasn't going to like the answer.

Cameron took a deep breath before giving him the news. "Thirty-eight dead, forty-two injured."

Nathan fell into his seat. "Thirty-eight? Oh my God," he muttered. The first thought that crossed his mind was how many of those deaths had occurred *after* he assumed command. It was a small point, insignificant to those who had perished. But it meant everything to Nathan. "How many injured?"

"Forty-two," she repeated. "But twenty of them are minor and can still man their posts."

"So we've only got forty people to run this ship?"

"That's it." Cameron could see that Nathan was devastated by the news. But as bad as she felt for him, if he was going to be captain, he was going to have to get used to such news.

"We can't run the ship with forty people, can we?" It didn't seem possible to him, but he wasn't sure.

"Technically, no. But there are several departments that either were not online yet, or are too damaged to be of any use right now, so we might be able to squeak by. There are some areas that are going to present problems, especially if we have to go into battle again."

Nathan looked at her, a confused look in his eye. He was still stuck on the number of crew he had lost and was not yet thinking clearly.

"We can fly the ship, and we can fight with her, but we won't have anyone for damage control."

"Maybe we can get some more help from these rebels." Nathan suggested off the top of his head.

"Nathan, I'm not sure we should trust them too much just yet," she warned. Like Jessica, she was far more suspicious of the rebel's motives than Nathan seemed to be. And his eagerness to trust them worried her.

Nathan considered her warning. "Yeah, you could be right about that. I just don't see that we have much choice given the circumstances. I mean, badly damaged, barely enough crew to fly the ship, and God knows how far away from home."

"Oh, and low on consumables," Cameron added.

"What?"

"Food, water. We weren't loaded for an extended voyage you know."

"Oh, great. You see, that's what I'm talking about. We're gonna need friends out here if we're gonna survive long enough to find a way home."

"You're right. I agree. I'm just not sure that *these* people are the type of friends we *want*, Nathan. That's all I'm saying."

"And on *that* we agree," he conceded, "but until we're presented with other options, we're gonna have to utilize what we've got. For now, that means *these* people."

"Just be careful," she warned him.

"Look, sooner or later, we're gonna need to find a safe harbor. I mean, we can't very well conduct repairs while hiding out in an asteroid field. Once we find a populated world, we're bound to find some other people and make more friends. Hopefully ones that are not so quick to throw themselves into the jaws of death."

"Make more friends, huh? That's your plan?"

"Hey, we've gotta play to our strengths," he smiled. "Now speaking of consumables, I think it would be wise if we tried to get everyone something to eat while it's still quiet around here. Any ideas?"

"With all that's happened, you're thinking about food?"

"We've gotta eat, Cam. We don't want the crew we have left passing out from low blood sugar, do we?"

Cameron knew he was right, as she herself was a bit hungry. "There are about a hundred lunch kits down in the galley, along with the leftovers from breakfast. What would you like?"

"Surprise me."

"I'll get someone on it right away," she promised as she turned to leave.

"And make sure everyone eats, even if they have to eat while they're working."

"Yes, sir."

"And when the food comes, have Jalea come in. I think she and I need to talk."

"Yes, sir," she answered as she left. She wasn't sure if she liked the idea of Nathan and Jalea meeting in private. It wasn't that she didn't trust him. She was sure that he wouldn't intentionally do anything wrong. But she had already noticed that Nathan had a tendency to act on impulse, especially in conversation, instead of thinking things through first. In the case of a conversation with Jalea, she was twice as concerned. She had noticed the way that Nathan had looked at the woman. Jalea had unusual eyes that seemed to catch your attention and hold it. Jessica had noticed it as well and had also voiced her concerns about Nathan's judgment in regards to Jalea and the rebels.

CHAPTER EIGHT

"You wish to speak with me?" Jalea called from the doorway.

"Ah, yes, Jalea, please come in," Nathan told her. He stepped out from behind the desk and pulled up a chair for her. "I thought we might talk a bit," he explained, returning to his seat. "I would like to know more about you and your people." Nathan began opening the two lunch kits that Cameron had sent in earlier. "Are you hungry?"

Jalea nodded tentatively, unsure of what the packages contained. "What do you want to know?"

Nathan handed her one of the open kits and a small bottle of water. She looked at the contents of the kit. It contained several different vegetables in varying shades of green, red, and orange, along with some small pieces of fruit and several slices of some type of meat and cheese. She watched as Nathan picked up one of the red fruits from his kit and popped it into his mouth. She picked up the same red fruit from her kit, placed it carefully between her teeth, and began to bite down.

"Be careful, those can..."

Jalea bit down on the small tomato, which split open, juice squirting out onto the desk and down her chin. She tried to catch the dripping liquid with her hand but was too late.

"...squirt a bit," he finished. "Yeah, it's better if you pop the whole thing into your mouth." He watched as she chewed her small tomato and swallowed. She gave no indication as to whether or not she liked it.

"So, where are you from?" he asked as he continued eating.

Jalea watched Nathan, waiting for him to eat something different before she tried it herself.

"Parule. My world is Parule."

"I thought you were from Bakara?"

"Bakara where we lived now. Parule is home, is my place of birth."

"I see. Is Parule far from here?"

"Yes, it is far. Not in Takaran space."

"It's not? How did you end up here then?" Nathan had already noticed that she was only eating what he was eating and purposefully tried everything at least once so that she would be more comfortable. So far, other than the radishes, she seemed to like everything.

"My husband is from Takara. I came to be with him."

"Oh, I didn't realize you were married."

"He died many years ago."

"I'm sorry. How did he die?"

"He fought like us. He died bravely."

"He fought the Takarans?" Nathan felt like he was starting to get somewhere.

"Yes."

"Why do you fight them?"

"The Takaran leaders, they are very bad." Jalea thought for a moment, trying to decide how to express her thoughts in English. "They want only for money, power. If you have money, if you can pay, life is very good for you. If you do not have, if you not pay, life is very bad for you. They are..." she struggled for the right word, mumbling what Nathan assumed was the appropriate word in her language.

"Corrupt?" he offered.

"Yes, corrupt. They only want money. No right, no wrong, only money."

Nathan smiled. "Yeah, that's the definition of corruption on our world as well." He took a drink of water as he watched her pick out what to eat next. She was quite an attractive woman, with long black hair and an olive complexion. Her eyes were so captivating; they just sucked him in. But he had seen a cold, dark side to her just before they had jumped away from the incoming Takaran reinforcements. Despite the fact that her eyes seemed softer at the moment, that side of her still worried him.

"It is same on your world?" she asked him as she tried a piece of cheese.

"Sometimes. Not as much as before, but still some. Is that why you fight? You fight corruption?"

"We fight to be free," she corrected him. "We fight to remove them from power."

Then it is a rebellion, Nathan thought. "How do you fight?"

"We steal weapons and ships to fight."

"Ships like this one?" Nathan asked, afraid that he might not like the answer.

"No. Such ships are very difficult. This is how my husband died."

"Trying to steal a large ship?"

"Yes. It is very dangerous to steal such ships, so we only take small ships. Much easier, but not so strong. So we make better." Nathan noticed a hint of pride in her last statement.

"How do you make them better?"

"We take to secret places," she explained. "Places where we can work on ships. Better, stronger, faster."

"Like a base of operations?" Nathan was becoming quite interested.

"No. Not so big. Usually on farms, in shelters. Sometimes inside mountains. Even rocks in space."

"But where do you live? What do you eat? Where do you get supplies?"

"The people, they give us food, shelter, clothing, what they can to help. But they afraid of Takaran soldiers."

Nathan leaned back in his chair, taking another drink of water as he thought about what Jalea had revealed to him. The rebels were fighting a guerrilla war rather than a large-scale organized conflict. They were stealing ships and supplies, making changes to them to fit their needs, and getting covert support from the locals. They certainly sounded like freedom fighters rebelling against a corrupt and repressive government. But Nathan had been a student of Earth history, and he knew that there was often a fine line between revolutionaries and terrorists. More often than not, the difference only became apparent after it was too late.

"So how did you hear of Earth?" Nathan felt it was time to change direction, and he had been curious about what she knew of his home.

"On my world, there is legend. Long ago, our people came to Parule from another world. The legend says, the people on that world once came from Earth," she explained. It was apparent by the tone of her voice that she had never truly believed the legend. "But, it was only story, told to young children. Many believe. Many still speak Angla and teach children. My father was such man."

"Really?" Nathan had finished his lunch and

closed up the container. "What did your father teach you of Earth?"

"Earth is where all humans came from. But long ago, they leave quickly. Terrible evil on Earth. It came to all her worlds. So people, they go to stars. They hope evil will not follow." Jalea ate the last piece of food in her kit and followed it with a drink of water before continuing. "Sometimes, parents tell children to behave, or evil will find them too."

"Does the story say what kind of evil?"

"No, but it is only story. No one truly believes this," she asserted.

"Do you believe it?"

"Maybe a little," she confessed, a tiny smile on her lips.

"Do many others believe?"

"Some. But they not say. They afraid."

"Afraid of what?"

"Takarans not believe. They say all come from Takara, not Earth. If you not believe as Takarans, you not live."

Then they are fighting against religious persecution. Suddenly, they were starting to look more like terrorists than revolutionaries. He was beginning to wonder how far he could trust them. Perhaps Cameron had been correct. Perhaps these were not the kind of people they wanted as friends.

"Do others in your group speak Angla?"

"Yes, some. Those from other worlds. But Takarans not learn Angla. Not safe."

"What about on Parule?" Nathan was hoping to find a world where they might be able to communicate without having to use the rebels as an intermediary.

"Yes, most people on Parule learn Angla. It is language of all worlds."

"A universal language. Of course." Nathan remembered from history that English had been the standard language spoken throughout the core at the time the bio-digital plague had struck.

"Is this not why your people speak Angla?" Jalea looked intrigued.

"Sort of, I guess. There are many different languages spoken on Earth, but we all learn English so that we can all communicate..." Nathan stopped in mid-sentence, noticing the look in her eyes had changed.

"Then you *are* from Earth?" Nathan didn't notice that her English syntax had suddenly improved.

"Well, yes, I thought we explained that..." Nathan stopped abruptly once again, noticing another change in her eyes. The intrigue had suddenly vanished, replaced by that same cold determination he had seen earlier on the bridge.

Jalea relaxed slightly, leaning with her elbow on the arm of the chair in which she sat. "Then I must ask you, Nathan, are you evil?"

Her question had been asked in near perfect English, and Nathan felt a chill go down his spine. So overwhelming was the sensation that Nathan was startled when Cameron entered the room with Abigail hot on her heels.

"Nathan, we need to talk," Cameron insisted. She noticed that Nathan seemed a bit shaken, yet Jalea was calm and relaxed. "Nathan?" she repeated.

He looked up at Cameron, seeing the urgency on her face. He looked back at Jalea, recomposing himself. "If you would excuse us a moment, Jalea."

Jalea bowed her head respectfully, rose from her chair, and strolled out of the room. Cameron watched her curiously as she exited, wondering what she had interrupted.

Cameron was about to start talking when Nathan held up his hand indicating that she should wait. Finally, when he was sure that the door was closed and Jalea was out of ear shot, he spoke. "What's wrong?"

"We've calculated our position, Nathan, and it's not good."

"And I'm supposed to be surprised?" he responded sarcastically.

"You will be," Cameron promised him. "We're more than a thousand light years from Earth."

There was a moment of silence. Nathan looked at Cameron with disbelief. He looked at Abigail and then back at Cameron again. "You're kidding, right?" Cameron didn't speak, but her expression gave him his answer. "No, I guess you wouldn't be, would you."

"Certainly not about this," she assured him.

"A thousand light years?" he repeated.

"Yup."

"You have *got* to be kidding me!" Nathan exclaimed. "Please, Cam! Tell me you're kidding me."

"Sorry."

Nathan couldn't believe his ears. After all that they had been through, to learn that they were so much farther away from Earth than anyone had ever thought possible.

"There's gotta be some kind of mistake here," he pleaded. "I mean, come on, a thousand light years?" Nathan turned to Abigail. "Abby, how the hell could we jump a thousand light years?"

"There's no mistake, Captain," Abigail apologized. She felt that it was somehow her fault that they were stranded so far from home. "I checked the calculations several times. We are onethousand seven light years from Sol. Of that I'm sure. As to how, my best guess is that it had something to do with the shock wave from that antimatter explosion. Maybe it somehow added additional energy into the fields. I just don't know yet."

"Well, now how long is it gonna take us to get home?" He already knew he was not going to like the answer.

"That's at least a hundred and ten jumps, maybe more. If everything goes well, maybe three or four months. But..."

"Fat chance of that," Nathan squawked, "I mean, considering how our luck has been so far!"

"You have to remember, Captain, that this is only a prototype model. I cannot guarantee that we'll get ten jumps out of it, let alone a hundred."

Nathan thought hard. There had to be a way out of this problem, he just had to think of something. "What if the FTL field emitters were operational? How long would it take us then?"

"About a hundred years," Cameron reminded him, knowing that he should already be aware of that fact. "We're only rated for ten times light, remember? Besides, it would take weeks to get those emitters back online and we'd have to take the jump drive offline in order to do it."

"What about the comm-drones the Takarans use? Jalea said they can do a hundred times light. Maybe we could adapt their technology into our systems."

"That's a bit of a reach, don't you think?" Cameron was getting tired of Nathan's desperate scramble for an immediate answer. "You might as well face the facts, Nathan. We're stuck out here for a while."

"There has got to be a way to get back," he

insisted. "I mean, we got here in a single jump, so there must be a way to get back in one. Isn't that right, Doctor?"

"If our assumptions about *how* are correct, then yes it is possible. But figuring out how to do that could take even longer than it would to make the hundred jumps home."

Nathan leaned back in his chair, thinking. He was the captain now, and Captain Roberts' last orders had been to get the jump drive back to Earth as soon as possible. Not only was the fate of his crew resting on his shoulders but also quite possibly the fate of his entire world as well. He hoped his lunch wasn't going to come back up.

"Nathan," Cameron began, "if we're going to get through this, we're going to have to get organized; we're going to need a proper chain of command. And I hate to admit it, but we're also going to need help, and lots of it."

"You're talking about Jalea and company, right?" Cameron just nodded. "I don't know, Cam. I'm starting to think you might have been right about them after all."

"Well, until we find somebody else..."

"Better the devil you know, huh?" Nathan took a deep breath and let it out slowly. "Who all knows about this?"

"Only the bridge crew," Cameron assured him.

"Not Jalea?"

"No, she was in here with you when we figured it out."

"Good, let's keep it that way. In fact, let's not tell anybody just yet. I'll figure out when to tell the crew." Nathan rose slowly from his seat as if standing tall to face the new challenge. "Very well. Doctor

Sorenson, if you could devote all your attention to keeping the jump drive operational, it would be greatly appreciated. Until we find a way to get our FTL systems functional, that prototype of yours is our only way to get around."

"Yes, Captain," Abigail answered.

"And if you can find the time, I wouldn't mind if you did a little research into possibly increasing the range of that prototype." Abigail nodded her agreement.

"Ensign Taylor," he said, addressing Cameron in a more formal tone than usual, "I'm going to need a full damage assessment, as well as a proposal for a working crew roster as soon as possible. You'll have to prioritize positions and maybe even retrain a few people. But one way or another, we need to be able to fly, and maybe even fight, with this ship. It looks like the Aurora is going to be our home for a bit longer than we expected."

"Yes, sir," Cameron acknowledged. Despite the fact the she had never thought Nathan was fit to be in command of anything, let alone the entire ship, she was happy that he was stepping up to the challenge.

"And one last thing, I'm going to need to meet with Jalea and Marak as soon as possible. And make sure Jessica is here as well," he added as he sat back down.

"Yes, sir!" Cameron stood at attention as Abigail left the room, raising her hand in salute. After a moment, Nathan looked back up at her. "Oh, please," he protested as he returned the salute. "Dismissed."

* * *

Jessica entered the captain's ready room, assuming a slightly relaxed stance in front of Nathan's desk. "You wanted to see me, sir?"

"Yeah, I'm afraid the situation has changed somewhat."

"How so?"

"You might want to sit down, Jessica," he warned her. Nathan rose from his seat and walked around to the front of his desk, sitting on its edge in the same manner as Captain Roberts had always done. "It seems we're a bit farther away from Earth than we originally thought."

"How far?" she asked suspiciously.

"About a thousand light years."

"No fucking way," she responded without thinking, quickly adding an embarrassed, "sir."

"Yeah, that was my reaction too."

"How the hell are we gonna get home?"

"We don't know yet; we're working on it, but it could take some time. So we're going to need to start making friends out here. We're gonna need help, and lots of it. At least until we get the ship up to snuff. I'm gonna need you to handle intelligence as well as ship's security. You up to it?"

"Hell yes, sir."

Nathan noticed she was grinning more than expected, considering the news. "What's so funny?"

"Nothing. I was just thinking about how when I first got assigned to this ship, I thought it was going to be a *boring* tour of duty."

"Funny, that's exactly what I was *hoping* it would be," Nathan chuckled.

"Then I guess we were both wrong."

"Listen, Jess. In a few minutes we're going to be meeting with Jalea and Marak. I'm gonna need to negotiate some kind of an arrangement with them. We need a safe harbor to make repairs, and right now they're our only option."

"I'd advise proceeding with caution, sir. I've got a hunch there's more going on with these people than they're telling us."

"Yeah, I got the same feeling," he said, remembering his last conversation with Jalea. "I can't tell if they're revolutionaries or terrorists."

"Exactly, so don't give them any more information than necessary. The less they know about us and our situation, the weaker their position."

"Makes sense. Anything else?"

"And watch what you say around them. I'm pretty sure Jalea speaks our language a lot better than she lets on. Hell, I wouldn't be surprised if they all speak *Angla* for that matter."

Nathan had already realized that Jalea spoke English better than he had originally thought, but he hadn't considered the possibility that the others spoke it as well. "You've got a suspicious mind, Jessica," he complimented her.

"It helps when you're in spec-ops."

The comm beeped twice, and Nathan pressed the button to answer. "Yes?"

"*Jalea and Marak are here, Captain,*" the communications officer reported over the comm.

"Send them in." Nathan got up and went back behind his desk, Jessica rising to stand beside him as their guests entered the room.

Jalea entered looking more poised and confident than she had the last time he spoke with her. Marak was close behind, the difference in him being that he was a little more unkempt after several hours working on damaged engineering systems. Nathan noticed Marak's appearance and chose to use it as his opening.

"Looks like you've been hard at work, Marak. How is it going in engineering?"

Jalea translated Nathan's words to Marak. Nathan wondered if Marak really didn't speak English, or if they were just keeping up a front. If they were, then they obviously were not ready to reveal that fact just yet, so Nathan would have to cautiously play along.

"Marak says that everything is going well and that your chief engineer is a very clever man."

"Yes, he is. Please, have a seat." Nathan waited for his guests to sit down before taking his seat. Jessica remained standing, leaning slightly against the counter behind her.

"What may we do for you, Captain?" Jalea was again speaking far better English than before, apparently feeling that the charade was no longer required. And her sudden improvement did not go unnoticed by Jessica.

"Your English has improved, Jalea," Nathan commented. He wanted her to know that her sudden improvement had not gone unnoticed.

"It is all coming back to me now," she lied, a polite smile on her face. Nathan had a feeling that she was probably very good at deception, especially with her hypnotic eyes. Nathan wondered if she had been chosen for this assignment specifically because of her unique attributes. He wondered if she had abruptly changed her personality after realizing that playing the beautiful, demure widow with broken English wasn't going to get her what she wanted. Yet in this role, she was just as convincing, if not more so.

"I'm sure it is." Nathan thought for a moment,

unsure of what to say next. He could dance around the issue, as Jessica had suggested, or he could come clean and lay his cards out on the table. Keeping in his usual character, he chose the latter.

"Look, I'm not going to waste your time dancing around the table here. The fact is, we are a long way from home, and our ship is in need of repair. We need a place to hide out for a while, a safe port, if you will, where we can make repairs and maybe pick up some supplies as well. Once that's done, we plan on returning to Earth as quickly as possible. So my question is, What do *you* require from us in exchange?"

Jalea was still translating Nathan's question to Marak as Nathan finished. He looked over to Jessica, who was glaring at him, obviously not happy with his straightforward negotiating tactics. Jalea finished her discussion with Marak and then returned her attention to Nathan.

"Marak only wishes to repay his life debt to you, Captain," she stated coldly. "He will see to it that you receive all the help that you need in order to get you started on your journey."

Nathan stared at Jalea, unsure if he could believe her. It had been a precisely worded response, which made him suspicious. "That's all?"

"Yes."

Nathan wasn't sure if they were telling the truth or if they were the universe's greatest liars. But he wasn't going to give them the chance to take advantage of him.

"Look, Jalea. No disrespect intended, but I find it hard to believe that it's *that* simple. I mean, by your own words, you people *are* fighting a war and, from what I hear, you're losing. And all you want is to repay a life debt?"

"I understand your reluctance to believe us, Captain. You do not understand us, so I would not expect you to take our word so easily. You would be foolish to do otherwise."

"Then you won't be insulted if I don't fully trust you right now?"

"Like I said, you would be foolish to do otherwise." Jalea could tell that Nathan was having a difficult time believing her and decided to offer more of an explanation. "Captain, your ship saved us not once, but twice. First you appeared, as if by magic, to stand as a shield between us and our enemy. Then, again as if by magic, you carried us all away to the safety of this asteroid field. In truth, you saved us not once, but twice. So indeed we owe you much, probably much more than we can ever repay."

Nathan looked them both over before deciding that he had little choice but to take them at their word for now. And he had no doubt that Jessica would keep a close eye on them while they were on board. "Very well," he stated as he rose. "On behalf of the Aurora and her crew, I thank you for your help."

"Just as we thank you for yours." Marak spoke a few words to Jalea as he rose. "Marak wonders if he might return to continue his work with your chief engineer."

"Yes, of course. Jessica will accompany you."

Jessica took the cue from Nathan and led Marak out of the room, leaving Nathan alone with Jalea.

"Captain," Jalea spoke, "may I offer you another bit of information that might ease your concerns?"

"Please do."

"What you said before is true. We are losing our

war with the Takarans. In fact, had they defeated us this day, it is likely that the few remaining '*Karuzari*', or '*rebels*' as you call them, would've disbanded forever, and the revolution would be over. So you have done far more than save our lives this day. You may have also saved our cause." Jalea bowed her head slightly, then brought her eyes back up to his, their fierce determination showing brightly. "It is for this that Marak feels indebted."

"Thank you for sharing that with me." Nathan looked at her intently. "Is there anything else?"

"You should understand, Captain, that a life debt is a very serious thing to the Karuzari, and Marak would gladly sacrifice his own life to honor that debt."

"Let's hope it doesn't come to that," Nathan stated in a tone that indicated he had nothing further to say on the matter.

Jalea bowed her head again, took a step backward, turned, and strode confidently out of the room, leaving Nathan alone.

"*Captain to the bridge!*" the comm officer's voice called over the comm. Nathan immediately rose and followed Jalea out of the room.

"What's up?" he asked as he entered the bridge.

"We've got a contact, Captain," Cameron reported. "It just left the Takaran outpost on one of the gas giant's moons. It's headed toward the asteroid field."

"Did you power down the reactors?"

"The moment they appeared," she assured him.

"Are they headed for us?"

"Not yet. They appear to be headed to a different part of the field."

"Let me know if they change course," Nathan ordered before turning to Abigail. "How much of a charge did we get?"

"Eighty-seven percent."

"So we can jump, what, maybe eight and a half light years?"

"I would try to keep it under eight, if possible."

Marak and Jessica entered the bridge having turned back when Jessica heard of the contact on their way to engineering. Marak immediately began talking excitedly with Jalea in their language.

"Comm, find out how much longer until we get maneuvering and propulsion back online."

"Captain," Jalea interrupted, "Marak has told our ships to monitor all transmissions from the Takaran ship. We will provide translations of any communications that we intercept."

"Thank you."

"Captain," the comm officer called out, "engineering reports maneuvering is restarting now. It should be online in a few minutes. Main propulsion will take longer."

"So we can crawl out, but we can't run."

"We do have rail guns back up. At least we'll be able to fight back," Cameron suggested, hoping to alleviate some of Nathan's frustration.

"I do not believe they will find us," Jalea assured him. "The rocks are an excellent place to hide."

"She's right, sir," Ensign Yosef chimed in. "With all the metal in these asteroids, and the distortions and echoes caused by their gravitational fields, they'd have to be able to actually see us in order to find us. I'm having a hard time tracking them, and our sensors are pointed away from the field."

"Okay. What else can we do?" Nathan was getting anxious.

"We can preload the forward torpedo tubes,"

Cameron suggested.

"Yeah, but we can barely turn the ship toward the targets," Nathan reminded her.

"They do have their own guidance systems, Nathan," she explained. "If they come so much as thirty degrees of our bow line, we can fire on them—as long as they're in range that is."

"Okay, make it happen."

"Might I suggest that you take steps to reduce any signals coming from your ship, Captain?" Jalea advised.

Nathan did not yet fully trust Jalea, but as long as she was on the same ship as them, their immediate motives were still the same—to survive.

"Ensign Yosef, please see to that," Nathan ordered, distracted by the continuing conversation between Marak and Jalea.

"Yes, sir."

Jalea broke from her discussion with Marak to speak to Nathan. "Captain, I do not understand. Can you not do as before? Can you not bring our ships on board and then simply disappear?"

"But to where?"

"Captain," Abigail interrupted, "we'll need to get clear of the gravitational influences of the asteroid field before we can safely jump."

"How clear?"

"Well clear, I'm afraid." Nathan didn't much care for the thought of wandering out into open space with a Takaran warship out there looking for them. In their current state, he doubted they would stand a chance.

"What would happen if we jumped from here?"

"I really do not know," she admitted. But Nathan could see on her face that she didn't want to find out.

"The minute we run, that ship will come after us," Cameron warned him.

"But they're not coming toward us now."

"No, but that could change at any moment," she reminded.

"Well, let's not wait around for that to happen. Work with Jalea to find us a new place to hide, preferably somewhere within eight light years. And let's start moving those rebel ships back inside. No use in waiting until the last moment."

Marak suddenly received another communication from his ships and immediately began giving Jalea instructions.

"We have intercepted a message," Jalea translated.

"From who?" Nathan's gaze was focused on the two of them, as if staring at them would make him able to understand what Marak was saying before she translated it.

Jalea listened in on Marak's conversation with their ships, translating what she heard. "From another Takaran ship, directed to the first one, the one that is searching for us," she explained. "They will soon join them."

"How soon?" Nathan asked.

"Contact!" Ensign Yosef reported.

"That soon!" Nathan exclaimed, throwing his hands up.

"Just dropped out of FTL! Transferring track to tactical!"

Cameron studied the tactical display. "It's another Takaran ship, sir. It's about the same size as the first one. They must've sent the message just before they arrived."

"There is more to the message, Captain," Jalea warned. "More ships will be arriving to join in the search."

"I'm afraid to ask how soon," Nathan admitted.

"The next one within the hour."

"Great," Nathan mumbled.

"Every ship they add to the search increases their chances of finding us," Cameron pointed out.

"Really?" he replied in a sarcastic tone.

"Marak says we must leave now," Jalea warned, interpreting Marak's words as he spoke, "or we will not leave this place alive."

"Damn it!" Nathan swore. "We can't crawl out of here. They'll be on us in seconds!" Nathan looked around the bridge. His outburst had startled more than one of his crew, and he knew that he shouldn't have lost control that way. But frustration had gotten the better of him. "We're gonna have to jump from here," he resigned.

"Nathan..." Cameron began.

"Captain," Abigail interrupted, standing to protest, "I cannot allow that! It's too risky!"

"I don't see that I have much choice, Doctor!"

"You don't understand; this system is the only one in existence."

"Don't worry, Doctor. I'm sure the fleet will start building another one as soon as they figure out we're overdue."

"No, they won't," Abigail disagreed. "You don't realize how secret this project has been. There is no evidence of its existence anywhere on Earth. The research it was based upon was erased from the Data Ark, and we brought all of our research with us when we came on board. Our leaders could not take the chance that it might fall into the hands of the

Jung. Captain Roberts even had standing orders to destroy the entire ship if captured. There are only a few people on Earth who even *know* that the project exists. If we don't get this system back to Earth, they *will* have *no* defense."

Nathan stared at Abigail. Other than Jalea's constant translations to Marak, the room was quiet. Nathan Scott had come aboard the Aurora as an ensign fresh out of the academy just three weeks ago. Since then, he had become the primary helmsman, a lieutenant, and now he was captain. Not only was his ship badly damaged and half his crew dead, apparently now his entire homeworld was depending on him to somehow quickly cross a thousand light years in order to save them from invasion. And he had hoped that this would be an *easy* assignment.

At least now he finally understood things more clearly. This had been the reason that Captain Roberts' demeanor had changed so drastically during their flight to Jupiter. This is why he had attacked that Jung patrol ship in the Oort without provocation. This was the reason he had so adamantly ordered Nathan to get the jump drive home. It *was* their only hope.

After what seemed like an eternity, Nathan looked at Cameron. She was always so calm, so confident. But now, he saw something different in her eyes. She was looking to *him* to decide what to do. They all were. For once in his life, he was determined not to let anyone down.

"All right," he started calmly, "we're going to need a diversion. We need to draw them away from us if we're going to get far enough out to jump safely *before* they open fire."

Marak began speaking into his communicator.

"Captain," Cameron reported, "two rebel ships just began accelerating away from us. They're on a course out of the asteroid field."

"What the hell are you doing?" Nathan sputtered at Marak, forgetting that he didn't understand English.

"Marak is sending ships to draw the Takarans away from us," Jalea explained.

"Are you crazy? They'll be slaughtered! Tell him he cannot do this!" he ordered.

Marak continued speaking to Jalea as she spoke for him. "We need a diversion; you said so yourself. This is the best way to achieve both our goals."

"You're just going to send them to their deaths?"

"It is what soldiers do," she translated.

"You fucking bastard!" Nathan screamed as he violently grabbed Marak by his tunic with both hands, quickly drawing him in closer and yelling in his face. "You can't do this!" In the blink of an eye, a small but deadly blade appeared in Marak's right hand, pointed at Nathan's throat. Just as quickly, Jessica, who had been quietly observing, had her sidearm out, safety off, with the weapon sighted on the back of Marak's head. Both the marine guards at the doors had done the same with their close-quarters weapons.

"Drop it," Jessica ordered in no uncertain terms, "or I drop you!"

Jalea translated Jessica's warning to Marak, repeating the translation at least two more times before he began to relax and bring the knife slowly away from Nathan's throat.

"He was only defending himself!" Jalea insisted. "It was a reflex! He will not harm your captain!"

As Marak's right hand slowly withdrew from Nathan's neck, Jessica stepped up and swiftly snatched the blade from his hand.

"We're clear!" she instructed the two marines, holding the knife up high for them to see. "It's all over. Everybody just calm down."

Marak said something else in a tone that could only be described as arrogant.

"What did he say?" Nathan asked after releasing his hold on Marak. Jalea was hesitant to answer. "What did he say?" Nathan repeated more sternly.

"He said, 'It is already done.'"

Nathan continued glaring at Marak, who stood confidently beside Jalea. He could tell by the rebel leader's steely eyes that he was not one to back down when challenged. Nathan knew that the man had made his decision and there was nothing he could do to change it. The only question was how he could make this work in their favor?

"Is there another place we can go?" Nathan was asking the question of Jalea, although his eyes were still locked with Marak's for the moment. "Some place where we can make repairs, get some supplies?" Jalea translated his request to Marak. For a moment, Nathan sensed that Marak was pleased that Nathan still sought his assistance. He had no doubt that Abigail's words had been clearly and accurately translated to him by Jalea. And now Nathan had to wonder if Marak somehow felt like he had power over them because of their desperate situation. However, there was nothing in Marak's expression or demeanor that might reveal his intent.

"There is a world," Jalea translated, "that still supports us. Not openly, but covertly. They are just beyond Takaran space. We have contacts on this world. Through them, we may find the assistance you require."

"Please give the location of this world to Doctor Sorenson," Nathan requested coldly.

"As you wish," Jalea nodded, turning toward Abigail.

Nathan stared at Marak a moment longer until the tension was broken by the communications officer.

"Sir, message from engineering. They can give us limited forward propulsion, but no more than ten percent thrust."

"Thank you, Ensign."

"That should be enough for now," Cameron noted.

Nathan finally broke eye contact with Marak, turning to Cameron instead. "Can you handle both helm and navigation?"

"Shouldn't be a problem, especially not at that speed."

"Good. I'll back you up on navigation if I can."

"Thanks, but I've seen your navigation skills," Cameron jabbed, finally getting a smile to crack Nathan's serious expression.

"Jess, I assume you trained for tactical at some point?"

"You bet," she answered. Spec-ops was a branch of the Security division. All spec-ops applicants had to have graduated as rated security officers before they could get accepted into the spec-ops training course. Jessica stepped up to the tactical station and looked it over like she was being reunited with a long-lost favorite toy.

"What's the plan, Skipper?" Jessica asked, giddy at being back behind the tactical console.

"First, we get the hell out of here and jump to

someplace safe," Nathan explained. "Then we beg, borrow, or steal whatever we need to get our ship fixed. Then we find a way to get this ship, and that jump drive, back to Earth as quickly as possible. If that means we have to deal with the devil, then so be it." Nathan stepped away from the tactical station and moved forward, taking a seat in the command chair directly in front of the station. Cameron traded looks with Jessica before taking the helm directly in front of Nathan.

"Sound general quarters."

CHAPTER NINE

"The rebel ships have exited the asteroid field," Jessica reported from the tactical station.

"Any change in the Takaran ships?" Nathan could feel the tension in the room as they waited to see if the diversion would have its desired effect.

"Nothing yet, but there's still a lot of the field still in their way. They may not see them yet," she pointed out.

"Captain," Ensign Yosef called, "the rebel ships are generating an unusually high radiation output from their propulsion systems."

Nathan spun his chair around to look at Jalea. "They're lighting themselves up?"

"To ensure that they will be noticed," Jalea explained.

"Isn't that an obvious tactic?" Jessica asked.

"To you and me, perhaps," Jalea answered, "but the Takarans do not usually win their battles through intelligence. They prefer overwhelming force."

Jessica smiled. "I like the sound of that."

She knew it was usually much easier to outthink an opponent than to outgun them, especially if they had a tendency to think *with* their guns.

"I don't," Nathan added. They had already been through a pounding by Takaran guns, and he didn't care to go through it again anytime soon.

"Well, it worked," Jessica reported. "The closest Takaran ship just lit up their mains and is giving chase. At their current speed, they should intercept the rebel ships in three minutes."

"What about the second ship?" Nathan asked. If they were going to make their escape, they would need both of the enemy ships to take the bait.

"No change."

Nathan was becoming nervous and had to fight to hide it from his crew. He knew that although they might be able to slug it out with one Takaran ship, there was little chance of defeating two of them, unless they got really lucky with a few torpedo shots.

"Doctor Sorenson," Nathan said, "how long do you need to calculate our jump?"

"Maybe five more minutes. But it will take twice that just to manually key it into the event sequencer."

"Sounds like something that should be done automatically," he commented.

"This is just a prototype, remember?"

"How long will it take us to reach a safe jump distance?" This time he was asking Cameron.

"About ten minutes at ten percent thrust."

"That's going to be cutting it close."

"The ship finally reports ready for battle, sir," Jessica reported.

"Good. Make sure the forward torpedo tubes get loaded."

"I'm on it," Jessica answered. "The Takaran ship is launching missiles at the rebels. She's launched four, two per target. The rebel ships are breaking formation. They're launching countermeasures and jamming. They're performing evasive maneuvers."

"At least they're not going down without a fight," he observed.

"Whoa! I'm seeing four rebel contacts now!"

"What? Where'd they come from?" Nathan stood

in alarm at the news.

"Beats the hell out of me!"

"They are decoys," Jalea reported calmly, "impossible to distinguish from the real ships."

"And they're working, sir!" Jessica added. "If I'm reading this right, it looks like the decoys continued on course and the original ships veered away sharply! And the missiles are tracking the decoys! Damn! That was slick!" Jessica cheered, pounding the console with her hand. "Missile impacts! All four. And I'm pretty sure they only destroyed the decoys."

Nathan was impressed by the ingenuity that the rebel pilots were displaying. He couldn't help but wonder if those decoys were one of the improvements that Jalea had alluded to earlier. "We'll know in a moment," he mumbled. Either the rebels were really good tacticians, or they had grossly underestimated their opponents. "Can those decoys maneuver?"

"Yes, nearly as well as the ships that launched them," Jalea assured Nathan.

"The rebel ships, or decoys—I don't know which yet—they're turning to engage the Takaran ship," Jessica continued. "The Takaran ship is opening up with her cannons. But it doesn't seem to be slowing down the rebel ships."

"I'm picking up new signatures from the rebels' ships, Captain," Ensign Yosef reported. "They're enveloped in some kind of an energy barrier. EM mostly, but highly charged."

"Some kind of shielding?" Nathan surmised. He looked at Jalea, who simply nodded, seemingly surprised that Nathan understood the concept so easily. The Aurora was designed to use shielding herself, but it was reflective in nature, designed only to reflect energy weapons away from them. They had nothing to stop solid projectiles from striking their hull. If these rebels did, then that was something that would be quite useful in the defense of Earth. It made Nathan wonder what other technologies this region of space might hold that would be useful back home.

"Holy shit!" Jessica cried out, immediately turning red as she realized she had let the inappropriate expletive fly. "Sorry, sir, but the rebels' ships just unleashed a hellish barrage of something!"

"Cannon fire?" Nathan hadn't noticed any cannons on the rebel ships.

"No, sir, too big for cannon-launched projectiles. They're like mini-missiles, or flechettes or something. Whatever they are, they're pounding that Takaran ship!"

Nathan was standing now, as was Cameron. If two of the rebel ships could possibly take out a Takaran warship, then they might be able to escape without further damage. "Can they actually take him out?"

"I doubt it, sir. They can't possibly keep up this level of bombardment long enough."

Nathan again looked at Jalea, who simply said, "They will not need to."

"The second ship is changing course, Captain!" Ensign Yosef announced.

Nathan felt another surge of hope well up from inside him, despite his best efforts to stay focused and keep his emotions under control.

Jessica checked the second ship's course, quickly plotting the ship's probable destination. "She's right. Looks like they're taking the bait as well," Jessica reported.

"Yes!" Nathan exclaimed excitedly, not caring if

he did show emotion. "Time to intercept?"

"Five minutes," Jessica reported instantly, having anticipated his request.

Nathan looked at Abigail, "Doctor?"

"I'll be done with the transition plot in a few minutes," she answered. She was not accustomed to performing such complex computations under pressure. The original jump plots had taken her nearly a week to complete and even longer to verify. Now she was having to do them in minutes—a task she would've considered impossible only a few days ago. She cursed to herself in her native tongue as she waited for her algorithms to process, unable to continue with each step until the previous step had been completed. The computer systems used at this station were not designed for the kind of multi-spatial algorithms she was running.

"The rebel ships have begun alternating fire," Jessica reported, sounding a bit surprised.

Nathan looked to Jalea for an explanation, which she offered without having to be asked. "They have expended their primary loads. They will have to reload often from this point forward," she explained.

"How much longer can they keep this up?"

Before Jalea could answer, Jessica offered an update. "The first ship is withdrawing! She's backing away!"

Nathan moved quickly, bounding the few steps to the tactical station to stand beside Jessica so that he could see the displays for himself. It wasn't that he didn't trust her interpretation of the data. He was just so excited at the idea of the rebels defeating one of the enemy ships that he had to see for himself.

"The rebels are staying with her!" Nathan exclaimed. He watched with Jessica as the rebel ships continued to pound their target, taking turns firing as the other reloaded their flechette pods.

"One minute until the second ship joins the battle," Jessica said.

"Right." Nathan stood up straight, taking his attention away from the tactical display and leaving it to Jessica. "Helm, prepare to get under way," he announced as he returned to the command chair.

"Yes, sir," Cameron acknowledged.

"Second Takaran ship has engaged the rebels," Jessica reported. "The rebel ships are breaking off their flechette attack and are maneuvering wildly."

With both the Takaran ships engaged by the rebel diversion, they finally had the only opportunity they were going to get. While there was a remote chance that the rebels' ships could beat one Takaran ship, it was doubtful they could defeat two of them. Nathan knew that, despite the risk in revealing their location, this was their only chance at escape.

"Take us out, Cam," Nathan ordered. "All available speed," he added, knowing it would not be much.

Cameron tapped a few buttons on her console, "Mains coming online. Thrust at ten percent."

The Aurora began to slowly move forward, her two remaining rebel escorts keeping pace beside her. Inside, without the inertial dampeners operating at full efficiency, the crew could feel the ship as it began to accelerate. The force was not enough to knock anyone off their feet, but it was enough to cause a slight misstep for anyone not expecting the sudden shifting of the decks beneath their feet as they walked.

For the last few hours, the bridge crew had been looking at the surface of the asteroid in front of them as it slowly rotated. Now, as they flew up and over the massive rock, light from the system's red dwarf star spilled over its jagged horizon, lighting up the interior of the bridge with its reddish-amber glow. The rock quickly passed under them as they left it behind, the red star glowing in the distance. Cameron immediately dipped the nose of the Aurora down slightly and dove under the next asteroid in their path, rolling slightly to starboard as she did so in order to better hug the surface of the massive rock as they passed under it. She knew that the closer she stayed to these rocks, the less chance the enemy had of detecting them. And she wanted to make sure that they did not show up on the enemy sensors until the last possible moment.

Although ten percent thrust was considered a slow speed, in a dense asteroid field it still required intense concentration. Cameron had piloted the ship through far more difficult simulations, but that had been with Nathan at her side offering constant navigational assistance. As poor as she had always felt his navigational skills to be, at that moment, she wished he was there, just in case.

"That's it; keep us tucked in close," Nathan encouraged. She wondered if he could tell how tense she was at that moment.

"Those rebel ships are coming awfully close to us," Cameron reported. Every time one of the rebels moved too close to the Aurora, a proximity warning light would flash on the helm display. She knew that the rebel pilots were not going to inadvertently smash into her, but it was distracting nonetheless.

"Don't worry about it, Cam. They're just trying to maintain a single contact profile in case we're spotted."

"I know. They're just irritating me."

"You're doing great," he reassured her.

A few minutes and about a dozen dodged asteroids later, the Aurora exited the asteroid field into open space, headed on a course directly away from both the field and the conflict still raging between the Takaran ships and the rebels' ships acting as decoys.

"We're clear," Cameron announced proudly, an obvious relief in her voice. After tapping a few buttons, she added, "Ten minutes to safe jump distance."

"Captain," Jessica yelled in shock, causing Nathan to spin around to face her, "one of the rebel ships was just blown apart! A single shot, right in her reactor!" Nathan's heart fell as he looked at Jalea and Marak. Jalea showed no emotion, just the same cold, determined eyes. Marak was muttering some unintelligible commands into his communicator.

"The second rebel ship just changed course and is accelerating!" Jessica continued. "I think he means to ram them!"

Nathan continued watching Jalea, but there was no change in her demeanor. Marak however had begun muttering some sort of chant, over and over, in a rhythmic fashion as if he were praying. "He's making a suicide run," Nathan realized.

"Both ships are targeting him! They're firing! The rebel ship is breaking apart! I'm not sure if he's going to..."

The bridge filled with a bright white flash of light reflecting off the forward sections of the ship that were visible through the main view screen. It only lasted a moment, but it was sudden and blinding during its brief presence.

"I'm reading a nuclear detonation!" Jessica announced. "At least ten megatons!"

"Why would they fire a nuke?" Nathan asked, baffled at what had just happened.

"I don't think the Takarans fired it, sir," Jessica warned.

All the pieces fell into place in Nathan's mind. He turned back to Jalea, who stood unwavering, unaffected. "Do your ships carry nuclear weapons?"

Jalea looked at Nathan for a moment, contemplating her response before she spoke. She could no longer hide this fact from them. "Our ships do not *carry* nuclear weapons, Captain. They *are* nuclear weapons."

Nathan stared at Jalea again. "You mean to tell me that all your ships are basically nuclear missiles? Even the one still in our hangar deck?"

"Yes, but it is only used as a last resort. And it has proven effective on several occasions."

"It makes sense, sir," Jessica told him.

"Are you kidding? How in the…"

"No, seriously," Jessica tried to explain. "I mean, when all else fails, use yourself as a nuclear torpedo. At least you won't miss."

"What is the disposition of the Takaran ships?" Jalea asked indignantly.

Jessica looked at her tactical display. "I'm only picking up one ship, sir. And it's sustained quite a bit of damage as well."

Nathan's shock suddenly faded at the idea of the incoming threat possibly being diminished. "Is it still a threat?"

"I'm not sure. We're way out of her range at the moment, but if her main propulsion is still operable, she might still be able to catch us before we jump."

"They will not be able to prevent our departure," Jalea insisted.

Nathan turned halfway back toward Jalea and Marak. "You know, I've got half a mind to shoot the both of you once we get out of this mess!" he stated angrily, turning to completely face them. "You both knew damned well that this was the way it was going to play out from the beginning, didn't you?"

"New contact off our port beam!" Ensign Yosef interrupted. "Just dropped out of FTL! Transferring track to tactical!"

Jessica began analyzing the new contact as Nathan turned back around to look for himself. "Crap," Jessica swore. "It's another Takaran warship," she announced, her optimism falling along with everyone else in the room, "and it's bigger than the last two."

"How long until they can..."

Nathan didn't have a chance to finish his question. "We'll be inside their weapons range in two minutes," Jessica said.

"Time to safe jump?"

"Eight minutes," Cameron answered. A split second later, Marak spoke through his communicator and the two remaining rebel ships that had been flying alongside the Aurora suddenly pulled ahead of them and angled to port on an intercept course with the third Takaran warship.

"You know, you could at least act like it was difficult to send your people off to die," Nathan remarked, obvious anger in his voice. As expected, there was no response.

Nathan felt emotionally and physically exhausted. They had all been working for nearly eighteen hours now, and during that time his emotions had bounced from one end of the spectrum and back again at least half a dozen times. But he knew that he couldn't give up now. He couldn't ever give up. The stakes were just too damned high.

"Helm, turn us into the new target. Let's bring our tubes to bear and give the enemy as little silhouette as possible," Nathan ordered.

"Coming to port, ten degrees and down slightly," Cameron announced as she changed course. "Same speed, Captain?"

"Same speed," he confirmed. "Jess, make sure all the rail guns are ready to fire as well. The only chance we've got is to blast our way through."

"Yes, sir."

Moments later, the rebel ships got close enough to launch their long-range missiles at the third Takaran warship.

"Rebels' ships are launching missiles," Jessica announced. "Enemy is spinning up her point-defense screen. Eight rebel missiles are on their way," Jessica reported. "Impact in thirty seconds."

"How many missiles do they carry?" Nathan asked Jalea.

"Four each."

"They just fired their whole load," he told Jessica.

"Takaran ship is firing missiles, but only two."

"They're either more conservative, or they have better missiles," Nathan decided.

"Rebels are launching decoys again," Jessica announced. "We have got to get us some of those," she whispered. "Rebel missiles have reached the enemy perimeter." Jessica paused a moment before continuing. "Only two missiles made it through. Impact in five seconds."

Nathan watched the tactical display as the two lines representing the paths of the rebel missiles eventually connected to the symbol representing the

Takaran warship.

"Impact." Jessica checked her readouts on the enemy ship. "Only minor damage."

A small orange and yellow fireball erupted on the main view screen. "One rebel ship has been destroyed. The other one is still advancing and is firing her flechettes."

"Do you think our torpedoes will work any better?"

"Sure, if they get through. But that bastard's got great point-defense systems."

"Get firing solutions for all four torpedoes, Jess."

"Yes, sir. Suggest we fire them consecutively, sir." Jessica could see by the confused look on Nathan's face that he didn't know what she was talking about. "If we fire them all at once, they have to spread out to avoid knocking each other off course. That means they all hit the same point-defense flak wall at the same time. If we fire consecutively, with each one following the one in front of it, they all go through the same hole. If the first torpedo gets nailed, its blast will make a whole in the flak field for the next one to get through. Theoretically, that is. I mean, I've never actually done it before," Jessica admitted sheepishly.

"Sounds good to me," Nathan agreed.

"They're firing missiles again," Jessica added.

"Are we in weapons range yet?"

"Yes, wait..." Jessica double-checked her readouts before continuing. "Inbound ordnance! That last missile launch was at us! Tracking four!"

"I thought we weren't in range yet!" Nathan snapped.

"Guess I was wrong," Jessica admitted. "Not like I've seen a whole lot of Takaran warships before.

Impact in two minutes."

"Launch torpedoes!" Nathan ordered. "Then bring the turrets online, point-defense mode!"

"Firing one!" Jessica announced. Everyone watched as the first torpedo appeared on the left side of the forward view screen as it streaked past, turning to port as it departed.

"Firing two!" The second torpedo streaked across from the right side.

"Firing three!"

Marak leaned in closely to Jalea, giving her hand a squeeze as he whispered something in her ear. For the briefest of moments, the cold, pragmatic look in her eyes softened, turning sad. She turned and looked at him respectfully as he let go of her hand, after which he turned and left the bridge.

"Firing four!" They watched as the last torpedo streaked away. "Rail guns coming online, point-defense mode. Firing all turrets."

On the outside of the Aurora, in eight different locations along the upper side of the ship, doors slid open and rail gun turrets popped up into view. Once fully deployed, the turrets once again raised their barrels and pivoted until they were pointed in the proper direction and began rapidly firing the special point-defense rounds. The turrets danced back and forth as they attempted to fill in the gaps in the defensive field of flak left by the turrets that had either been damaged, or had not yet been installed.

"Point-defense perimeter established!" Jessica announced. "Torpedo one is shot down. Torpedo two, also shot down."

Nathan could feel his hope fade with each torpedo that was intercepted and destroyed before reaching its target.

"Torpedo three... damn!"

Nathan closed his eyes as he waited for the report on their last torpedo.

"Torpedo four... has made it through! Impact in five!" Jessica exclaimed. Suddenly, a warning indicator flashed on her tactical threat display. "Oh shit. Brace for impact!"

Jessica had been paying such close attention to their own torpedoes, she had failed to notice that one of the enemy missiles had made it past their own point-defense field. The missile streaked past the forward section of the ship, striking the upper portion of the main drive section just above the starboard torpedo tubes.

The force of the explosion rocked the ship, causing her stern to suddenly drop down sharply. On the bridge, it had nearly knocked them all off their feet. Nathan couldn't help but wonder how Vladimir and his men were doing in engineering, which was far closer to the point of impact.

"Impact! Starboard edge of the drive section! Torpedo tubes two and four are damaged!"

"Propulsion is down!" Cameron alerted. "The impact is pushing us into a lateral spin! Attempting to compensate!"

"Bridge to engineering!" Nathan called out over his comm-set. "Vlad!"

"We've still got maneuvering!" Cameron added. "Course and speed are unchanged! ETA to safe jump, two minutes!"

"Captain, we've lost most of our rail guns!" Jessica reported.

"That torpedo must've knocked out at least one of our reactors!" Nathan exclaimed. "Abby!" he shouted, spinning his chair around to face her. "Do you still have power?!"

"Yes, all systems still show ready. I've almost got the sequence entered."

"Captain!" Jessica reported. "Our torpedo! It took out their missile battery!"

Nathan looked at Jessica. "Nice shootin'." He glanced at Jalea behind her and noticed that Marak was no longer standing next to her.

"The last rebel ship made it through their defense perimeter!" Jessica announced. "He must've followed our last torpedo through the gap in their flak field!"

Nathan spun back around to face forward. He could barely make out the rebel ship as it plunged toward the Takaran warship. The enemy's flak exploded all across the screen in front of them as they drifted closer, their main engines still offline.

"He's making a suicide run!" Nathan exclaimed.

"Captain, another rebel ship just launched from our flight deck!"

Nathan spun back around to look at Jalea. He thought he saw her nod her head slightly in confirmation, but it might have just been the violent vibrations as they began taking hits from the enemy ship's rail guns.

"We're taking fire!" Jessica announced.

"Time to safe jump?"

"One minute!" Cameron answered.

Suddenly, the room lit up in a brilliant white light that came from the center of the main view screen. Seconds later, as the light began to die, Nathan thought he could see the last rebel ship, piloted by Marak, dive toward the Takaran warship.

"He's using the detonation from the first ship to slip in undetected!" Jessica deduced. Nathan turned back to look at Jessica. "Clever little fucker," she added.

Nathan wondered if they had planned it this way all along. "Time to safe jump?"

"Forty-five seconds!" Cameron announced.

"Jess, how long till Marak impacts the Takaran ship?"

"Fifteen seconds!" Jessica answered, tension starting to creep into her voice.

"Helm, quick as you can, show them our belly."

"Pitching up," Cameron announced, as she pulled the control stick back and slightly right.

The Aurora began to roll onto her right side as her nose pitched back. A few seconds later, she ended the maneuver, leaving the ship drifting forward belly first toward the enemy.

"Impact," Jessica announced. "Detonation."

With their belly pointed toward the detonation, there was no blinding flash this time, just a good deal of turbulence as the shock wave from the nuclear detonation struck them.

"Kill the main view screen," Nathan ordered. He waited a few more seconds for the shock wave to subside before giving the next order. "Abby, jump the ship."

Doctor Sorenson quickly tapped in the commands and pressed the execute button. "Jumping," she announced.

The Aurora again seemed to glow a brilliant blue-white for a fraction of a second before disappearing in a bright flash of white light. The vibrations from the shock wave instantly stopped, leaving the bridge quiet once again.

"Jump complete," she announced, having fully adopted Nathan's parlance.

"Viewer on," Nathan ordered, turning back

toward the front. The screen that surrounded the entire forward section of the bridge flickered back to life, resolving into a black star field with a small star directly ahead of them that was significantly brighter than all the rest.

Nathan looked confused. "Are we facing the wrong way?" he asked Cameron. "I thought we were jumping into a system."

"I took the liberty of jumping us to a point just inside the target system," Abigail explained. "Considering how the last three jumps went, I thought it best that we didn't jump into the middle of everything this time. I hope you don't mind."

"Not at all," Nathan assured her. "Good thinking."

"We are still adrift, Captain," Cameron pointed out.

"Sir, engineering reports the two scrammed reactors are coming back online, and main propulsion should be back up in approximately ten minutes."

Nathan looked around the room, cocking his head in strange positions and looking about the bridge, as if he were looking for some sign of trouble.

"How far out are we?" he asked no one in particular.

"About two days journey," Cameron answered. "Assuming we're still only able to run the mains at ten percent."

"Any contacts?" he asked.

"No, sir," Ensign Yosef reported. "We're the only ones out here."

"Finally," Nathan observed, "some peace and quiet."

CHAPTER TEN

Nathan sat watching the surf crash onto the tropical beach. The sound of the waves as they broke over the reefs, the seagulls overhead—it was the sound of life to him. It was the sound of peace.

The peace was interrupted by the door buzzer.

"Enter," he called.

Cameron entered the ready room. "Morning, sir," she greeted.

"Would you knock off the 'sir' crap?"

"You are the captain," she reminded him, "which means you outrank me by, what, five steps?"

"Yeah, about that. I'll make you a deal," he said as he reached into his shirt pocket. "You promise to stop calling me sir, at least in private, and you can have these." He tossed her a plastic packet containing something shiny.

Cameron caught the packet with ease and looked at it. It contained a pair of rank insignia pins. The rank was commander. A smile began to grow across her face. "It's about time," she muttered. Her smile was now fully developed, going from ear to ear.

"So you can smile, eh, Commander Taylor?"

"I've got the crew roster ready." She handed him the data tablet to look at.

"Well, put them on," he insisted as he took the tablet and began to read the report. "We lost two more?"

"They were injured in the first battle out in the

Oort cloud. Doctor Chen said they didn't have a chance. She was surprised they had hung on as long as they did."

Nathan tried to put their deaths behind him, but Cameron could tell that he had not yet developed that crucial command skill.

She turned to look at the ocean view displayed on the large screen that covered the forward-facing bulkhead of the captain's ready room. A beautiful and energetic little border collie ran out from the bottom of the screen, scampering out onto the beach to run freely and chase the birds. "What's this?" she asked, pointing to the screen.

"It was in Captain Roberts' personal documents file in the computer system. I think it's the view from his beach house back on Earth. It's a long file, probably at least forty hours' worth. He must've run it while he was in here working, to feel like he was back home." The two of them watched in silence for a moment before continuing their conversation.

"So, did you figure out a way to run the ship with a crew of thirty-eight?" Nathan asked as he picked up the remote and shut off the screen.

"We can fly it with thirty-eight, but if we get into another fight, we're not going to have anyone for damage control, let alone backups in case someone gets injured."

"I guess we'll just have to steer clear of any more trouble, then. Speaking of the crew, how are they taking the news?"

"They're all pretty shaken," she admitted as she sat down across the desk from him. "I mean, after what we went through, and now stranded so far from home... but they're all well trained, and they all joined the fleet for the same reasons, so they'll pull through," she insisted. "How are you doing?"

"Leg still hurts a bit, but it was only a hairline fracture. It'll heal in a few days."

Cameron looked him in the eyes. "That's not what I meant."

Nathan leaned back in his chair, exhaling slowly. He had tried not to let himself wallow in his own emotions after the crisis had finally resolved. But he knew that it was going to catch up to him sooner or later. They were going to be away from Earth for a long time. Other than Vladimir, Cameron was the only other person on board he could trust.

"I'll be honest, Cam; I've been better." Cameron said nothing, waiting for him to finish his response. "Hell, I've been through more in the last few days than I expected to go through in an entire career." Nathan felt his emotions bubbling up from deep inside as he looked down at the crew roster. "I look at this list, and I can't help but wonder how many of them *I* got killed."

Cameron felt sorry for him but knew that coddling him wouldn't help. "You wanted command," she said.

Nathan chuckled. "Actually, no, I didn't. I just didn't wanna roll over and let *you* have it."

"In that case, it serves you right," she jabbed.

Nathan laughed even harder. "You really are a bitch; you know that?"

Cameron smiled and shrugged her shoulders. "Hey, we all gotta play to our strengths." Cameron stood to leave. "Listen, Nathan, if it will make you feel any better, truth be told, you did all right."

Nathan looked up at her, a grin creeping across his face at her compliment of his performance.

"But I'll deny ever saying that," she added as she

turned to walk out of the room, nodding at Jalea who was just entering.

"Good morning, Captain." Now that the situation had calmed down, Jalea's demeanor had returned to the warmer, more soulful one that he had first met. Although he definitely preferred this persona, he doubted he could ever forget the other side of her.

"Good morning. How may I help you?"

"I've spoken to one of our contacts in the system," Jalea informed him as she took a seat across the desk from him.

"What did you tell him?" Nathan asked suspiciously.

"Only that we needed to smuggle in a ship to be repaired. It is not the first time we have made such a request of this person."

"And this person can help us?"

"He is more of a facilitator," she explained.

"Like a middleman?"

"Yes. He will bring the proper transponder and codes out to us. We can then use these to travel throughout this system without raising suspicion."

"When can he get here?"

"It will take him about two days to reach us. I would request that you take no hostile actions upon his approach. It might lead to unfortunate results," she stated carefully.

"I'll alert Jessica to expect him."

Jalea respectfully nodded.

"Just one question, though. What's it going to cost us?"

"These people are also repaying debts."

"Life debts?"

"Correct."

"But these debts are not owed to my people,

Jalea. They're owed to yours."

"True. But we owe you far more than we can ever repay."

"Is that why Marak sacrificed himself, to repay us?"

"Marak did what he felt was in the best interest of both our people."

"And how is saving this ship in the interest of your people?" Nathan had been curious about this question for a while now.

"The name of your ship," she smiled, "do you know what it means?"

Nathan was a bit embarrassed to admit that he did not. As far as he knew, it was the name of some pretty lights seen at the northern latitudes on Earth.

"No, I'm afraid I don't," he admitted.

"It means 'New dawn'," she told him.

Now Nathan smiled. "That's just a coincidence," he assured her.

"Perhaps." Jalea turned and headed for the door. Before she reached the exit, she paused and turned back around to face him again. "And your name, Captain, what does 'Nathan' mean?"

"If I remember correctly, it means 'Gift from God'."

"Another coincidence?" she asked.

Nathan smiled. "Perhaps."

Thank you for reading this story.
(*A review would be greatly appreciated!*)

AVAILABLE NOW

"THE RINGS OF HAVEN"
Episode 2
of
The Frontiers Saga

Visit us online at
www.frontierssaga.com
or on Facebook

Want to be notified when
new episodes are published?
Join our mailing list!
http://www.frontierssaga.com/mailinglist/

santa clara
county
library district

Renewals: (800) 471-0991

www.sccl.org

12/18 ① 11/17

Made in the USA
San Bernardino, CA
27 July 2017